MAGIC IN THE WEAVE

MAGIC IN THE WEAVE

Alys Clare

SEVERN
HOUSE

First world edition published in Great Britain in 2021 and the USA in 2022
by Severn House, an imprint of Canongate Books Ltd,
14 High Street, Edinburgh EH1 1TE.

Trade paperback edition first published in Great Britain and the USA in 2023
by Severn House, an imprint of Canongate Books Ltd.

severnhouse.com

British Library Cataloguing-in-Publication Data
A CIP catalogue record for this title is available from the British Library.

ISBN-13: 978-0-7278-9010-8 (cased)
ISBN-13: 978-1-4483-0727-2 (trade paper)
ISBN-13: 978-1-4483-0726-5 (e-book)

All Severn House titles are printed on acid-free paper.

Typeset by Palimpsest Book Production Ltd.,
Falkirk, Stirlingshire, Scotland.
Printed and bound in Great Britain by
TJ Books, Padstow, Cornwall.

Dedicated to everyone else who has found refuge in imaginary worlds over the last eighteen months.

ONE

Late October 1604

'Why is he *believing* all this?' my sister hissed, angry tears in her eyes. 'Is he stupid? *Mad?*'

'Sssshh!' A cross-looking man standing nearby spun round and scowled at her. As he turned to look down towards the players again she stuck her tongue out at him.

'His lieutenant is clever,' Judyth Penwarden whispered back. 'He perceives that his general is insecure. He cannot quite believe in this miraculous thing that has happened, and thus he is vulnerable to having the doubts planted.'

'But *why* is the lieutenant doing it?' Celia persisted.

Judyth shrugged, and I could tell from her rapt expression that she wanted to give her full attention to what was happening down in the inn yard.

I felt the same, and I hoped Celia would take the hint.

We were standing in a row, the four of us – Jonathan Carew, Celia, Judyth and I – on an upper gallery looking down onto the yard of the Saracen's Head in Plymouth. We had secured a spot at the front so that we could lean against the wooden railing, which was just as well as it was the only means of support. A small amount of warmth permeated out from the rooms at the rear of the gallery, which, although the day was mild, was welcome in view of the necessity to stand still. There was nowhere to sit and the play was rumoured to be some two and a half hours long. I had anticipated that I might find this excursion trying, for I'd been very busy of late and my own hearth, with a pipe of tobacco and a glass of port to hand, had more appeal than standing over an inn yard watching a band of players. But I hadn't managed to resist the invitation, because for one thing the players were a London company with a fine reputation, and for another, the outing had been Judyth's suggestion.

I did not have it in me to refuse an opportunity to spend an afternoon with Judyth. And, as I was discovering, the players were worthy of their reputation.

There was plague in London – hardly a rare occurrence – and the theatres were closed. This particular group had abandoned the dangers of the capital and set off to keep the wolf from the door by touring the towns of the West Country, sensibly getting as far away from the lethal infection as they could. I'd heard someone refer to it as the Plague Tour, and the word was that the Company – that appeared to be the name they were known by – had at least half a dozen plays in their repertoire and probably more.

The play that was currently enthralling the entire audience told the story of a battle-weary general who, well into middle age, fell deeply and overwhelmingly in love with the innocent, sheltered daughter of a Venetian merchant. He discovered to his absolute amazement that she returned his ardour in full, and the pair were secretly married immediately before the general was commanded to sail off to defend the island of Cyprus from attack by the Turks. His evil second-in-command took it into his head to make his general believe his beautiful young wife was unfaithful to him, and so successfully did he worm this falsehood into the older man's anxious mind that, with terrifying haste, almost straight away he began to plan how to kill her.

The evil lieutenant played on the general's inexperience. The general – his name was Othello – was a black man, a Moor, in a sophisticated society where people of that race were uncommon, and the very words employed by Iago – that was the name of the villainous subordinate – carried the clear suggestion that sex and marriage between the middle-aged Moor and the young Venetian girl were abhorrent; bestial, almost. *An old black ram is tupping your white ewe* was an example of the sort of remarks that Iago yelled out to the girl's horrified father; as well as *you'll have your daughter covered with a Barbary horse*; and *your daughter and the Moor are now making the beast with two backs*.

As the play continued towards its tragic and inevitable outcome, it seemed to me that the whole powerful work was throbbing and thrumming with sex. The actors portraying Othello and the young bride Desdemona could, at the start, hardly keep their hands off each other, and Desdemona's first dramatic entrance was at a limping pace, the clear innuendo being that she was suffering from an excess of passionate lovemaking in the bridal bed. She – although of course it was really *he* – was slim and straight, not over-tall, with a long neck and sloping shoulders, and her hair was a dark mane. Her eyes were startling: light hazel in colour, they seemed to shine with gold when the light caught them, and I had the impression of huge and densely black pupils, as reflective as mirrors. Her bridegroom was a big, tall, heavy, handsome man, dark-complexioned and with black hair turning grey, and it was all too easy to imagine that his ardour would be uncomfortable for his pale, frail bride.

As if the visual impressions were not enough, there was the language. *O, blood, blood, blood!* the general moaned at one point, and, later, *yet I'll not shed her blood.* And there was the business of the handkerchief, a gift from Othello to Desdemona and made of some pale fabric dotted with red: *spotted with strawberries*, according to the dialogue, although when this was accompanied by talk of a *bed lust-stain'd with lust's blood spotted* and the bride's mention of her wedding sheets, it was all too easy to see that the handkerchief represented the bloodstained bedding of fervid wedding-night consummation and a virgin's ruptured hymen. And then the handkerchief ended up in the possession of a man observed wiping his beard with it, and everyone in the audience knew what was meant in a play when *beards* were mentioned.

Trying to distract my mind from these arousing images, I wondered if this had been the playwright's intention, or whether this interpretation was the idea of whoever was putting on this particular production.

The trouble was, of course, that I'd had sex on my mind anyway, for I was standing next to Judyth, pressed against her by the crush of people, and I could feel the warmth of her beautiful body through our clothes.

Less than a month ago, in the course of an enquiry of mine, she had been put in danger and injured. Before we knew

whether or not this injury was serious – thankfully it hadn't
been – she had rushed into my arms and I had held her tightly
against me, resting my cheek on the top of her head and
smelling the sweet scent of her glossy black hair. I had already
been fiercely attracted to her before that precious moment,
and now the thought of her was with me all the time. We had
spent not a little of our rare leisure hours together, but always
in company. I had yet to be alone with her, and did not know
if I yearned for or dreaded it . . .

But there were other aspects of this play that were even
more disturbing than its preoccupation with sex. As it drove
on inexorably towards what was surely going to be a tragic
final scene, I realized uneasily that it was a work full of obfus-
cation, of hinted-at secrets, of unspoken dangers. Of magic. I
kept sensing that I was being presented with one version of
the truth, whereas in fact what was really going on was deeply
hidden under increasingly impenetrable layers. The actors
seemed intent on confusing us – on fooling us, even – and
much use was made of a rather beautiful mirror. It was about
four feet high and perhaps three across, its top a graceful
semicircle and its frame a geometric pattern constructed out
of pieces of bronze, gold and silver. The reflecting surface
was pitted and spotted with age, so that images could only
be faintly made out. It was as if ghostly figures were moving
on the other side of a gauzy veil.

It was used to shocking effect in the scene when the general's
emotions finally overcame him and he suffocated his wife. I
had no idea how the Company contrived it, but it looked as
if dead Desdemona was looking out from the mirror at the
man who had just killed her. Othello, already in an agony
of guilt, lunged towards her, a cry of anguish breaking out of
him, only to slump back in despair when her image faded
away.

The play had ended, and the actors, bowing gracefully, had
acknowledged their well-deserved applause. Now the four of
us were squeezed in among the crush in the Saracen's Head
taproom and we each had a mug of ale in our hands, regularly
topped up by the jugs that were being passed round.

Jonathan had just remarked on how affecting the ending had been, and Celia reverted to her protestation that Othello had been too easily led into his fatal jealousy. Now Judyth was expanding on her explanation that it was because of his insecurity. 'He was too old for her, too unpractised in the arts of society, of wooing,' she said, 'and when Iago suggested so slyly that she was unfaithful and that the urbane and sophisticated Cassio was her lover, it seemed only too likely, and—'

Celia waved an impatient hand. 'Yes, yes, I realize that, but it still doesn't explain why Iago was so vicious towards him. And,' she pressed on before anyone could respond, 'there's that wretched handkerchief!'

The one spotted with red like drops of blood on a wedding sheet, I thought, uncomfortable all over again and feeling the heat rise up in my face.

I caught Judyth's eyes on me, a slight smile on her generous mouth as if she understood only too well. 'What of it?' she asked.

'It was all wrong!' Celia exclaimed. 'The way it was described suggested something fine, made by a two-hundred-year-old witch from beautiful silk produced by special silkworms and—'

'Hallowed worms,' Jonathan put in helpfully. 'Meaning holy, or perhaps magical, since Othello said there was magic in the fabric.'

'Yes, quite,' Celia said, 'and it was dyed with some sort of liquid obtained from dead virgins' hearts and then embroidered, and yet the object in the play looked like a tatty old scrap of coarse linen with dots of red paint on it!'

Her voice rose with indignation and I almost hushed her, for members of the Company had joined us in the taproom and I feared one of them would overhear. But you didn't hush my sister.

And anyway I realized it was too late.

A slim, elegantly dressed young man with bright, light grey-blue eyes, smooth dark hair and, despite the dashingly trimmed beard, a slight air of the feminine about him, was standing right behind Celia, a rueful smile on his handsome face.

'You are quite right, madam,' he said, and as Celia spun round to face him, her cheeks flushing with embarrassment, he took her hand and, bending over it, kissed it. 'The handkerchief has indeed been a bone of contention, for the original is mislaid – left behind, I dare say, in Barnstaple, where last we played – and this poor substitute was the best we could do at short notice, the absence only being discovered just before we began.' His bright gaze went to Jonathan, to Judyth and to me, and with a courteous bow he said, 'Fallon Adderbury, playwright, player of small and insignificant roles and manager of the Company at your service.'

His clear eyes had gone back to Celia, and I noticed he was studying her gown. It was new: she had finished hemming it only that morning, and it was made from a generous length of one of the finest of the silks she had brought with her from her old life to her new one. Her late husband, Jeromy Palfrey, had been a silk merchant, or to be exact he had been in the employ of one, and had presented his wife with bale after bale of fabric, including not a few of the finest Venetian *seta reale*, the true silk that is unwound from the intact cocoon. Celia's new gown was of this silk, in a particularly subtle shade of pale aquamarine that mirrored the colour of her eyes and made them shine like jewels.

Jonathan too had observed the focus of this Fallon Adderbury's glance. And so had Celia: with her prettiest smile she blinked fetchingly and said, 'There is surely someone in your costume department who could make a better one?' and I was quite sure I wasn't the only one to detect the rising intonation that turned it into a question.

Fallon Adderbury put out his lower lip like child deprived of a treat. 'I fear not, madam. Costume repairers, shoemakers and leather-workers I have in plenty, but even had I a length of suitably gorgeous silk, nobody in the Company is capable of embroidering strawberries fine enough to grace the handkerchief that Othello gave to Desdemona.'

And my sister said, as I'm sure we all knew she would, 'I could make it for you.'

He made a good pretence at surprise; well, he was an actor.

'Madam, I could not possibly put you to the trouble!' he exclaimed.

She dimpled and a faint flush rose in her cheeks. 'No trouble, I assure you, for I love to sew and embroider.'

'Well in that case,' Fallon Adderbury said with a beaming smile, 'let us call that settled! Now' – he spun round to include the rest of us – 'please let me replenish your mugs and you shall tell me what you thought of the play.'

In short time we all had full mugs, and Celia raised hers and said, looking at Fallon, 'To your play!'

'Did you write it?' Jonathan asked when we had drunk the toast. Fallon cast down his eyes with a modest smile but did not reply. 'Well done,' Jonathan went on, taking this for silent assent. 'It was extremely good.'

Fallon looked at him, one well-shaped eyebrow raised. 'Bloody, violent and over-full of sex for a man in holy orders, I would have thought?' He twinkled a smile.

Jonathan considered him, head on one side, and after a pause simply said, 'Not at all.'

Fallon Adderbury's ebullient confidence was dimmed, but only briefly.

Judyth, who had been watching these exchanges without comment, broke her silence. 'Was it the intention not to explain Iago's motive in driving his general mad with jealousy?' she asked.

Fallon turned to her. 'Did you not, then, detect his reason?'

She frowned, then said, 'There was a throwaway comment suggesting he thought Othello might have seduced his wife, but it was not pursued. He also mentioned that Michael Cassio was a man damned in a fair wife – I believe I have the wording correctly?' Fallon nodded. 'Possibly that suggested Iago mistrusted and disliked beautiful women, believing them incapable of fidelity.'

I expected Fallon to have commented; to have replied in a way that would extend the discussion. But he merely smiled and said, 'Possibly, possibly.'

I thought that perhaps he had enough of the whole business of writing when he was sitting at his desk, or wherever he worked, and did not wish to continue with it in his leisure moments. I could readily understand, having grown weary of being accosted in the street, in the inn, when I was simply riding along, by men and women saying, *Oh, Doctor, I've been meaning to come to see you about my earache/sore throat/ bellyache/piles/ingrowing toenail, and since you're here, you may as well have a look and tell me what you think.* Once a man in a yard where I was leaving my horse got as far as lowering his breeches to show me the boil on his buttock, but I tiptoed away while he was giving me the graphic details and left him standing alone with his bum in the air.

Smiling at the memory, I brought my attention back to the moment.

We had been joined by two more of the Company, the big dark-skinned man who had played Othello and the willowy boy who had been such a beautiful Desdemona. The boy's face was scrubbed clean and the wig of thick, glossy dark brown hair was absent, and but for the long neck and the elegant set of his head, I might not have recognized him. Seeing him close to, I saw that I'd been right about the wide pupils. They were still dilated, and I suspected he'd used belladonna drops.

Celia began to question the two actors about the play, and, unlike Fallon Adderbury – who had slipped away – they were more than happy to discuss it. Judyth and then Jonathan joined the conversation, and it seemed to me the players were gratified by their intelligent and perceptive remarks.

I did not contribute. I was still affected by the mood of the piece; not only its strong sexuality but also the sense of something dangerous in the air. There had been too much talk of magic: Desdemona's father, horrified at the rumour of her marriage, accused the Moor outright of having enchanted her; Othello spoke of conjuration and mighty magic; of drugs and charms, even of witchcraft. And then there was the hand-kerchief, supposedly imbued by its impossibly aged maker with a spell to ensure that the woman who possessed it would always be loved by her husband and keep him faithful to her.

In these times in which we lived, such talk was perilous, even in the context of a play.

More of the Company were shoving their way into the taproom. They brought a bright vibrancy with them, their heads turning this way and that as their restless eyes scanned the crowd, perhaps seeking the group most likely to offer stimulating conversation. They had just come from a glittering, powerful performance and were undoubtedly even more affected by the violence, the powerful emotion, the heartbreak, than their audience. They were, I thought, hardly likely to meekly retire to their beds with a soothing hot drink.

All of them were good-looking, or at least arresting, they held themselves well, and the majority were young. A quartet of older, grey-haired players stood a little apart from the throng, quietly talking, occasionally smiling wryly as if at the excesses and the follies of youth. One of them caught my eye and gave me an ironic smile; I recognized the tall, elegant man with the silver hair and the carefully trimmed beard who had played Desdemona's father, Brabanzio. Beside him, chuckling at some private joke, stood a stout, balding actor who had taken the role of the Duke of Venice.

Then I became aware of someone's eyes on me. Turning, I picked him out. He was older than the others; older, even, than the quartet in the corner, with a lean, intelligent face and a cerebral look about him. He was dressed more like a scholar than an actor, in a long, black, slightly shabby robe, and with a dark cap over his fine, shoulder-length white hair. He had played the minor role of Graziano, kinsman to Desdemona's father, who had popped up in the final, tragic scene to inform the surviving characters – and indeed the audience – that the old man was dead. He had not been particularly impressive, but the role offered scant opportunity for high drama. He smiled and I smiled back, and, taking this as encouragement, he elbowed a way over to me and said, 'I trust you enjoyed the play?'

'Very much,' I replied. 'Full of – er, full of passion.'

'Full of sex,' he corrected with a grin.

And far more dangerous things, I thought.

It was almost as if he read my mind, for abruptly his grin disappeared and he fixed me with an intent look from narrowed dark eyes. 'It was but a play, my friend,' he murmured softly.

'Of course!' I replied, my tone bright.

He regarded me for a moment, then held out a long, slim hand. 'Francis Heron,' he said.

I took his hand. It was cool, the skin dry and fine as silk.

'Gabriel Taverner, physician,' I replied.

'I trust we shall not be requiring your professional services, Doctor,' he said lightly. Then he nodded and slipped away.

I was overcome with the strange sensation that I had just been released from a spell. Shaking it off, I forced myself to glance around the taproom, searching for something – anything – to bring me back to the here and now . . .

And, to my relief, I spotted Celia. Her lovely face was flushed and she had gone over to talk to one of her friends, a young woman by the name of Sidony who, widowed a year ago, had returned to her elderly father's house here in Plymouth. She was a year or two younger than Celia but it always seemed to me that she was barely more than a child, for she was inclined to silliness and undoubtedly her old father spoiled her. He was a merchant who had made himself extremely wealthy, having perceived the Englishman and woman's insatiable taste for Spanish wine and making it his life's work to attempt to satisfy it. His house was elegant and, according to Celia, full of beautiful objects, and he kept a large staff of servants that included a nursemaid and a personal servant for Sidony's three-year-old son, the pair of them so diligent and doting that Sidony was largely able to ignore his presence and, thus absolved of any sort of responsibility, revert to giddy girlishness.

I watched Celia and her friend whispering and giggling, reflecting not for the first time that Sidony did not bring out the best in my sister. I was about to turn away – Celia was her own woman, and it was not for me to choose her friends – when I caught a particular expression flash across her face.

She had been laughing, nudging Sidony and saying something about the plays that the Company were to put on over the next few days and, with a glance at Fallon Adderbury, speculating on who might take the lead roles. And then, just for an instant, her bright eyes narrowed and her smiling mouth straightened, and I recognized her scheming expression. It was the one that had tightened her face when, as children, she was planning how to deflect responsibility for some mischief from herself and onto me, or when she was calculating how to wheedle an extra biscuit from some stern cook who had just said firmly, *No more, Miss Celia.*

Now, wearing her most winning smile, she spoke earnestly to Sidony, but the noise level had suddenly increased – somebody was laughing loudly – and I could not catch the words. And Sidony clapped her hands and, her face bright with excitement, leant close to Celia and said something that made my sister smile in quiet satisfaction.

I did not know why, but I was filled with misgiving.

All at once I was weary of the crowd, of the loud voices, of the spilled beer and the smell of hot bodies, and wanted to be out in the cold night air. Jonathan was beside me, his watchful eyes on Celia, and I surmised from his expression that he was not enjoying this latter part of the evening any more than I was. I looked round for Judyth, caught her eye and mouthed, 'Time to go?' and she nodded.

I leaned close to Jonathan and said, 'I will fetch our horses, if you are ready?' and he too nodded. I stretched over and touched my sister's hand and, spinning round from her lively conversation with Sidony and the youth who had played Desdemona, her face fell. But before she could protest, I said, 'It's getting late, Celia, and I have a busy day tomorrow.'

She drew a swift breath as if about to reply, but then abruptly she closed her mouth. After a short pause she gave a curt nod.

I shouldered a way through the crush, aware of Judyth right behind me, and together we crossed the now-deserted yard. I knew the stable lad to be swift and efficient but I was in a hurry to be gone, and it was only with reluctance that I let him help prepare our horses; and, of course, the task was achieved far more swiftly with two, for he knew his job.

Judyth was already mounted on the chestnut gelding, I was trying to hold an impatient Hal and the stable lad had the reins of the grey mare and the cob when Celia and Jonathan emerged. I couldn't read my sister's expression. I had the impression that she was very excited about something and trying to hide it.

I hoped very much that this something was not the prospect of making a beautiful embroidered handkerchief for the dashingly handsome Fallon Adderbury. But I very much feared it was.

We rode together, and largely in silence, to the spot where Jonathan's path down into Tavy St Luke's branched off to the right, where he bade us a polite farewell. We went on to Rosewyke, and Celia turned her mare onto the track up to the house. I wanted very much to ride on and escort Judyth home to her cottage by the river – above the place where the ferry departs – but she dissuaded me.

'Thank you, Gabriel, but I am well used to riding these paths and tracks alone,' she said firmly, softening the reply with a lovely smile. 'Besides, I have a middle-aged woman coming to term who is in truth a little old for childbearing, even with a fifth baby, and I intend to call on my way home. Farewell' – she turned to smile at Celia – 'and thank you for such an interesting and entertaining outing.'

'Thank you for suggesting it,' Celia replied courteously.

Judyth kicked the chestnut gelding to a trot, then a canter, and she was gone.

Celia and I rode on to Rosewyke.

She was smiling to herself, excitement still brightening her eyes. I wondered if she was mentally going through the contents of the large wooden chests up in her room, making up her mind which particular piece of fine white silk she would select for the wretched handkerchief, which precise shade of bright blood-red thread she would choose for embroidering the strawberries. I wanted to say, *It's not too late to change your mind, Celia.*

I wanted to ask her if she hadn't had enough – far, far more than enough – of dangerously good-looking, beautifully dressed and very slightly androgynous young men. Her husband had been such a one, and nobody with the wits they were born with could say *that* marriage had turned out well . . .

But then I thought how dull her life with me was; how little of novelty and diversion it contained; how each day was much like the one before and the one after. Would it really do any harm for her to involve herself with this company of players for a short while? They'd be gone soon, when all was said and done.

And this thrilling new interest was putting roses in her cheeks so that she looked lovelier than she had in months.

So I kept quiet.

TWO

It was over breakfast the next morning that Celia announced her plan.

'I wish to see the remainder of the plays that the Company will be putting on,' she said, buttering her bread, 'and to avoid the inconvenience of journeying repeatedly to and from Plymouth, Sidony Scrope has very kindly invited me to stay.'

'Sidony *Scrope*?'

Celia made an exclamation of impatience. 'It's her married name. She was Sidony Baynton before.' She frowned severely at me. 'Stop prevaricating, Gabe.'

She was quite right, that was precisely what I was doing. I needed time to understand why my sister's proposal had aroused such a strong reaction in me. But it seemed I was not to be allowed even a few moments.

Leaning forward, Celia said, 'Surely you cannot object? Staying with Sidony and her father in Plymouth will save me many weary journeys to and fro, at a time of the year where the weather is uncertain to say the least, and darkness falls a little earlier each evening. It is a very *kind* invitation' – she laid heavy emphasis on *kind* – 'and it would be churlish to refuse, would it not?'

I gave her a long look. 'Heaven forfend that you should be churlish,' I murmured.

She sat back in her chair, slammed her fists down on the table and cried, 'You're so *bossy*, Gabe!' Before I could protest, she went on, 'You keep me shut up out here in the wilds of the countryside' – we're only a few miles from Plymouth! I wanted to shout – 'and you absolutely *hate* it if I have any fun, and if you had your way I'd stay a withered old widow till the day I die and nobody would ever make me laugh or bring me little gifts or tell me I'm pretty and it's just *so unfair*!'

The last two words burst out of her at such volume that

Sallie came running in from the kitchen to demand what was wrong.

Ignoring her, I got up and went to stand behind Celia's chair, wrapping my arms round her and dropping a kiss on top of her head.

'Celia, please don't,' I said gently. I met Sallie's worried eyes and jerked my head in the direction of the door to the hall. She picked up the message and, not without a backward glance or two, went out again. I put my cheek against Celia's. 'I don't want you to be a withered old widow, I'd like you to have fun every single day of your life, I wouldn't dream of even attempting to keep you shut up here, I'll make you laugh as, indeed, you do me, and I'll try to remember to bring you gifts now and then if that's what is necessary to convince you that I treasure your company, and that your insight and your intelligence have been invaluable to me on many occasions and in many contexts.' I let the words of her outburst play again in my head. 'Oh, and you're not just pretty, you're beautiful.'

She didn't say anything for a few moments. Then – and I could tell from her voice she was trying not to smile – she muttered, 'That's all very well, Gabe, but you're my brother and you don't really count.'

I sat down again, taking her hand across the table and holding it tightly. 'No, I appreciate that,' I said. 'Of course you must go and stay with Sidony, and see as many of the Company's plays as you wish. It is indeed a kind invitation, as well as a practical one.' I paused.

'But,' Celia said.

'Hmm?'

'But,' she repeated. 'You're going to say *but* and come up with some trite objection, aren't you?'

I sighed.

'I'm just a little concerned that these theatre people may not be—'

'*Oh!*' she exclaimed, abruptly removing her hand from mine. She glared at me. 'I *knew* you didn't like him, I could tell from the way you were eyeing him up and down with that disapproving look on your face!' I opened my mouth to speak but she yelled, 'And don't you *dare* say *Didn't like who?* or I'll *punch* you!'

My sister's frequent punches during our childhood had always been uniquely painful. She had a way of extending her bent middle finger so that it dug deep into the muscle she was aiming for, and she had an exceptionally good aim.

'You're right, and I admit I didn't warm to Fallon Adderbury,' I said. 'You were at your vivacious and lovely best, and it was very obvious he found you very attractive, and—'

'Why shouldn't he?' she demanded.

'No reason at all,' I said soothingly. 'What I'm trying to say is that I thought he was rather too eager to accept your offer to make the silk handkerchief, and he appeared to think that his well-practised smile was sufficient payment for what will amount to a costly piece of fabric and many hours' work, which—'

She leaned towards me, her eyes narrowed in triumph.

'What you do not know, Gabriel' – I winced at her use of my full name, which she only employs when she's furious with me and a victory is imminent – 'is that Fallon *is* paying me.' She paused, the sudden silence as dramatic as any on the Company's stage. 'He has promised a pass for the performance today, not only for me but for Sidony too.' She smiled a very smug smile and nodded, as if to say, *So what do you think of that?*

What I thought was, *Fallon Adderbury is shrewder than I thought.*

I took her hand again. 'That's as it should be,' I said after a moment. Even to myself I sounded unbearably prim. There was so much more I wanted to say, but now, apparently accepting my reply as an indication that all my misgivings had been satisfactorily answered, her smile was warm and genuine, and I couldn't bear to see it distorted once more into anger.

I pushed back my chair and stood up, giving her hand a final squeeze before letting it go. 'When do you ride down to Plymouth?' I asked, in as normal a voice as I could manage.

'As soon as I have packed a small bag,' she replied. 'Sidony expects me by midday, and we shall attend the play this afternoon. It's *A Midsummer Night's Dream*, and I really love it – remember, we saw it in London a few years ago?'

Her face was full of excitement. 'Yes,' I replied, returning her smile. 'Bottom the Weaver and the Queen of the Fairies.'

'Everything will be all right, Gabe,' she said gently. 'Don't worry, because I won't enjoy myself nearly as much if I know you aren't easy.'

'I won't,' I assured her. 'Now, go and pack your bag, and if you're quick I'll wait for you. I have to call on a patient near the north gate of the town, so let's ride together.'

Celia prepared to bid farewell to Gabe at the north gate with considerable relief. As they had ridden down from Rosewyke she had kept up a stream of light chatter, and he had responded. The topics had ranged from the likelihood of a hard frost that night via Sallie's painful knee to whether or not Celia should work on a new tapestry to hang over the fireplace, and she didn't think he was any more interested in what they'd talked about than she was. She'd maintained the conversation purely to stop either of them bringing up what was uppermost in their minds, and she knew her brother well enough to recognize that he too was glad to have light matters to discuss.

They drew rein and he turned his big black horse's head to the right, onto the track that led to his elderly patient's dwelling. She turned to him, and his eyes were fixed on her, his expression lowering. But then he too smiled.

'I hope you enjoy the plays,' he said. She knew full well it wasn't what he wanted to say. 'And Sidony's undiluted company,' he added with a grimace.

She grinned. 'Not undiluted! Her father will be at home, and you always say you like old Gilbert Baynton.'

'I do like him,' Gabe agreed. 'He strikes me as a man who had adjusted to his solitude after losing his wife, and indeed had grown to enjoy it in a quiet way, only to have it—' He broke off.

'To have it rudely interrupted when Sidony's husband died, so that now he shares his beautiful house with a restless young woman and a small boy. Yes, Gabe, I know. But it's a big house, and everyone is very careful to tiptoe when they pass his rooms.'

Gabe nudged Hal with his heels. 'I must go. Remember me to Master Baynton.'

'I will.'

He touched his cap to her and rode away.

As she went in through the gate she wondered why, when she'd had to work quite hard to arrange this visit – Sidony was not the brightest of people and it had taken several increasingly heavy hints before she had picked up what Celia wanted and issued the invitation – the greater part of her was wishing she would be riding home this evening to a quiet evening beside the fire with Gabe.

I am unaccustomed to such pleasant diversions, she told herself, carefully guiding the grey mare through the thronged streets. I spend my days in the quiet of the countryside and it is far too long since I have been in the company of people of the town and enjoyed their colour, their sophistication and their wit.

Into her mind came an image of Jonathan Carew, his grave face brightened with sudden laughter at something she had just said. The pleasures of the town faded a little, and she fought down the thought that Sidony couldn't really be called sophisticated, even by her best friends.

With uncomfortable honesty, Celia admitted to herself that she wasn't making the visit because she wanted to spend time with Sidony; on the contrary – the inspection of her conscience sharpened its focus – being with Sidony for the next few days was the price she was paying in order to get what she really desired. And automatically her hand went to rest on the bag she had fastened to her saddle, in which, in addition to her personal necessities, she had carefully folded a square of the most gorgeous pure white Venetian silk, hemmed with tiny, perfectly even stitches and in a corner of which there were three strawberries, so perfectly depicted in the bright blood-red embroidery thread that you felt you could almost bite into them.

She had sat up late into the night working on the handkerchief and finished it in the light of dawn. It was, she considered, one of the loveliest things she had ever made.

She pictured Fallon Adderbury's expression when, with a carefully nonchalant 'I thought this might suffice', she handed it to him. She would give the impression that it was something she'd found in the bottom of a chest; that the giving of it was no great matter.

She felt a sort of shiver deep inside her belly.

She drew a breath, and another, and arranged her face in the blandly cheerful expression suitable for being welcomed into her hostess's house.

The Baynton house was tall and narrow and set in one of the quieter streets leading up from the quayside. Four storeys rose up, each with generous windows made of small panes of glass set in lead, and the upper storeys jutted out over the street below. The frontage was heavily ornamented with timbers, the gables beautifully carved. Everything appeared to be in very good order; this was a wealthy household.

Sidony was looking out for her. Her head and shoulders extended far out of one of the windows in the jetty, so that she was directly above Celia as she dismounted and looked up.

'*Celia!*' Sidony shrieked, leaning even further out and stretching out her arms as if to embrace her guest, making the flesh of her upper breasts swell out over her tight-laced gown.

'Careful!' Celia called back. She glanced to her right, where a pair of men on a wagon loaded with beer barrels had stopped to ogle.

Sidony waved a dismissive hand. 'Oh, don't nag, you're as bad as Father! I always do this, it's quite safe and I am in no danger of falling!'

The risk of Sidony falling was not what Celia feared, and she was quite sure Gilbert Baynton felt the same.

'Someone's coming for your horse,' Sidony continued, 'I sent word when I saw you turn into the street.' She straightened up, clapping her hands like a child promised a toffee apple. 'Isn't it *exciting*? We're going to have such *fun*!'

There was the quiet sound of a male clearing of the throat.

Turning, Celia saw a man in late middle age, sombrely dressed in shades of brown and wearing a heavy sacking apron. 'Shall I take the mare, ma'am?' he suggested. 'Stabling's round the back, and we'll take good care of her.'

'Yes please, and thank you.' Celia handed over the mare's reins. Looking faintly surprised – perhaps his employers didn't often remember to thank him – the old man led the horse away.

The imposing front door was flung open and Sidony stood at the top of the short flight of broad steps. She grabbed Celia in the sort of embrace people more usually exchange after long absence, and Celia felt slightly awkward as she returned it.

'Come in, come in, you must be quite exhausted!' Sidony cried.

'Hardly,' Celia said. 'I have only ridden from Rosewyke, and—'

Sidony was not listening. 'Come up to my floor and we can lay out your gowns – you did bring plenty? Enough to have a different one each day?'

'Well, I—'

'That's Father's study, and his private quarters are beyond' – they were passing the rooms of the first floor – 'and I'm up here!' The beautifully-carved staircase flowed on upwards, but Sidony had turned off and was leading the way through a wide arch to a corridor off which three – no, four – doors opened.

'What is up there?' Celia asked. She could hear voices: two women talking, quite loudly, and someone screaming persistently and deafeningly. The other two seemed to be trying to placate whoever was in such a terrible temper.

'Oh, don't worry about them, that's just Katharine and Maria trying to stop Myles breaking all his toys.'

'Goodness,' Celia said faintly as a bellow like a small and very angry bull blasted down from above. 'How old is he now?'

Sidony shrugged. 'Four, I think. Now this is your room!' She flung open a door, and Celia was dazzled by the autumn sunshine streaming in through the window. 'Isn't it heavenly?'

Celia had to agree that it was. Someone – Katharine or Maria? – had gone to considerable trouble to prepare it. The dark wood framework of the high bed had been polished to a sheen, the linen was crisp and the soft wool blankets looked thick and costly. A large chest stood open, and there was a posy of flowers in a small pot on the little table beside the bed.

Sidony had grabbed Celia's bag and was already unfastening it, her every move swift and abrupt as if she could not contain her impatience. 'Come, let's be quick, I'll help you, and then we shall join Father below and take a light meal with him – he doesn't like me to go out until I have eaten – and then we can go to the *play!*'

Throughout the walk from Gilbert Baynton's house to the Saracen's Head, Celia had been concentrating almost exclusively on keeping calm, on steadying her breathing, on trying to ignore the pounding of her heart. Fortunately Sidony's incessant chatter was light, if not to say frivolous, and Celia was not required to do more than laugh at the silliest of the silly little jokes and say, 'Yes, how I agree!' or 'Really! How utterly wonderful!' when Sidony paused for breath.

They had an escort: Master Baynton must know his daughter rather better than Celia had surmised, for he had commanded a tall and taciturn manservant to accompany his daughter and her friend. The man was middle-aged and nondescript-looking, and went by the name of Phillips. To Sidony's scowling disapproval, Phillips was to attend them until they returned home. 'I'm *really* sorry, Celia,' Sidony had complained, not troubling to lower her voice even though the dignified manservant was standing right behind her, 'it's such a frightful nuisance, but Father won't hear of my going anywhere *near* an inn unescorted, even if it is to see a play! Really, he is so dreadfully *rigid!*' She correctly interpreted the question in Celia's eyes and, leaning close to whisper, added, 'But do not be dismayed, nothing will stop us going into the taproom when the play is over – after all, it is only courteous to congratulate the players!'

It would have taken far more than Phillips's discreet presence to dampen Celia's spirits. It was a very long time since she had felt this breathless excitement at the prospect of imminently seeing a certain person, this tremor right through the middle of the body at the thought of a certain face, a certain pair of knowing eyes and a certain luscious mouth.

Stop it, she commanded.

Sidony was pushing on ahead through the crowds massed round the inn, Phillips right behind her, and Celia followed in their wake. Would Fallon be there looking out for them? Would he escort them into the tavern and up the steps to the balcony? *Oh, please let it happen that way*, she prayed silently. But surely he would be too busy, fully occupied in whatever duties fell to him in this hectic time just before the performance? The beautiful silk handkerchief was tucked into the purse she wore at her belt, and for at least the twentieth time she wondered if she should present it to him before the play – if indeed he materialized to greet her – or whether it would be better to wait until afterwards, when he could give her and her gift his full attention, when he would examine it with an expression of incredulous delight slowly spreading across that handsome face and, looking right into her eyes, murmur, 'But my dear lady, this is *exquisite!*'

'Come *on*, Celia!' Sidony yelled, her loud, raucous voice jerking Celia out of her daydream. 'Where are we meant to go? You said he'd leave passes for us, but this fool's demanding I *pay* him, and—'

The man on duty at the foot of the steps flushed with anger at being called a fool, and Celia leaned towards him and said quietly, 'I am *so* sorry, my companion is a little distressed by the crowds, but that is no excuse for rudeness. I believe she and I are expected? Fallon Adderbury' – she felt the hot blood flood up into her face as she spoke his name – 'said he would arrange for our admittance, and—'

The man's face cleared. 'He did,' he agreed. His right eyelid lowered in a suggestively lewd wink, and instinctively Celia backed away. 'You're the lady what sews?'

She inclined her head in a gesture designed to reprimand him for his coarseness and remind him she was a person of quality. 'I am,' she said coolly.

He grinned. 'Up the steps here, then. Quick now, and find yourselves a space right at the front by the rail. Enjoy the play!'

She drew in her wide skirts and swept past him, hoping to imply by the gesture that she did not want to soil her garments by having them brush against him. For that one dirty little wink had spoiled the moment, with its suggestion that Fallon always gave away a free pass or two to the prettiest women and undoubtedly had a reputation in the Company for extracting payment for his generosity between the tatty and not very clean sheets of whatever poor hovel he was putting up at.

It's not true, she thought. It's just that vulgar man's filthy mind. I must not pay him any attention.

Numbly she followed Sidony along the balcony to a prime spot with a good view of the open yard, where the action would take place. Without really noticing, she took in the scenery: trees cut out of wood, brownish-grey trunks, brilliant green foliage. A backcloth with impossibly blue sky, sunlit hills and a distant view of a city full of white buildings, temples and pillars that suggested it was a long way from Devon. Sidony's voice gabbled on like a lively, bubbling stream. Briefly but intensely, Celia wished the woman was somewhere else.

And then suddenly the play was beginning.

There were Theseus and his fair Hippolyta, four days before their wedding and very clearly hardly able to wait. A compelling, handsome Theseus, despite the silver-white hair . . . Celia recognized the stately and commanding actor who had played Brabanzio yesterday, surprised to find him so attractive today when yesterday he'd just been – well, he'd just been Desdemona's father. And here was the old man Egeus, whose daughter would not have the man he had chosen for her but insisted that she loved another, and – *oh*, and there was Fallon Adderbury in the role of Lysander, tall and fine, his long legs elegant in fine hose and a *very* short doublet, his dark-complexioned face and glossy black hair in sharp contrast to the pure white linen of his shirt, moving with the grace of some great sinuous feline such as those legendary beasts that illustrated Gabe's books of foreign lands and the wonders they contained, and Celia stared down at him and drank him in.

*   *   *

The play flashed by in a rapid succession of frustration at the
lovers' spell-induced confusion, wonder at the fairy king and
queen and their ethereal attendants, and laughter at the
Mechanicals and their play, and the audience showed their
appreciation with full voice. During the scenes in which Fallon
did not appear, Celia found herself waiting impatiently for
his return, especially once he had located her in the crowd
and began sending her the occasional sly look from under his
long dark eyelashes. In the woodland scene where Lysander
and Hermia lay down to sleep – *One turf shall serve as pillow
for us both* – Lysander made his intentions all too clear as
he tried to persuade Hermia to lie closer, and Celia was quite
sure he briefly put his hand on her breast. And later, when
he declared his love for Helena – *Helen, I love thee; by my
life, I do* – the bright grey-blue eyes seemed to burn with
fervour and Celia ached to be standing in Helena's place.

It was only when the play was over, and Puck had delivered
his benign blessing on the audience to a tumult of applause,
that a cool little voice in her head pointed out that Fallon
Adderbury wasn't actually much of an actor . . .

'You said yesterday when you introduced yourself that you
were a player of small and insignificant roles.' Celia tapped
her fingers on Fallon's wrist as if in admonition. 'Your role
today was scarcely that.'

He looked into her eyes and smiled a slow smile. 'My
apologies, my dear lady,' he said. 'I was torn between wanting
to impress you and not wishing to sound like a braggart.' He
paused. 'Did you like the play?'

'Very much. It was beautiful to look at, and there was
such a sense of—' Abruptly she stopped. She had been on the
point of remarking on the strong sexual power that drove
the play on, for, just as in *Othello* yesterday, this version of
A Midsummer Night's Dream shouted out loud and clear that
it was all about people desperately wanting to bed each
other, and the sooner the better. 'Er, the emphasis on magic
and the unearthly qualities of the fairies made such a good
contrast with the bumbling Mechanicals, and I *loved* Bottom's
ass's head!'

Fallon gave her a knowing look, and she was quite sure he knew exactly what she had held back from saying. Before he could comment, hurriedly she reached inside her purse and held out the neatly folded and carefully wrapped handkerchief. 'This is for you. For the next time you put on *Othello*,' she added hastily.

He opened the package and unfolded the square of soft, gleaming silk. He turned it this way and that, peering at the tiny hem stitches, running a delicate finger over the strawberries. He looked up and met her eyes. 'It is a work of art,' he said very softly. 'And how fitting, that something so exquisite should come out of the hands of so beautiful a seamstress.'

Exquisite! she cried silently. *He said exquisite, just as I knew he would!*

Fallon was still looking at her. Very gently he reached out and put his fingers on her cheek in a touch as light as a cobweb. She trembled. His eyes seemed to burn into hers, and she had the strong sense that he was waiting for her to say something.

She thought she might know what it was.

Almost imperceptibly he nodded, as if encouraging her to go on.

'I have a store of silk, of ribbons, of brocade and lace,' she whispered. He leaned closer to hear her, and her lips brushed against his smooth hair. 'If there should be other items of costume with which I could help, I would be happy to?'

She noticed she had turned the offer into a question.

He held his chin in his hand, his head on one side. And after an interminable pause, he said, 'I cannot think of anything I should like more.'

THREE

I spent some time with my elderly patient. He lived in a very pretty cottage on the fringes of the town, and the garden still showed clear signs of his long years of tending it after he had retired from the sea. His wife had died long before I got to know him and now he was cared for by his daughter, who with her husband and two children had moved in specifically for that purpose. And, as I had perceived the first time I visited the house, because the two of them, father and daughter, loved each other very deeply and she couldn't have borne to be anywhere else.

He was dying. He knew it as well as I did, and nowadays my visits were more to sit by his saggy old chair set in the window and talk to him than for any medical treatment. His lungs were rotting away, and all I or his daughter could do was alleviate the symptoms.

He was anxious this morning.

'I'm worried about Beth,' he said as soon as I sat down. There was no danger of his daughter overhearing; we could both see her at the end of the garden draping wet washing over the lavender bushes.

'Is she unwell?' I asked.

'No, no.' He sighed. 'It's just—' He didn't seem able to go on.

It's just that you will leave her soon, I thought, my heart hurting, *and you are anxious about how her life will be without you.*

Beth's husband wasn't a bad man; it was simply that he was his first and largely his sole concern. As long as he was comfortable in mind and body, then the world was a good place. When he was ailing – and I had rarely met anyone who could conjure up such a variety of conditions, each one of them apparently the direst threat to his health, if not his life – then Beth had to put up with his complaints, his dozens of little worries, his petulance and his total disregard for anyone else, including her. The two children, a boy and a girl, weren't bad but they were young, with the self-absorption that typically goes with it.

Her refuge was her father. Many times I had observed a look they exchanged when Beth's husband was being particularly tiresome or the children refused to stop their bickering: it spoke of shared humour and an understanding so profound that they had no need of words. She relied on him, it was clear, and for his part, I had tended him once when he was lost deep in delirium, and his sole concern had been her. 'I must find my daughter!' he kept saying as I tried to make him return to bed and lie down. 'She is here somewhere, *I have to find her!*'

They had the great gift of being in total sympathy, and I fully understood the old man's anxiety.

I thought for a few moments.

'She will miss you very much, Enos,' I said eventually. 'They all will, although Alard and the children do not know it yet.'

All too frequently I come across households where the next generation barely manage to disguise their impatience for the old father or mother to die so that they can clear away their bed and belongings and expand into the house that they have just inherited, ruthlessly rearranging it without a backward glance.

This was not one of them. Enos had his son-in-law and grandchildren's respect, and in my view they depended on his quiet, serene presence more than they knew.

He was looking at me, his expression tense.

Some patients in his position want a priest, but Enos had chosen to speak to his physician. It wasn't up to a man of my calling to reassure him about God's promise of life eternal and assure him that he and his beloved daughter would be together again in paradise one day.

'You will still be with her,' I said. 'You will be here.' Leaning forward, I touched him gently over his heart, and then on the forehead. 'She is your child, your flesh and blood, and she has your strength and certainty. You will be gone in body, but your spirit will remain with her as long as she lives. She will be all right, Enos.'

He swallowed once or twice, and his eyes were wet with tears. Then he said, 'Thank you, Doctor T.' He sat up a little straighter, cleared his throat and then said in almost his normal voice, 'Going to rain later, d'you reckon?'

I had two other errands in the town – the apothecary had an order waiting for me to collect, and a very large woman recovering from the effects of a heavy fall needed to have her dressings changed – but neither took much time. I could go back to Rosewyke, and spent a diligent afternoon making up my notes. I could call on Jonathan Carew, ask him if he intended to go to another play. Neither idea appealed. I was too restless to sit at my desk with my books, and, most unusually, I wasn't keen to see Jonathan.

I made myself admit the reason: it was because I had noticed the way he looked at Celia when he thought himself unobserved, and my sister was even now giggling and plotting with her silly friend Sidony over how to make herself as attractive as she could for chasing after Fallon Adderbury.

Angry suddenly – with Celia, but much more with myself, for I was being severe and judgemental and also, undoubtedly, very unfair – I turned Hal towards the quayside and set off to find myself a mug of good ale and a slice of pie for a much belated midday meal.

The day's performance was well into its stride as I passed the Saracen's Head afterwards on my way to collect my horse. I had run into an old shipmate in the tavern and time had passed on wings, as it usually does once two former colleagues get talking. Attracted by the laughter coming from the inn yard, I went over and stood on tiptoe to peer over the wall. From what I recalled of the play, it seemed it was in fact approaching the conclusion. I spotted Celia leaning on the balcony rail, her face alive with merriment, and Sidony beside her. Letting my eyes roam on round the audience, I saw my friend Theophilus Davey and his comely wife Elaine, their three children crammed into a narrow space on the bench between them. They too seemed to be enjoying the play, although I thought Theo had an oddly watchful look . . .

I decided to wait and talk to him. I'd have to be careful not to let my sister see me, for if she thought I was keeping an eye on her in case she threw herself bodily at Fallon Adderbury and decided to join the Company and run off with him, I'd suffer from the sharpest edge of her sarcastic tongue for the next month or more.

I went to stand by the wide arch through which horses, carts and people entered and left the inn yard. The laughter ceased and in the sudden quiet I heard Puck's clear tones speaking the final words. There was a great burst of applause and some cheers, and presently the audience began to emerge. I peered down the passage into the yard, but I didn't see either Celia or Sidony: would they nerve themselves to go into the taproom? It was unlikely behaviour, for Celia anyway, but that was where we had all met the members of the Company yesterday, and I was quite sure her aim today was to see Fallon Adderbury again. But then – and I realized I should have thought of this before – Gilbert Baynton was not a man to permit his daughter to attend a performance in an inn yard accompanied only by another young woman, even if they were both widows, and he would undoubtedly have provided a male escort.

All the same . . .

I gritted my teeth and waited for Theo.

I heard his family approaching before I saw them: from the midst of a knot of people I heard his elder son Carolus's delighted voice crying with delight, 'Bottom! That man was called *Bottom*!' His sister Isabelle and the little brother Benjamin joined in the chorus, all three yelling, '*BOTTOM!*' at the top of their voices, and I had a moment's pity for Elaine and Theo, having to extinguish this joyful vulgarity at some point between now and bedtime.

I fell into step beside Elaine and said to the children, 'So you enjoyed the play, then?'

Elaine turned to me, a happy smile on her lovely face. 'Oh, yes! Such exuberance! Did you see it? What did you think?'

'No, I wasn't in the audience. I went to *Othello* yesterday,

though.' I wasn't quite sure why I told her that, unless it was
to demonstrate that I wasn't totally without artistic sensibility.

She nodded politely, but I could tell she was trying to keep
a close eye on the children and it wasn't really the time for
polite conversation, so I moved to walk beside Theo and
said, 'Good to see you enjoying an afternoon's entertainment,
Master Coroner.'

He spun round, and I saw from his face that he'd had no
idea I was there until I addressed him. 'Gabe! What are you
doing here? Were you at the play?'

'No,' I said for the second time.

He was frowning, brows drawn tight above his bright blue
eyes, and I had the sense that something far beyond my
failure to appreciate comic drama was bothering him. He put
out a hand and grabbed my sleeve. 'Will you come back with
me? I have to help Elaine get the children home – they're
all wildly over-excited and I truly think a sheep dog would
be a good idea – but I need to speak to you.'

'Of course,' I said.

We were out in the street now, in a crush of cheerful people,
not a few of them quite well gone in alcohol; I had noticed
the previous day that the Saracen's Head did a grand trade in
jugs of ale during the performance as well as after it.

I glanced back just once – my sister was undoubtedly in
the tavern, even now perhaps resuming her flirtation with a
man I mistrusted so profoundly that it made my fists curl
with the urge to punch him – but there was absolutely nothing
I could do about it.

So I fetched my horse and walked home with Theo, his
wife and children, and accepted his invitation to go and
wait in his office while he herded his children upstairs to
the family's private quarters.

He did not keep me waiting long.

He emerged into the room like a clap of thunder, swung
round his wide desk, as usual littered with documents, and
flung himself into his chair.

'I looked over the wall and saw you in the audience,' I said.
'Everyone around you was laughing with varying degrees of

enthusiasm, but you were looking over your shoulder and not laughing at all. What is it?'

He sighed, then rubbed his hands over his face. Meeting my eyes, he said, 'I expect I have an overly suspicious mind, but . . .' He stopped.

'Tell me what happened,' I said firmly. Something had occurred which disturbed him sufficiently to ask me to come here and talk to him, and if one of us didn't initiate a frank discussion I would be there all night.

'We were well into the play when I noticed Benjamin wriggling and I knew he needed a piss – excitement affects him that way.'

'In common with most children of his age, I dare say,' I put in.

'I was going to take him to the privy out behind the stables but it was rank, you could smell it from ten paces away. So we went out into the street and doubled back into that dark little alley that runs behind the inn, and someone was talking – well, whispering, but in that audible sort of hiss that implies intense anger. Then someone else replied, and he too sounded furious, and the first man interrupted and the argument rapidly grew more intense. I looked around but I couldn't see anybody, although the alley runs right under the corridor where the inn's guest accommodation is, such as it is, and I thought the voices probably came from there.'

'You overheard two people having an argument,' I said. 'Not an unusual occurrence, and many people in the Saracen's Head have undoubtedly been drinking all afternoon.'

'Yes, I'm sure. It wasn't the fact of two men arguing, it was what they were arguing about,' Theo said darkly.

I felt a shiver of apprehension. 'Which was?'

He frowned again, then shook his head. 'That's the trouble – I can't be sure.'

'Tell me what you heard,' I suggested. 'Word for word. Then we will see if I react in the same way that you did.'

He nodded. 'Yes, that's sensible.' He closed his eyes and I thought he was probably putting himself back in that dark little alley, the better to remember. 'The first man – he sounded as if he was quite old – said, "Do not threaten me, for I will not tell you what you so desperately want to know until I am ready," and the second, younger man said in a sort of suppressed shout, "Until you feel safe, you mean, and you are so solicitous of yourself that I shall wait until hell ices over before that happens!" Then the older man muttered something about having already done his companion a great service by getting him and the other players out of London, and the younger man said, "Aye, that's true, and the rampant pestilence in the city means that nobody questions our flight." They both lowered their voices to a mutter for a few moments, and then the younger man said in an aggressive and deeply unpleasant tone, "There are other reasons than the plague for a man to flee the capital," and the old man replied with a sort of sob in his voice, "I know it only too well! I fear for my life, Daniel, and the death that stalks me is a particularly awful and long-drawn-out one that haunts me by night and day! Do you wonder that I am so careful, damn you?"' Theo stopped, opening his eyes wide at the memory what he had heard. 'Well?' he prompted. 'What do *you* think?'

But something else was troubling me. 'Did your little son hear all this too?' I asked.

'No, thank God, for he had finished his business and was already back at the entrance to the alley, telling me to hurry up because we were missing the funny bits.' Looking a little sheepish, he muttered, 'Thought I'd take the chance to empty my bladder too while I was there. That ale runs through you like an overflowing pump.'

'Very wise,' I murmured. Then: 'They call this the Plague Tour, you know; the Company, I mean. The younger man seemed to be saying that the pestilence provided an excuse for them – the two of them, or perhaps the whole Company – to flee the city. And whatever the real reason for their flight might be, this secret they carry with them – whatever it is the older man won't reveal to the younger one till he feels it's safe to do so – is a deadly one.'

Theo looked at me intently. 'One that carries the threat of a particularly awful and long-drawn-out death,' he said very softly. 'I do not think he meant death from the plague.'

'Nor do I,' I agreed.

We went on looking at each other. I had the sense – and I'm sure Theo did too – that a spectral figure had crept into the room; one that watched us with cold judgemental eyes and listened with fearsome intensity to every word we spoke and everything we tried to hold back.

Eventually Theo said, 'Death by execution, I judge.'

Slowly I nodded. It was what I too had been thinking.

The late Queen's operatives had refined their methods of prolonging agonizing death. Hanging, drawing and quartering usually comprised the final act, but before that a condemned man – or woman – would have endured long and desperate hours, days, weeks and sometimes months of torture. At times Elizabeth's fury with a man who had plotted against her rose to ungovernable heights, it was said, and she would rail at her torturers and executioners, screaming that surely there was more they could do, some new variation they could try. On one unforgettable day, the endless spectacle of bloody and ghastly deaths paraded before the public on Tower Hill had turned even the hardened stomachs of Londoners, many of whom had walked away, sickened.

Another monarch sat on England's throne now. So far King James had not shown signs of his predecessor's appetite for brutally vicious revenge, for blood, guts, mangled bodies and the spectacle of a man watching his entrails and genitals burned before him. But it was early days yet.

Theo looked sick, as if he too was seeing the images that raced through my mind.

'So, Gabe, what do you make of this?' he asked.

'Had I been in that alley with you and your boy, my ears too would have pricked up at that whispered conversation,' I said.

'But what does it *mean*?' he insisted.

My instinct was to yell, *How should I know? I'm a country physician, not a city courtier on the run from a plague-ridden city and bearing a terrible secret!* But I held back. Theo was my friend, and he was absolutely right to be worried.

'It seems certain that these men you heard belong to the Company,' I said eventually. 'The reference to the other players would appear to confirm it. So we may conclude, I think, that

among their number is someone who is using the Plague Tour
for his own ends. Perhaps this man is not a regular member
of the Company?' I shook my head violently, trying to make
sense of the vague mist of suspicion. And to dislodge the fear,
for I could not stop seeing those terrible images . . .

'What should we do?' Theo demanded.

'What *can* we do?' I replied sharply. 'Nothing but watch
and wait.'

'Wait for what? Watch for whom?'

'Theo, I have no more idea than you!' I said.

He emitted an expression of impatience. 'Let us hope that
this old man keeps his blasted secret until the Company have
moved on,' he said crossly, 'when whatever it leads to is no
longer my problem.'

'Amen to that,' I muttered.

I stood up, and Theo rose as well to see me out. We went
into his yard and I took Hal's reins from his stable boy. Theo
came out on the road with me.

'I will keep my eyes and ears open,' he said quietly. 'I
have contacts in most of the inns in the town, and Jarman
Hodge has more and better ones. We shall see what can be
uncovered.'

'Good. Please inform me of anything that emerges.'

'Of course. Good evening to you, Gabe.'

I touched my cap and put my heels to Hal's sides.

As I rode home I could not stop thinking about a company
of London players who had come here to my town, one of
them in possession of a frightening secret.

And about the fact that my beloved sister appeared to have
temporarily lost her normally intelligent and sensible head
to a very handsome, flamboyant and no doubt unreliable, ruthless and perhaps very dangerous stranger who happened to be
a member of that company.

Celia couldn't remember when she had last had such a
wonderful, thrilling evening. Everywhere she looked she saw
lively, handsome, talkative, sophisticated people who threw
witty, frequently barbed remarks at each other, so swiftly that

they might have been glittering juggler's balls. On this her second evening with the Company she was learning to identify who had played which role in *Othello* and *A Midsummer Night's Dream* – or *the Dream*, as she was rapidly learning to call it – and usually in both. Her sharp eyes and quick mind were putting names to the actors: the beautiful boy who had played Desdemona and Titania was Raphe Wymer, the handsome, silver-haired man who had played Theseus was Thomas Lightbodie – they all seemed rather in awe of him – and the dignified, elderly man who was the oldest of the Company and had played Desdemona's father's relation and one of the Rude Mechanicals was Francis Heron, the dark-complexioned Othello who today had portrayed the King of the Fairies was Harry Perrot. Then there was Oliver, Verney, Barnaby, Gerard . . . oh, and a red-haired man with dancing brown eyes and the most wicked grin was called Quentyn Barre and today he had been a scintillating, magical, quicksilver Puck. It had fascinated Celia that none of these qualities had been evident the day before, when he had taken the role of Cassio, and – so very glad she hadn't voiced this thought aloud to Fallon or anybody else, come to that – she realized, in a moment akin to scales dropping from before the eyes, that this was what actors *did* . . .

And beneath all the delight and the sheer *fun* of it, there was the knowledge that Fallon Adderbury had accepted her offer to make some more contributions to the Company's collection of costumes and properties. Well, he had done much more than accept it; he had put his fingers to her cheek in the softest of touches, stared deep into her eyes and said, *I cannot think of anything I should like more.*

Celia caught her breath, lost for a moment in a happy vision of herself in some hectic and busy room where the contents of huge wicker baskets of brilliant garments and extraordinary accessories were all bundled together and she sat perched amid the chaos, needle and thread in hand, pincushion on her wrist, tiny, delicate scissors hanging on a cord from her belt and her new friends queuing up and shoving each other aside to say, 'Celia, I am sure you can arrange this

collar better!' and, 'I hate this shade of green, is there time
before tomorrow's performance for you to contrive something
more becoming for me?'

She was standing in a corner of the taproom. Fallon was
some distance away, separated from her by quite a crowd of
people and deep in conversation with Quentyn Barre. He raised
his head, caught her eye and mouthed, *Sorry, I will be back
as soon as I can!*, making a comically exaggerated face of
distress.

She grinned back and mouthed, *I'm quite all right!*

She was. After the huge excitement of talking to so many
new people, one after another with no pause, it was rather
nice now to have a short pause so that she could catch up
with herself. She looked around for Sidony, but before she
could spot her she heard her, as Sidony's shrill bray of laughter
rang out over the throng and she screeched at the red-haired
man, '*Oooh*, what an impudent fellow, to ask such a question!
I'm not going to tell you, you cheeky jester, and I most
assuredly will not grant you what you ask!'

Celia smiled to herself. Sidony seemed to have had one
or two more mugs of ale than was wise. Phillips, standing
glowering behind her like a disapproving shadow, was looking
more and more miserable.

She let her eyes run on round the big room. She was just
wondering if anyone was going to arrange anything to eat or
if they'd all go on drinking till they fell over, when she heard
a very strange sound from somewhere near at hand.

It sounded like . . . yes, it sounded like a fist punching flesh.

It was followed by another identical sound and a cry, so
swiftly muffled that it had probably only been Celia, standing
so close, who had heard and correctly identified it. There was
a sob, and the slap of a hand over a mouth.

'Hush your noise or you'll get more of the same!' a harsh
male voice hissed. 'You'll forget you saw me, you won't
mention me to a soul, else I'll take a whip to you and let you
know what pain really feels like!'

Distressed, angry – for she loathed anything that suggested
bullying – Celia looked around, trying to see where the sounds
had come from. Everyone in her corner of the taproom looked

cheerful and happy, and although there was quite a lot of rail-
lery and some good-natured pushing and shoving, it really
didn't seem as if anybody was being menaced and assaulted.
Noticing a low archway that was hidden in the dark beneath
a flight of wooden steps, she edged towards it and peered
through. There was a short passage, then another archway that
seemed to open onto a cramped little scullery where there was
a big barrel of water and rinsed mugs and jugs set on a shelf
to dry.

A young man lay hunched on the dirty stone flags of the
passage. His bright hose and the hem of his lovely velvet
doublet were soaking up the puddle of spilt beer, as was the
shoulder-length silky blond hair. His body was curled in on
itself and one arm was clutching at his belly, as if it pained
him. His chin was resting on his chest, and his other hand
cradled his mouth and jaw. Blood was running quite fast
through his thin, pale fingers.

With a soft exclamation of distress, Celia hurried over to
him and crouched beside him. 'Oh, you are hurt!' she said.
'What has happened? Who did this?'

The youth shook his head violently and said something
that could have been 'Tripped,' but the word was muffled and
indistinct.

He's afraid, Celia thought. He cannot say who hit him and
reduced him to this, because he's scared they'll hurt him more.

She put her arm round his shoulders and very gently took
his hand away from his lower face. Turning him slightly so
that she could see what had been done to him, she saw blood
flooding out of a mashed nose and – as if this was not enough
– a dislocated jaw.

Suppressing her dismay – she'd always observed that Gabe
was calm in the face of dramatic injuries – she said in what
she hoped was close to her normal voice, 'Sit very still, and
I shall fetch a cloth and cold water to bathe your nose.' His
eyes – dark brown and huge with fear – stared up at her and
she nerved herself to tell him the rest. 'I'm afraid your jaw
may be dislocated, but I shall find someone who will be able
to help and you will be mended in no time!'

She got up and he shot out a hand as if to detain her. She

saw tears in his eyes, and realized that he was only a boy. 'I
will not be long,' she assured him. Then she hurried out into
the taproom.

The bowl of water and the cloth were swiftly acquired, and
the man skilled in reducing dislocations did not take much
longer. Plymouth was a port, after all, and the Saracen's Head
not far from the quayside, and there were two ship's surgeons
in the taproom enjoying a quiet pint. One of them agreed to
attend the boy, and he put back the jaw with a brutality whose
only virtue was its speed.

Wanting to give his fat backside a vicious kick as he
crouched over his patient, Celia wished with all her heart
that this had happened the previous day, and that Gabe had
been here. The reduction would probably have hurt nearly
as much – Gabe had told her that putting back dislocations
was always painful – but he would have treated the boy with
kindness.

'I won't charge you,' the fat ship's surgeon said, straightening up and giving Celia a lascivious look, 'but you can fill
up my mug and give me a kiss.'

'I shall do neither,' Celia said frostily. Reaching in the
little purse at her waist, she extracted a couple of coins. The
surgeon glanced down at them and grinned. Then he touched
his forelock and muscled his way back into the taproom.

Celia bent over the boy.

'How do you feel?' she asked. She hoped he felt better
than he looked, for his nose was a fat red bulb and his jaw
looked puffy and swollen.

He struggled to his feet and gave her a graceful bow. 'Oliver
Dauncey,' he murmured. 'Better, my lady, thanks to you,' he
added, and now his diction was not only perfectly clear but
rather beautiful, and she guessed he was one of the players.

'I did little,' she replied. 'But now, if I may, I will give you
some advice?'

'Of course!' He tried to smile, instantly wincing.

'My brother is a doctor, so I am not without experience,'
she said, 'and he would advise going straight to bed and trying
to sleep. Oh, and wring out that piece of cloth in cold water

again and keep it pressed to your face, for it will help the swellings to subside.'

He frowned briefly, his expression anxious. 'I will.'

'What is it?' she asked.

'A swollen face will bring me more trouble,' he muttered, 'for the day after tomorrow we present *Romeo and Juliet*.'

'Oh, dear,' she said, understanding. 'And you're playing Juliet?'

He nodded. 'I am. And Quentyn's my Romeo, and he won't—' Abruptly he stopped.

She waited, but he didn't continue. 'Go and rest,' she advised. 'Sleep. Bathe your face.'

He bowed again, then spun round in a dancing movement and hurried away.

Celia stared after him. She could not forget that harsh, hissing voice. Someone had threatened the boy, someone had bullied him into doing what they wanted, and to force the message home they had driven a fist into his belly and hit him so hard that his nose had squashed and his jaw had been driven out of its socket.

She was still anxious and troubled when Fallon Adderbury returned to seek her out. Although her heart rose at the sight of his handsome, smiling face, and it would undoubtedly have been a comfort to tell him what had just happened, nevertheless when he said, 'You look glum! What is wrong?' she smiled, gave a little laugh and said brightly, 'Nothing!'

FOUR

I had planned to work at home all the next morning. After an early breakfast I shut myself away behind the kitchen and devoted an hour and more to making up some of the more potent of the potions and powders I habitually use, replenishing wherever my supply was running short. I told Sallie what I would be doing and warned her to keep away, and she gave a *humph!* of impatience and said if I thought she had the least inclination to come anywhere near the back scullery when I was insisting on poking and prodding and meddling about with substances that could kill a man stone dead soon as look at him, then I'd another think coming.

'Of course I don't think you'd interrupt my work, Sallie,' I said, having extracted her meaning from the flow of words. 'You have been a doctor's housekeeper for several years now and you have learned much concerning the sometimes perilous nature of potions and remedies. Besides which,' I added hastily, noticing that she was looking affronted at the suggestion that she only learned about potions after she came to my household, 'you have always had more than the usual measure of good common sense!'

She went *humph!* again, and shot me a sharp look, but I reckoned I'd got away with it.

When I was done, and a neat little row of small glass bottles and tiny phials filled the high shelf up in my study, I washed my hands very thoroughly, rolled down my sleeves and put on my doublet, then sat down at my desk to make up my inventory. It makes sense, I always believe, to maintain an accurate record of my stock of medicines, especially those where a few drops too many can prove fatal. Like the preparation of the substances itself, this too required total concentration. Besides, with Celia's bright presence absent from home, it was good to have a task that occupied my full attention.

I had just closed my ledger and had stood up to put it away in its place when I heard the sound of a fast-ridden horse. There was a scurry of hooves and jingle of harness as it was drawn sharply to a halt, and then the pounding of a fist on the heavy door. Sallie's footsteps hurried across the hall and I heard the rapid exchange of words. I was already out of my study and running down the stairs, and as I heard Sallie say, 'Wait, I will fetch him,' I leapt the last few steps and strode to the open door.

A man not long out of boyhood stood there, cap in his hands, face taut with worry.

'What is it?' I demanded.

'It's the Mistress. She's had her baby but it's slow to breathe and the midwife cannot lay it aside for so much as an instant. But the Mistress, she's bleeding bad and midwife says you're to come.'

I grabbed my bag and flew out of the door, pushing the youth before me. Sallie had already raced round to the yard, and Samuel and Tock were both busy with Hal, their four hands working so efficiently together that my horse was ready even as I ran towards them. I swung up into the saddle and clattered out of the yard behind the young man.

'Is it far?' I yelled.

'Hooper's Oak,' he yelled back, naming a smallholding some three or four miles away.

My mind buzzed with more questions. Is there no grand-mother or older servant who can help stem the blood? Is it from a tear or something more grave, such as a prolapse? If it is a complicated matter, how shall I manage to acquit myself satisfactorily under the critical eyes of a woman skilled in such matters? What is the midwife's name?

Is she Judyth Penwarden?

I didn't ask any of my questions. I would find out the answers soon enough.

It was a tear, but a bad one. There was no one present other than the young father – white with horror at the blood issuing out of his even younger wife and at his inability to do anything about it – and the midwife was indeed Judyth.

She had a small, limp, pale body in her arms, its lips blueish, no sound emanating from it. She looked up just once, quickly, and said, 'Thank you for coming so quickly. I believe it is a matter of pressure and then sutures, but I cannot stop what I am doing and you were nearest.'

Then she bent her dark head over the naked infant and resumed her efforts to make it take its first breath.

The silence seemed to pulsate through the small, dark, foetid room. The husband had slumped down on the doorstep, one knuckle pressed between his teeth, his eyes wide and unblinking. The lad who had ridden to fetch me had disappeared. I didn't blame him.

The mother was barely conscious, lying splayed across the blood-soaked bed almost as limp as her newborn child. I made use of the bowl of hot water on the floor beside her, alternately bathing away the blood and putting pressure on the tear, which was long and jagged, almost as if the emerging infant's finger or nail had caught in the tender flesh. Presently I realized, to my great relief, that the blood was all emanating from this tear; the poor woman was not suffering a postpartum haemor-rhage. The flow began to slow down, and I reached in my bag for the suturing needle and thread. This was a procedure I had only carried out once before, and for a moment I was very conscious of Judyth's presence, aware how very much better a job she would do. But a stitch was a stitch, and this young woman was in need.

I worked swiftly, careful to keep the line of stitches neat and regular, the flesh as flat as possible. She was far gone in distress and pain, and barely moved, and I was finished in short time. I wrapped her in the soiled bedding, then gently rolled her to the far side of the big bed, spreading out fresh sheets on the straw-filled mattress. I plumped the pillows and, removing her bloody wrappings, helped her into a clean nightgown and laid her down once more, drawing up the sheet and blankets to keep her warm. I was brushing her sweaty hair off her forehead when abruptly she grabbed hold of my wrist, her fingers like an iron clamp.

'You are in pain?' I asked anxiously.

'*Ssssh!*' she hissed. Her face was alight.

And I became aware that a soft little sound I'd been aware of right on the edge of hearing for the last few minutes was all at once growing a lot louder. Spinning round, I saw Judyth, a broad smile on her lovely lips, the rapidly reddening infant now wriggling in her arms, its mouth wide open as it let loose its first full-lunged scream.

'What did you do?' I asked her as, some time later, we rode away. The husband had recovered his usual confidence, not to say bumptiousness, as soon as we all knew his little son was no longer in imminent peril, and had insisted on opening what proved to be a singularly potent bottle of ale to wet the child's head. Judyth and I had taken a polite glass, but after only a few sips I'd felt my head spinning – it was a long time since breakfast – and I'd surreptitiously put it down on the floor.

'The usual,' Judyth replied, answering my question. 'The birth was rapid and the child's mouth and throat were both blocked and, I believe, had in addition been crushed during delivery by its fist, tucked right in under the chin. I cleared all that could be cleared, then breathed some very small and gentle breaths into its mouth, and quite soon it – he, I should say – understood what was needed and took over.' She paused. 'You did a good job,' she said. 'A tidy repair is important for a woman.'

I decided to leave that comment unremarked upon. We were two professionals riding away from a successful case, I knew that well enough, but she was also the woman to whom I was very strongly attracted.

We had reached the place where our paths diverged. She looked at me. 'Well?'

I smiled sheepishly. 'Well what?'

Her eyes were full of laughter. 'When shall we see each other next? I would like very much to suggest you ride home with me and I make dinner for us both, but I have three other women to visit today and I do not have the time.'

'I would have liked that too,' I said quietly. 'Very much.' I raked through my mind for some attractive suggestion of my own, for now that she had raised the possibility of our imminently spending time together, I could not just let it lie. An idea occurred to me, and although it wasn't what I really wanted (for I was desperate to be alone with her) it was the best I could come up with. 'Er – I believe the players are to perform *Romeo and Juliet* tomorrow,' I blurted out. 'Shall we go together, you and I? If you can spare the time, of course, and you don't consider a tragic romance unsuitable entertainment?'

Her face fell. 'Oh, is it a tragedy? I had no idea, and now the ending won't be a surprise.'

'Judyth, I am so sorry!' I exclaimed, cursing my gaucheness. 'I've spoiled it for you, and I truly didn't mean to.'

But she was laughing. 'Of course I knew, Gabe,' she said. Her silvery eyes on mine, she added gently. 'You haven't spoiled anything, and I'd love to go with you.'

She raised her hand and waved, then she was gone.

I rode back to Rosewyke singing.

Celia's day began far too early and rather acrimoniously. She was violently awoken by Sidony's son Myles screaming with the full force of his lungs apparently from somewhere about a foot away, and she shot up in bed with her heart thumping in anxiety.

Myles was not in fact in her bedchamber but out in the passage and the far side of a closed door. His furious yells were joined by other voices, one of them trying to mollify him (the nursemaid, presumably) and the other shouting at him with such wild fury that it only served to make him scream the louder (and that voice was unmistakably Sidony's).

A ewer of hot water had been left for Celia, and now, since the possibilities of having another brief doze until it was fully light seemed slight, she thought she might as well get up. She washed her face and hands, dressed, then used the remainder of the water and the wash cloth to sponge the hem of the gown she had worn yesterday, still damp with spilled ale from where she had crouched beside the wounded boy.

Fortunately the gown was a darkish shade of gold-tinged brown – 'Ale coloured,' Celia murmured aloud – and she was more concerned to wash out the smell than any marks. The damage repaired, she finished dressing and perched down before a mirror with a very beautiful frame of silver to arrange her hair.

The mirror reminded her of the one the Company used. Twice now: in Desdemona's chamber, with her ghostly image seeming to reach out to her murderous husband even as he leaned yearningly towards it searching for her, and yesterday in Titania's bower, where its highly decorated frame had been concealed by a garland of foliage, berries and flowers made from muslin.

Celia was not at all sure she liked that mirror. There was definitely something disturbing about the way it seemed to reflect objects and people that it should not have been able to . . . Desdemona, and then yesterday poor Bottom in his ass's head.

'Do not be fanciful,' she told her reflection. 'Have you not enough to overcome with this child who will not be comforted?'

At that moment Myles's screams escalated to a higher pitch and an even greater volume, and with a quiet moan Celia put her hands over her ears. Unfortunately Sidony burst into the room just as she did so.

'Oh, that *wretched* boy, I shall have to—' Sidony began. Then she saw Celia, hastily dropping her hands into her lap, and her red, angry face froze into quite a different expression. 'I am sorry if the noise is too much for you,' she said with stiff dislike. Then, cruelty briefly flashing in her eyes, she added with a sugary smile, 'Of course, a childless woman such as you could not possibly be accustomed to the habits of small boys.' Then she spun round and lurched out, slamming the door behind her.

Torn between hurt and fury, Celia sat perfectly still waiting for her heart to slow down. Then she got up, went over to open the door and for a few moments stood listening. Myles was still crying, and Sidony was now screeching that life was not *fair*, why should she be burdened like this and why didn't somebody *do* something? Other women's voices were trying to soothe her, offering suggestions, but it was clear she wasn't in the mood to be pacified.

Noticing that there was no noise at all, raised voices, screaming or otherwise, from downstairs, Celia made a graceful descent and went across the hall to where a table was laid ready for breakfast. As if he had been waiting for her – perhaps he had – Gilbert Baynton appeared from a doorway on the far side and said courteously, 'Breakfast is ready, if you would like to join me?'

'I would love to, thank you,' Celia replied, smiling prettily.

Gilbert Baynton rang a small brass bell, and almost immediately maids and servants began to appear with loaded trays. 'And now,' Master Baynton said as dish after dish was put on the table, 'what would you like?'

Celia and her host had an uninterrupted breakfast; other than the occasional slammed door and scream of fury, they might have been alone in the tall, narrow house. They talked easily together on subjects ranging from the Company and the plays they were performing and the poor state of the Plymouth streets to how 'the Doctor' was settling down on land after a life at sea, and, given that the food and the lightly flavoured ale were both delicious, Celia felt more than content, the unpleasantness with Sidony put firmly behind her.

There was the sudden summons of the door knocker, and a servant slipped away to answer it. A man's voice murmured something, and Celia's eyes widened, for she thought she knew whose it was. The servant returned, bent to speak quietly to his master, and Gilbert Baynton looked at Celia and said with an amused smile, 'You have a caller, my dear, despite the early hour: a Master Adderbury. He wishes to speak to you on a matter of urgency, and if you have finished your breakfast' – he looked enquiringly at her and she nodded – 'then I suggest you receive him in the library, which is through there.' He indicated. 'Go on in, and your caller will be brought to you.'

What does he want? Celia wondered. *How does he know where to find me?*

Composing herself, she sat down on the edge of a satin-covered chair and folded her hands in her lap.

The door was pushed open more widely and the servant said through a mouth full of plums, 'Master Fallon Adderbury,' bowing with exaggerated elegance and backing out again, closing the door as delicately as if it were made of glass.

Celia looked up at Fallon Adderbury staring down at her. They maintained their formal, well-mannered expressions for a moment, then both broke into a smile.

'What do you want?' Celia asked, just as he said, 'Oh, I'm so sorry to seek you out like this, and so early too, but it truly is an emergency and you are the only person who can help!'

'Sit down,' she said, and he pulled forward a chair opposite to her. 'Now, what can I do?'

Briefly he studied her in silence. Then he said – and she noticed immediately that the flirtatious charmer of yesterday and the day before had gone, replaced by someone far more serious – 'You are a skilled needlewoman and you have a wonderful supply of luxurious fabrics and trimmings, and you offered to help the Company if we had need of you.'

'I did,' she agreed, her curiosity roused.

'Could you help me now, this morning?' he asked urgently.

'I – well, I could, but I think you had better tell me what you need.'

'Of course.' He shook his head. 'My apologies, dear lady. In truth, I am not myself . . .' Then straight away he launched into a flow of words: 'Today we put on a play called *The Demon's Glass* and it's particularly important to me because I wrote this one.'

'But I thought—' she began. Noticing his embarrassed expression, she stopped, waving her hand for him to go on.

'It's a bloody and very violent piece that always goes down well in a port, where people live tough lives, and it involves a man who barters with the Devil and acquires a second life to live in parallel with his own, through the medium of a magic – or perhaps a cursed – looking glass. I won't tell you the entire plot – there are, as I just implied, an awful lot of brutal dismemberments, slayings and at one point the cutting-up of a body so that it can be baked in a pie – and the piece culminates in the hero – if one can call him that – standing before the mirror and trying to fight his own hand as it slowly rises up from beneath his cloak to cut his throat.'

'Good Lord!' Celia murmured.

'Yes, I'm sorry to make you face all this so soon after breakfast,' Fallon responded wryly.

She grinned. 'What do you want from me?'

'The problem is the wretched cloak,' he said. 'It's far too light, and it won't stay in place and fulfil its purpose of concealing the mechanism that operates the spare hand. What is needed is a much more voluminous garment in a far heavier fabric, so that—'

'Weights,' Celia interrupted. 'I have lengths of the cloth you require, but in addition we need lead weights, sewn into the hem, twenty, thirty, fifty of them, and—' He was smiling again, a happy, natural, very attractive smile. '*What?*' she demanded, beginning to respond.

'*We*,' he said. '*We* need lead weights.' His light eyes were on hers. 'Does this mean, my dear Mistress Palfrey, that you are prepared to help me?'

Smiling, laughing now from sheer delight – for it was a task she knew she could do well, he was attractive and attentive, it was a fine autumn day and she was in robust health and had just eaten a delicious breakfast – she said, 'Of course I am.'

Gilbert Baynton was hovering in the hall when Celia emerged from the library, Fallon behind her.

Barely pausing to reflect, she said, 'Oh, Master Baynton, I have to go on an errand back to my house this morning. I have offered to help with some matters of costume, and Master Adderbury here will accompany me to guide the choice of cloth. I—'

She had been about to ask him to pass on some message to Sidony but he forestalled her. With a rueful smile, he said, 'I dare say you shall welcome a morning away from my daughter, hmm?'

'Well, I—'

He patted her arm. 'No need to explain, my dear.' Turning towards the passage leading to the back of the house, he called out, 'Landry? Prepare Mistress Palfrey's mare. Quick, now!'

Not long afterwards, Celia and Fallon were riding off through the streets of the town. The business of the day was in full swing, and it was not until they were outside the walls and out on the road that bent its way along the course of the wide estuary of the conjoined Tamar and Tavy rivers that the throng of traffic eased sufficiently to ride abreast. Kicking his staid cob briefly to a trot, Fallon drew level and said worriedly, 'Is it far?'

She glanced at him. He looked as anxious as he sounded, and she recalled with a faint shock that he was putting on his play later today. 'No!' she said bracingly. 'Provided I can lay my hands on exactly what I want – and don't worry, I arrange my chests of fabrics and my shelves of haberdashery with great care! – we shall be back at the Saracen's Head by mid-morning.'

He nodded, smiling weakly. 'Oh, good.'

Once again, she sensed the change in him. 'You're nervous, I detect,' she said.

'I am!' he agreed fervently. 'I have had a hand in the writing of several of our productions, but *The Demon's Glass* is the first play that is entirely my own work.' His mouth turned downwards in an exaggerated mime of dismay. 'Would you not be nervous?'

She didn't answer. Once again, she was recalling the afternoon they had met, when Jonathan Carew had asked him if he had written *Othello* and his only reply had been downcast eyes and a modest smile. 'I think you allowed us to believe a falsehood,' she said gently, 'my brother, my friends and I. Concerning the authorship of that extraordinary play about the Moor and his bride?' she prompted when he did not answer.

He sighed. 'I did, and I have been seeking a way to apologize, and to correct the misapprehension, ever since.'

'Did you write any of it?'

He shook his head. 'No. It is the work of Will Shakespeare. He is not among our number down here in Devon,' he added, 'but called away on a family matter.'

'And you try out his new play in his absence?'

'Yes, but on his orders.' He gave her a look in which nervousness struggled with pride. 'The play is to be performed at court this November next, at the Whitehall Banqueting Hall, and he would not take it before such an august audience untried.'

'Performed before the *King*?' Celia whispered.

And silently he nodded.

Samuel and Tock hurried out into the yard to greet her, taking the reins of her mare and the cob. Thanking them, Celia reflected that the cob would receive better care in the next half an hour than in a whole week in some inn yard in Plymouth. 'Is my brother at home?' she asked.

'No, Mistress Celia, called away some time ago by a lad in a muck sweat of panic,' Samuel replied.

Celia nodded, pleased – although she did not wish to ask herself why – to learn Gabe was out.

She led Fallon in through the yard door, calling out a greeting to Sallie in the kitchen. 'I have somebody with me and we are going to my rooms to look out some cloth,' she added, urging Fallon ahead of her now, across the hall and up the stairs. Faintly she heard Sallie call back, 'Very well, Miss Celia!'

Then they were emerging onto the gallery that ran along the back of the house, and she was hurrying him along to the little private sitting room and workroom that served as an antechamber to her bedroom. Much to her relief, the bedroom door was shut.

His nearness was making her skin feel shivery and setting off fingertip tremors in her belly.

We are here for a serious purpose, she told herself very firmly. *You must give no hint whatsoever of what you are feeling!*

'The fabric I have in mind is in this chest,' she said in a clear, businesslike voice. Opening one of the large wooden chests that lined the wall, she delved down through several layers of immaculately folded cloth and extracted a heavy bolt of velvet in a deep shade of smoky grey that shimmered with purple, bronze and crimson depths. The pile was so deep that running a hand across it made a wave like the turning tide. She held it up and spread it out. It measured some four yards by two, just as she had remembered.

Fallon stared at it. He took hold of the hem and felt the weight. 'It is perfect,' he said simply. 'But – how swiftly can you sew it into a cloak?'

She had been thinking about that. 'You already have a cloak? The garment that is unsatisfactory because it is too light?'

'Yes?'

'Then I propose to attach the velvet to it, using it as if it were a lining,' she said.

'The cloak has a high, rigid collar,' he said, frowning.

'No matter. A layer of velvet can easily be attached to it.' He was staring at her, eyes wide, but he did not speak. 'Well?' she demanded. 'Is it all right? Oh – wait, I'll find the weights.' And, leaving him holding the cloth, she flew across the room to her shelves and picked up a cloth bag heavy with the coin-shaped lead pieces inside. She turned back to him. 'Here, these will serve, and—' She gasped.

He had wrapped the beautiful cloth around him as if it was already the cloak it was soon to be. The complex thundercloud colour with its subtle undertones darkened his hair to black, and his eyes shone out pale, brilliant blue. The luxury fabric became him utterly, as if it had been made for him, and on impulse she said, 'It is the perfect shade for you.'

'Thank you,' he said softly. 'And thank you too, dear lady, for presenting me with precisely what was needed to turn me into the character I shall portray.'

He was looking at her steadily, smiling slightly. She stepped up to him, raising her hands to adjust a fold of velvet so that it lay more smoothly over his shoulder. 'You will look fine,' she whispered.

They stood staring at each other, and the moment seemed poised on a balance.

She had been aware of voices from somewhere below, but in that strange moment of time nothing from outside could reach her. She heard footsteps, someone calling out her name, but she let the interruption flow past.

But then the door that she had half-closed was flung wide open and Gabe burst into the room.

FIVE

The sight of my sister standing in that slick, smooth, self-satisfied actor's embrace made my anger flare up in me like a fierce, hot fire.

They sprang apart as I went into the room, the actor's expression alarmed, Celia's descending into a ferocious scowl.

'What do you think you're doing?' I shouted, shoving the actor away from my sister.

'*Gabriel!*' she said, and her voice cracked on the three distinct syllables of my name with icy fury.

I spun round. 'This is your *bedroom*, Celia! Have you no sense of decency?'

Her eyes narrowed into slits of chilly sea green. '*That* is my bedroom,' she corrected me in the same ice-cold tone, pointing a rigid finger at the closed door. '*This* is my workroom.'

The actor spoke up. 'I apologize, Doctor Taverner, if it is inappropriate for me to be here, but you have my word that nothing even hinting at impropriety has taken place, in fact—'

'Leave him, Fallon,' Celia said in a crushingly scathing tone. 'Because I live beneath his roof he believes he has control over my comings and goings, over whom I choose to spend time with, and he would lock me away out here in the deep countryside in veil and habit if he had his way.' I thought she was going to say more but abruptly she stopped. Turning from glaring at me to bestow an altogether kinder look upon the actor, she said in a completely different voice, 'Would you be good enough to wait downstairs?' She pulled the length of dark velvet off him as she spoke, swiftly rolling it into a long tube which she laid across his shoulder. 'I will bring the lead weights. I will join you directly, for I have not forgotten we are in haste.'

Without a word he edged out of the room and I heard his light footsteps running down the stairs.

'Celia, I—'

I got no further. 'How *dare* you!' my sister said with a quiet intensity that was far, far worse than shouting. 'You come crashing into my private quarters, you interrupt a professional matter that is theatre business and has nothing whatever to do with you, you assume the very worst and you assault a guest in our house. Have I left anything out?' She mimed deep thinking, one hand on the opposite elbow, forefinger to her cheek, frown of concentration. 'Oh, yes! You took against this same guest from the outset and you seem to have convinced yourself, on no basis whatsoever, that I am about to fling myself into his arms and admit him to my bed. *And don't try to deny it*' – now she was shouting – 'because I can see it in your face, I can *smell* the intensity of your dislike of him!'

She stood panting right in front of me. Her eyes were blazing, her jaw was set in a rictus as if she wanted to bite me. She used to do that when we were little, complaining bitterly, when punished for the toothmarks in my upper arm, that it was the one weapon she had that worked against a bigger, stronger opponent.

I couldn't deny it. What she said was absolutely right.

'Celia, please don't—' I began.

But she wasn't ready to listen.

Calm now, she picked up her cloak from where it lay across the chest under the widow. She collected a cloth bag whose contents emitted a dull clink, then walked past me – she contrived to turn her back to me as she passed, which hurt more than I liked to admit – and headed off along the passage, pausing at the top of the stairs.

'I am returning to the Saracen's Head now, where I have undertaken to work on a garment needed in this afternoon's production,' she said distantly.

'Will you come back?' I said.

She looked at me for a long moment. 'Tonight I stay with Sidony, as arranged,' she said, which didn't answer the question I was really asking.

Then she followed the actor down the stairs.

I went along the gallery and into my own bedchamber, hurrying over to the window that overlooked the approach to the house. After only a short pause I first heard and then saw them, two figures on horseback, riding hard and the horses already at a canter as they flew off down the track to the road.

Celia didn't look back.

I stood for some time after they had gone. Then I turned away and went slowly downstairs. Sallie came out of the kitchen into the hall. I had the strong impression she had been listening out for me.

I met her sympathetic eyes. 'Oh, Sallie,' I murmured.

She made a face I couldn't read. Sympathy was now modified by almost a scolding look.

'Mistress Celia and her companion only arrived home a few minutes before you did, Doctor,' she said, and yes, there was a definite note of reproof in her voice. 'They came in through the door from the yard and Miss Celia called out they were going up to her workroom to sort out some cloth. They'd only just gone upstairs, Doctor, and I was about to follow them and ask the mistress if they would like me to take up a mug of spiced ale and some little cakes.'

I nodded. No time, Sallie seemed to be saying, for anything untoward to have taken place.

Nevertheless.

'She had a man in her room.' The plain fact, baldly stated, still sounded abhorrent.

Sallie gave me a kindly look. 'Miss Celia's not some untried young girl, Doctor,' she said gently. 'She's been a wife and now she's a widow' – she shot me a glance, and not for the first time I wondered if she knew more about Jeromy Palfrey's death than I'd convinced myself to believe – 'and the rules are not so strict for her.'

'Perhaps,' I said grudgingly.

There was quite a long silence. Then Sallie said, 'Seems to me she's happy living here with you, and you like it too, unless I'm much mistaken.'

'I do like it,' I growled.

She nodded. 'Course you do, you're close, the pair of you, not like some siblings.' Another silence. Then: 'May I speak plain, Doctor?'

'You usually do, Sallie.'

She smiled faintly. 'She's young and she's lovely to look at, clever, sharp-witted, accomplished. She's recovered so bravely from her past, but she's not fully back to her proper self just yet. But it will happen. Indeed it's happening all the time, a little more each day, and when the process is done she will leave Rosewyke, Doctor, and become wife to some good man and mistress in her own home. And it won't be any footling actor, so don't you worry about that,' she added, giving me a sly grin.

How could she be so sure? I wondered. What had she observed about Celia's behaviour since the wretched players had come to town that allowed her to state with such conviction that Fallon Adderbury was no threat? I could not begin to fathom it. Perhaps it was an insight available only to another woman.

'If you want my advice,' Sallie went on – I seemed to be receiving it, whether I wanted it or not – 'then let her be. You nag her and try to control her and you'll only lose her. She'll go and live with the old folks at Fernycombe – your parents would be delighted to have her – or with your brother Nathaniel on his farm, although in truth I cannot picture her there . . .' A frown crossed my housekeeper's kindly, homely face. Then, as if this distraction had brought her back to herself, she gasped and said, 'My goodness, hark at me, going on at you! I am *so* sorry, Doctor, I can't think what came over me!'

Now she was flustered, blushing, and I went to take her hand.

'Nothing to be sorry about, Sallie,' I said, patting her plump shoulder, although in truth I too was greatly surprised at her outburst. But it had come from love, I realized; I had long understood Sallie's protective and deep affection for Celia, and it now appeared she cared about my happiness too. 'And you are quite right: I would indeed miss her if she stormed off to live with our parents.' Sallie nodded, still looking awkward, and, taking pity on her, I said, 'Now, I must ride into Plymouth later, so what about some dinner?'

'Right away, Doctor!' she exclaimed, as relieved, I thought, as I was that she was restored to her natural place in my household.

Watching her hurry away, I reflected that if I didn't want Celia to leave Rosewyke, I had better set about adjusting some of the more archaic of my attitudes towards her.

I called in on Theo on my way down to Plymouth that afternoon. He was in his inner office, looking as harassed as ever, the usual slew of documents spread across his desk.

'If you are busy I will not stay,' I said.

'I'm always busy, today is no worse than any other day,' he grunted. 'Sit down, Gabe, you always look so threatening when you're looming over me.'

I sat.

'I can guess why you're here,' he said. 'I haven't been able to drag my thoughts away from that whispered conversation either.'

'Any progress?' I asked.

He frowned, picking up his quill and turning it over in his hands. 'I sent Jarman out late last evening to see what he could uncover. Many of the players from the Company were still drinking in the Saracen's Head taproom when he got there, and not a few were readily persuaded to talk.'

'Did he discover anything useful?' I demanded.

'No, I don't think so, but certainly quite a lot of background, if you'll hear it?'

'Yes, of course!'

'If the older of the two speakers I overheard was one of the Company, as we both suspect, then from what Jarman told me it appears he was probably someone called Francis Heron, and—'

'Clever-looking fellow, dressed like a scholar, white hair under a dark cap. Yes, I've met Master Heron.'

'—and it appears he is something of an outsider in the Company rather than a central figure in its organization, and only ever called upon to play the lesser roles,' Theo continued, ignoring my interruption. 'Apparently he has furnished them with a fine supply of costly items to use in their plays – *properties*, they call them. The talk is that he's a man of wealth and influence, although there's some mystery about him and the players don't seem to know what he's doing down here in

Devon with them. They say he's no great shakes as an actor, which is no doubt why he only plays minor parts.'

'He delivered Graziano's few lines adequately,' I said mildly.

'I'll have to take your word for that. He was a notably unfunny Flute the Bellows-Mender.'

'What of the other man you heard? Daniel, didn't you say he was called?'

'I did. There isn't anyone called Daniel among the players in the Company.'

I swore under my breath. 'So how do we track him down?'

Theo held up a hand. 'Wait! Jarman doesn't give up that easily, as you very well know. He casually asked some of the players and the other members of the Company if Daniel was around, and although most of them said they didn't know any Daniel, one did respond.

'He said he thought there was a man by that name among the gang that pack and unpack the heavy luggage, and that most of them were lodging out on the edge of town where the accommodation's cheaper.'

'Did Jarman locate him?'

Theo watched me, smiling faintly. 'He reckons he knows where the man's putting up, but he wasn't there last night. Jarman's trying again today.'

It was something, I supposed. I stood up abruptly.

'Off now, are you?' Theo asked with a grin.

'I'm going to the Saracen's Head to watch the remainder of this afternoon's performance,' I said, 'and I know you're busy but I think you ought to come too.'

'Why?' he demanded.

I'd been hoping he wouldn't ask. 'Oh – because I have the strongest sense that something is about to happen.'

'Something is about to happen,' he echoed tonelessly. But already he was on his feet, reaching for the heavy sleeveless garment, a cross between a cloak and a robe, that he wears over his clothes when he goes out. 'I would dismiss that as the vague and useless comment it undoubtedly is, Gabe, except that I'm sensing exactly the same thing.'

*   *   *

A handbill was thrust into my hand as we strode into the yard of the Saracen's Head. It advertised the play as something called *The Demon's Glass*, and from the shrieks and gasps of horror coming from the audience – undoubtedly enjoying it hugely – it appeared to be going down well.

'It's halfway through,' said the man handing out the hand-bills, 'so I'll do you gentlemen a favour and let you in at a third off, which for two of you comes to—'

Theo drew himself up and thrust back his shoulders. 'I am His Majesty's coroner,' he said grandly.

Assuming that this was more than enough to admit us both for nothing – as indeed it was, for the man with the handbills instantly stepped back – Theo strode on and led the way to a corner from which we could watch both the action in the inn yard and the people drinking it in with such gusto. The members of the Company were using a big storeroom and workshop on the far side of the yard as their tiring room, and our position also allowed a sharply angled view into it.

The Demon's Glass was a weird, dark, scary, supernatural and deeply disturbing piece. It was quite extraordinarily violent: I had seen plays by Webster, and Kyd's *Spanish Tragedy*, and on one afternoon I'd rather forget a horribly bloody production of *Titus Andronicus*, and this play borrowed the most harrowing parts of all of them. Throats were cut open, with most dextrous and effective use of hidden pouches of animal blood; parents were presented with pies filled with the flesh of their own murdered children; hands were sliced off as readily as a man might shed his gloves. Theo leaned across and muttered, after a riot of limb-lopping and even a decapitation had brought an act to an end, that he was very glad he and Elaine had taken the children to *A Midsummer Night's Dream* and not this horror. I nodded, fully agreeing with him. But there were children in the audience; people are so used to horrors, and some parents seem to take the attitude that you may as well harden your children to them sooner rather than later.

I saw Celia, standing up in the gallery overlooking the yard. She was intent on the play.

Over on the far side of the improvised stage I recognized

the beautiful antique mirror that had been used to such haunting effect in *Othello*. Today it was the portal through which the hero communicated with his other self, the extra life given to him through the pact he had made with the demon of the title. Coming in halfway through as Theo and I had done, it was difficult to follow exactly what was happening, but it appeared that this man (he was called Alessandro DaCosta) had purchased the second life by promising to give the wicked-looking red-headed demon (whose name was Rigadoro) the bodies of quite a few of his relatives and close friends.

The part of Alessandro DaCosta was played by Fallon Adderbury. Dressed in a cloak made from the velvet my sister had given him that morning.

I had to admit it was a glorious garment. Celia must have worked at lightning speed, and she had done a fine job. The wide folds of the hem swept the stage to highly dramatic effect, and the cloak was so well made that it did what I took to be its main job – the concealing of the extra hand that materialized from beneath the folds of heavy velvet like a snake rising from a basket – so well that the illusion all but carried me. For a few horrible moments I let myself believe that a demon's hand had grown out of this poor cursed hero's reflection and was intent on vengeance.

And we all watched, quite unable to look away, as the doomed hero stood there in his heavy cloak in front of the mirror, and the Demon's ghastly hand slowly and inexorably rose up of its own volition and calmly cut his throat. As he slumped to the ground, pig's blood flowing out of the bladder hidden inside the neck of his shirt, there was a terrible scream from somewhere in the wings.

I thought – everyone thought – that it was part of the play. In the first shocked instant I wondered if the long, ear-paining shriek was the sound of DaCosta's doomed soul as it fled from his dying body. And I saw – thought I saw – an answering movement in the mirror: a cloaked figure, identical to the one now lying in a pool of blood on the dirty cobbles of the inn yard, the folds of its cloak billowing out like a pair of wide, frantically-flapping wings . . .

Then Theo grabbed my arm, hard enough to jerk me straight

back into reality. 'Come on,' he said gruffly right in my ear, 'something's happened back there.'

I followed him around the yard and into the tiring room, breaking into a run as I spotted what he had seen. It could have been a bundle of costumes or even a stack of old sacks, but I knew it wasn't. I crouched down over it, Theo right beside me.

It was a young man. He had fair hair, shoulder-length and very straight, and he was short and stocky, his chest like a barrel in the tight-laced rust-red doublet. I recognized the costume if not the actor: he, or someone wearing that costume, had taken the minor role of the hero's friend, who had tried ineffectually to warn him against the worst of his follies.

'What's the matter with him?' Theo demanded. 'He's not dead, is he?'

I ran my hands over the youth's body, searching for blood, and was about to tear open his doublet to feel for his heartbeat when a great roar broke out of the inn yard and there was the sudden sound of stampeding feet, the cries and yells that accompanied it suggesting something catastrophic was happening.

Theo had hold of my leather jerkin and was dragging me up, pulling me after him, and I went with him.

Two things struck me as we ran out into the daylight: the first was that the play was finished, the actors were lined up making their bows and the crashing noise was the audience showing their appreciation.

The second thing was the sight of Francis Heron, standing exactly where Theo and I had just stood, crouching forward with his torso at a right angle to his legs and holding his stomach, retching feebly and groaning, very obviously in great pain.

Nobody else appeared to have noticed him, for that section of the inn yard was set slightly apart from the main bulk of the audience and it was outside their line of sight as they gave their full adoring attention to the players.

Thinking rapidly, I said to Theo, 'Go and see what ails Master Heron there.' I nodded towards the slumped figure.

Theo spun round to stare at me. '*That's* Francis Heron? The older man of the pair I heard whispering?'

'Yes. Go on' – I gave him a shove – 'the poor bugger's suffering!'

I ran back into the tiring room.

The young man's body wasn't there.

I could hear Theo, asking over and over again: 'Who was the youth dressed in rust-red velvet?' I tried to ignore his question and the succession of answers as he approached each member of the Company milling around in the makeshift tiring room, shedding their costumes, wiping off the thick greasy make-up, carefully rolling up the sumptuous wigs and putting them in the cloth bags that kept them clean and untangled.

Briefly I wondered if Celia was still outside in the unruly throng. Then I knelt down beside my patient and forgot about her.

We had carried Francis Heron out of the inn yard and away from the sight of far too many pairs of curious eyes, into a tiny little passage running between the yard and the section of the inn where the guest accommodation was. There wasn't much light, it smelt fusty and unused, and I suspected it was not the main thoroughfare. My patient lay on a stack of sacks supplied by the innkeeper, who was hovering in the background looking anxious. 'Coxton,' he said, catching my eye, jerking a thumb at his chest. 'Innkeeper.' The frown deepening, he leaned closer and muttered, 'I don't want any sickness on the premises, what with it being so bad for business. You're a doctor, are you?'

'I am,' I replied.

He sniffed, then turned and strode away, roughly pushing past the figure approaching up the dank little passage.

As he advanced out of the shadows I recognized the tall, white-bearded man who I'd noticed on the first evening in the taproom. He was still in costume – a long dark robe and a silver wig beneath a close-fitting black cap, thick white make-up on his face and his eyebrows extended like black antennae. Behind him, in his shadow, was the plump actor who had played the part of the cook who made the deadly pie. He too still wore costume – female, in his case – and his make-up was streaked with tears. As I looked at him, he crept away.

The white-haired man stared down at the writhing figure. 'They said it was Francis who was unwell,' he said softly. 'Oh, dear.' Noticing my expression as I briefly looked up to study him, he said with a wry turning-down of his mobile mouth, 'Forgive the apparel and the eyebrows. I am come straight from the stage. Thomas Lightbodie,' he added, a hand to his breast. 'This is, as much as it is anybody's, my Company.'

And Fallon Adderbury had told us that first night that he was manager of the Company. Well, I never did believe him.

'Master Lightbodie.' I nodded to him.

'And who, if I may ask, are you?' he asked politely.

'Gabriel Taverner. I'm a doctor,' I replied.

Then I bent down over my patient.

I put my hand on his forehead. He felt very hot, and his heart was beating much too fast. He had closed his eyes with a moan of pain as he'd been borne out of the tiring room, but now his eyelids fluttered and his eyes opened. He stared straight up at me and he looked very frightened.

'You are in pain, Master Heron?' I asked him gently.

He nodded, flinching away from the sudden stab of agony. 'Aye, I am. My head.' He managed a very faint smile. 'I said I hoped not to require your professional attention, Doctor, and yet here you are.' He gazed down at himself. 'Here *I* am,' he murmured.

'Have you pain anywhere else?' I asked.

'My belly. I feel my guts churning, and I have an urge to void my bowels.' A horrified expression crossed his face. 'Aaah! I need to vomit!' He leaned over the edge of his pile of sacks and blankets and I threw myself to one side, managing to avoid the gush that surged up out of his mouth. Thomas Lightbodie, I noticed, had stepped back a few paces, and I didn't blame him. I extracted one of the sacks from the side of the pile and threw it down to cover the mess.

'My apologies, Doctor,' Francis Heron whispered. He was lying back again, his face deathly white. He groaned again, one hand held feebly to his forehead.

'Bind it with this,' a voice said from right beside me.

I spun round. The beautiful boy who had played Desdemona had come to stand quietly beside Thomas Lightbodie, still in the gown he had worn today in the role of a murdered noble-woman, the lovely fabric stained with stage blood. In his hand he held the white silk handkerchief spotted with strawberries that Celia had made and presented to Fallon Adderbury.

I looked questioningly up at him.

'It was Desdemona's prescribed remedy for her lord,' he said in a soft, musical voice that sounded almost like singing. 'Othello complains of his headache, and she says, *Let me but bind it hard, within the hour it will be well*, but Othello dismisses her loving solicitude, saying bluntly that her napkin is too little.'

'It is an ancient remedy,' I said.

'Try it,' the young man urged. He thrust the handkerchief at me, and, almost without my own volition, I found myself taking it.

I folded it corner to corner and then over and over until it was a strip about as wide as the middle joint of my thumb. Then very gently I raised Francis Heron's head and laid the silk across his forehead, tying the ends behind his coif. As I laid his head down again he said with a smile, 'Ah, how cool that feels!' Then he closed his eyes.

I studied him for several moments. He appeared to be asleep, and I reckoned it was as good a time as any to take him off somewhere quiet, away from the rest of the company.

I announced my intention to Thomas Lightbodie, who nodded and summoned four of the stronger-looking Company members. 'Bear our poor companion away,' he said, his voice calm and authoritative. 'Take care, now – he is sick and in pain.'

As they shuffled out, Thomas following, Celia appeared at the end of the passage. Fallon Adderbury was just behind her.

'What's happened, Gabe?' she asked, hurrying up to me and keeping her voice low. 'There are all manner of worrying rumours flying round! They talk of a dead body that's vanished and—' She didn't finish the sentence.

'I have little more idea than you,' I replied softly. 'I don't like the sound of all that angry muttering out there, though.' I met her eyes. 'You should leave. I'll come with you, make sure you reach—'

'I will look after her, Doctor Taverner,' Fallon Adderbury said quietly. 'I am well aware that you do not like me, but I like your sister, and I would not let any harm come to her.'

I glared at him, about to make a sharp reply, but Celia forestalled me. With a tut of annoyance she said sharply, 'Stop it, both of you. I don't need looking after, thank you, Fallon, and Gabe, there's absolutely no need for you to abandon your patient to see me home, or whatever it was you were about to propose.'

'But—' I began.

'I am leaving now, Gabe – I only sought you out to tell you so – and *if* it's any of your business, I'll be staying with Sidony tonight.'

'Let me at least escort you to your friend's house!' Adderbury implored.

She turned to him. 'Very well.' She turned back to me, wished me a frosty farewell and, turning, stalked away, Adderbury trotting behind her.

Suppressing a smile, I hurried off to follow the Company men bearing Francis Heron into the rear section of the inn.

I had told Coxton the innkeeper that he needed to be isolated until I discovered what ailed him, and he must have told them where to go. I caught up with them as they made their way through a maze of narrow, dark little passages until we came to the low door of a room set apart from the rest of the accommodation over in the rearmost wing of the inn, furthest from the noise of the street; we were, I guessed, in the most ancient part of the old building. The Company men laid him down on a low bed and I covered him up.

'Do you need anything, Doctor?' the oldest of them said, looking down compassionately at the sick man. I thought I recognized the dark, heavy-browed actor who had played Roderigo in *Othello*; his flustered indecision as Iago told him to put money in his purse had been gratingly irritating, not that he was being indecisive now.

'Good, fresh water, a mug, wash cloths. Oh, and a bucket,' I said. I had not forgotten that my patient had felt nauseous and said he had the urge to defecate. I should also need my bag, which I had left in the care of the stable lad looking after my horse. 'And send someone along to the Anchor – it's at the corner of the street going towards the harbour, if you don't know – and tell them to tell the stable lad that Doctor Taverner needs his bag.'

I was sitting in silent thought on a pile of old sacks beside my sleeping patient when there was a soft tap on the door. 'Come in!' I called in a low voice.

Theo crept into the room.

'How is he?'

'His headache seems to be a little easier.' I indicated the silk handkerchief round his forehead. 'The lad who played Desdemona suggested it,' I said, 'and although I've never really believed in its efficacy, it seems to have allowed him to go to sleep.'

Theo stared at the white silk. 'Hmm.' Then, seeming to shake himself, he said, 'He played Titania yesterday, too.'

'What?'

'The lad! The beautiful boy! Come on, Gabe, you were just talking about him!'

'Oh.' For an instant I seemed to hear a soft buzzing inside my head, and just a hint of distant voices singing a quiet and very sweet line of melody. I shook myself and it was gone.

Turning to Theo, I said sharply, 'What news?'

He looked faintly startled at my abrupt tone, then said, 'We've done a head count of the entire Company, players, producers, writers, stage hands, luggage-carters, scenery-shifters, and there's nobody missing.'

'So the lad in rust-red velvet has turned up? Is he all right? Unharmed? Has he any memory of what happened?' The questions shot out and Theo put up his hands as if to fend them off.

'One at a time! No he hasn't turned up, so I can't say if he's all right or not.'

I tried to work it out, but my mind still seemed to be affected by that strange moment when I'd heard the singing. 'But you just said all the Company members are accounted for?'

'Yes, that's what I've been trying to tell you! The lad who played the friend of the fool who made his deal with the demon

changed out of his rust-red costume some time back because
he had to put on a different outfit to play another character in
the last section of the play.' He glared at me. 'Are you
following? You're looking bemused, Gabe – come on, pay
attention!'

'Sorry. Yes, of course I am – the rust-red costume must have
been left in the tiring room, presumably to be put away by
the wardrobe master once the play was done, and—'

'And someone else found it and put it on,' Theo finished.
'Or possibly someone else dressed the young man in it?'

'It didn't fit him very well,' I said suddenly, remembering.
'The doublet was very tight, and the lacings didn't draw the
two edges together properly.'

Theo nodded slowly. After quite a long pause he said, 'He
was dead, wasn't he?'

'I can't say,' I said, 'I was about to feel for a heartbeat when
Francis collapsed and, at almost the same moment, there
was that great explosion of noise from the inn yard. I didn't
have the chance to examine him properly.'

Theo was still nodding. 'That tumult of shouting and
stamping could have been specially arranged to distract us,'
he said slowly.

'No!' I protested. 'It was the audience breaking out into
their appreciative applause at the end of the play!'

And Theo just looked at me.

Night had fallen. Still I sat with my patient, for I was becoming very worried about him. Fear seemed to stalk in the
dark little passage outside. Sometimes I heard the shuffle of
quiet footfalls; sometimes there were soft, whispered, anxious
conversations.

There was a knock on the door, and Thomas Lightbodie
came into the room. He had discarded his costume and his
stage make-up, and he was once more the graceful, elegant
figure I'd noticed that first evening, his snowy hair and beard
appearing to shine in the dim light. With him was the dark-
browed man who had hastened to fetch my bag and the items
I needed. I looked at him enquiringly, and he muttered,
'Barnaby Abell.'

Without preamble Thomas Lightbodie said softly, 'The Company members are starting to panic. There's talk he may have it.'

I did not need to ask what he meant by *it*. The same thought had crossed my mind.

'When did you leave London?' I demanded.

His lips moved silently as he calculated. 'Four, four and a half weeks ago.'

'And since? Have you been in any town where you heard there were cases?'

'Of course not,' Barnaby Abell said, an edge of defensive anger in his voice. 'That was the whole idea, Doctor Taverner, to keep us *away* from infection.'

I nodded. 'Yes, I understand that.' I thought for a moment. 'The incubation period is generally accepted to be four to six days. A week at the most. Where have you been most recently?'

'We arrived here in Plymouth three days ago, and gave our first performance the day before yesterday.' Thomas again. 'Before that we were in Barnstaple, and we stayed there for five days, then two days on the road to come here.' He paused, then said with quiet emphasis, 'But nowhere any mention of the sickness. Of that I do most emphatically assure you.'

If Francis Heron was suffering from the plague, then he must have contracted it in Barnstaple. Barnstaple was sixty, seventy miles away; people regularly travelled between the north coast of Devon and the south, and had there been an outbreak as near to us as Barnstaple, news would have spread with horrible rapidity.

Wouldn't it?

I looked from one to the other. 'I do not believe Master Heron has the sickness,' I said, with a lot more conviction than I felt. 'I shall stay with him and keep watch. If he develops the telltale buboes, then I shall be proved wrong. But I do not expect that he will,' I concluded firmly.

Thomas murmured, 'I am grateful, Doctor.' Then, with a polite nod, he turned and left the room.

Barnaby accepted the news in silence. His face was impassive: he looked neither relieved nor frightened.

After some time he said, 'What do you think ails him then, Doctor?'

I looked down at my patient, his breathing shallow and rapid now, a frown of pain on his white face even as he slept.

I was already beginning to think he'd been poisoned, but I wasn't going to say so to anybody else; not yet. So I just said quietly, 'Time alone will tell.'

SIX

Full darkness had fallen now. Some time ago I'd heard Coxton, or one of his staff, fastening the shutters and throwing the bolts on the doors, and now the sounds of the Company preparing for bed had finally died away. All was very quiet. I heard an owl from somewhere outside: it was a moonlit night, and good for hunting.

Francis Heron slept fitfully on the narrow little bed. Sometimes heat seemed to surge through him and he would throw off the covers; then he would start to shiver, so violently that I heard his teeth chattering, and I would hasten to tuck him up again. But the blanket was coarse against his skin, and, hoping to find some soft scarf or wrap, I opened the sturdy old leather bag that some kind Company member had brought along from Francis's previous shared accommodation. Overcoming the strong sense that I was invading another man's privacy – this is purely for his benefit, I told myself – I delved inside.

Spare personal linen, some well-darned hose, a small bag with a razor and a wash cloth. A very soft wool scarf, or possibly a shawl, for it was generously sized. I took it out, for it was just what I had hoped to find, and gently tucked it round Francis's neck and over his chest. His eyelids fluttered open and he looked up at me with a feeble smile.

'Thank you,' he whispered, his voice cracked and hoarse.

An earthenware jug of water had been left ready. I poured some into a cup and held it to his lips. 'No,' he protested, 'for I am still very nauseous and I shall only bring it up again.'

'Drink,' I insisted. 'You have been vomiting, and you've voided your bowels. Your body is dehydrated.'

Obediently he swallowed a few sips, then pushed my hand away. I let him sleep.

I looked down at him for a while, trying to still the deeply anxious questions racing through my mind. For all my brave words to Barnaby, I really could not be absolutely sure this was not plague. In my mind I went through the symptoms: fever, headache, alternating sweats and shivers. Well, Francis was exhibiting all of those, but then they were common to pretty much every sickness that produced fever. The symptom that confirmed the presence of the terrible disease was the buboes that swelled up so agonizingly as the poison spread through the body. Very carefully I put my hand inside Francis's robe and beneath his under linen, feeling for the nodes in his armpit.

I thought I detected a slight swelling.

My heart started to beat rapidly as fear ran through me. If this was the plague, then we were facing a catastrophe. Francis had been in close proximity to all the other players for days, weeks, and in addition had been performing before audiences in venues all through the region. There was no knowing how many people he might have infected.

And I had been sitting close beside him for hours now.

I fought down the panic and found some courage. Doctors developed resistance to diseases, I told myself firmly. If they didn't, bearing in mind all the terrible sicknesses I'd treated in my career, I'd have been dead a dozen times over, and without exception in a horribly painful way.

I felt in Francis's armpit again, and then felt my own. I smiled – although in truth there was very little to smile about – because I could feel very little difference. Either both of us had the plague or neither of us did.

To distract my thoughts, I went through the rest of his bag, in case there was some other personal item that might comfort him. I felt the worn leather binding of a small book, and drew it out. Holding it to the light of the lantern, I opened it. The pages were thin, much-handled, and covered in writing inscribed in black ink: page after page of dense script, broken only occasionally by a new paragraph, and continuing for perhaps two thirds of the book. Then came blank pages, and I thought there was no more. I flipped through the remaining pages, and discovered that the last three were filled with neat columns of words, the majority having five letters, occasionally interspersed with a shorter word. These lists – for that was what they looked like – were in a different hand. I brought the page closer to my eyes, but a better look only confirmed my first impression: the contents of Francis Heron's much-used little notebook were in code. It was comprised of letters and symbols, I'd never seen anything like it, and I did not begin to understand it.

I turned to the flyleaf, wondering if Francis had inscribed his name. He hadn't, but there was a symbol, strangely compelling, formed of a circle with a dot in the centre, through the top third of which was an upturned arc. A line ran down from the base of the circle, terminating in two more arcs, one either side as if they were feet. A short way down from the top, this line was crossed by another, extending a little beyond the circle's width.

A cross sitting on two arcs, a circle with a dot in the middle and another arc . . .

Beyond a vague idea that the circle might be the sun and the crescent above it the moon, I had no idea what it meant. Was it Francis's own symbol, in some way representative of his name? Was it a sign by which the members of some body of men recognized one another, rather like the staff of Asclepius, the serpent-entwined rod that since ancient times has been the symbol of those involved in medicine? I did not know.

The symbol captivated me. I ran my forefinger around the circle and the arc, down the vertical line, along the two arcs at the base and along the horizontal line. For an instant I thought I felt some other consciousness reach out eagerly towards mine, but then it was gone. 'Too much imagination,' I muttered aloud. Too long sitting alone in the dark, in that place that had become the temporary abode of storytellers and players who fudged and twisted reality for their own ends and persuaded their gullible audience – who after all were there purely to be entertained, taken out of their stolid lives into the world of fantasy – that magic was real and all around them . . .

I looked down at Francis, now apparently deeply asleep. I felt for his pulse. Still too fast. I considered feeling again for those dreaded swellings, but decided against it. I might disturb him, and he needed his sleep.

Replacing the little book, I settled more comfortably on my heap of sacks, drawing one of the spare blankets around me. I leant back into the corner formed by the junction of two walls, putting a sack behind my head as a pillow. Either my makeshift bed was a lot more comfortable than I had anticipated or I was very tired – I suspected the latter, for we must by now be into the small hours – for very soon I found myself starting to drift into sleep. The first few times I resisted – what if Francis's condition should suddenly deteriorate? – but then I muttered to myself, as I have so often said to others, 'You are no use to the person you are caring for if you are exhausted.' I drew the rough and mildly malodorous blanket closer around me and gave in.

How do you know if you're dreaming? Do you know at the time, or does the realization only come later, once you are awake and looking back into the colourful, bizarre, nonsensical and often very frightening world that your sleeping mind conjured up?

That night in the dark and dank little room at the back of the Saracen's Head, I dreamed more vividly than ever before.

I came up to consciousness from profound sleep. What had disturbed me? Some sound from my patient? I leaned down over Francis, but he was still asleep. He was hot, and had once again thrown off the covers. I put the palm of my hand just over his forehead, and I could feel the heat coming off him.

Some instinct told me that it had not been he who had awakened me.

I thought I heard a whisper. Very soft, barely audible; *pssst!*, the sort of hiss that people make to attract someone's attention. The character Alessandro DaCosta in this afternoon's play – no, yesterday's play, for it was surely well after midnight now – had made just such a sound. He had seduced the wife of a dignified and stately nobleman, the nobleman had found out and was pursuing DaCosta, vengeance burning in his heart. The little hiss had come at the moment when the viciously cruel villain wanted to attract the nobleman's attention; to make him turn round and watch as his wife's head was cut off.

Confused, alarmed, I leapt up, rushing out of the little room into the total darkness of the passage. I thought there was the faintest glimmer of light over to my right, where after many twists and turns the passage emerged into the tiring room off the inn yard, and without thinking I ran towards it, stumbling over uneven flagstones and bouncing off unexpected corners.

I was in the tiring room. It was lit by an odd greenish light whose source I could not identify. The costumes were carefully arrayed, cloaks and long robes hung up on hooks, skirts, bodices and doublets placed over wooden boxes. As my eyes circled the room it seemed that the garments were inhabited by bodies, and the bodies were moving.

I was about to investigate this strange phenomenon when something else caught my eye. Slowly, and with such powerful reluctance that I knew even as I did so that I was about to see something dreadful, I turned.

The magnificent mirror with the gold, silver and bronze-patterned frame stood right behind me, so close that I wondered why I had not noticed it before. *It crept up on you*, I heard a soft voice say, and this seemed perfectly reasonable.

It appeared to be inviting my total attention.

I looked right into its silvery, cloudy depths.

There was someone inside it.

I thought at first it was a woman, for the face had an extraordinary, haunting loveliness. Her skin was very pale, her long, lustrous hair as black as night, her eyes a brilliant, light-filled gold, shining like two little lanterns. The black pupils seemed to be vibrating gently, varying between tiny black dots and wide lakes that I almost felt I could dive into. For the space of one single heartbeat I thought she had two irises in each eye, one with the pupil wide open, one with it all but closed. I shook my head roughly and the illusion went away.

Her head sat proudly on a long, elegant neck that curved into rounded shoulders, the flesh white as snow above the black velvet of the gown. Her breasts swelled out over the tightly laced bodice, and I watched as my hand reached out for her.

But then abruptly I thought: *There are no women in the Company, for all the female roles are taken by boys and youths.*

I knew in that instant the identity of the person in the mirror. It was the beautiful young man who had been such a heart-breaking Desdemona; who had been a flirtatious, gorgeous Titania; who, in the role of the sad and beautiful noblewoman, had had his head struck from his body in *The Demon's Glass.*

And who, as Francis Heron lay gasping and groaning with the agony of his headache, had produced the silk handkerchief my sister had made, and offered it as a palliative.

I felt a sort of tug inside my head. It was as if she – he – read my mind and understood that he no longer had my total attention.

I heard a sound like an animal's snarl, then the swishing sound of a blade moving fast through the air. There right in front of me inside the mirror, the terrible scene in yesterday's play was acted out again and the head of the figure in black velvet was severed from its body. I *saw* that same scene now, only this time the decapitation was no clever stage trick. It was done right there, before my eyes, and in a moment of total horror I watched as the woman threw up her hands to the place where her head used to be.

In that moment of horrified confusion I thought, it's the handkerchief, something's been done to the handkerchief, and then abruptly, with no warning, someone was right up close beside me. With immense power I was pushed violently forward, straight into the mirror, and I cried out because it was full of blood. I banged my head hard, my vision started to go black and I fell to the ground.

As I fell, as my closing eyes swept past the section of the frame at the base of the mirror, I caught sight of a strange little symbol formed out of bright silver that interrupted the geometric pattern. It was surely too small and placed too far down to be readily visible.

But I saw it.

Saw it and recognized it.

It was the same arc-bisected, cross-formed figure I had seen on the flyleaf of Francis Heron's book.

*   *   *

I opened my eyes.

It was morning, and a spear of thin, cold light was permeating the dark little room from some unseen source.

In the first confused half-awake moments I thought that I would find myself on the tiring-room floor, covered in blood in front of the mirror. But I was slumped on my stack of sacks, my neck aching from the unnatural angle of my head, dribble on my chin.

And I thought, with considerable relief, *So it was just a dream.*

I sat up, turning instantly to my patient.

Francis had been sick again. He was groaning feebly, retching, his body heaving with the effort, and I hastened to position the bucket. Not that he had much to bring up, poor man. I dipped the wash cloth in the bowl of cold water and gently sponged his burning face and forehead, and he gave me a shaky smile.

'Still alive, Doctor,' he said, his voice barely audible.

'Indeed you are, Master Heron,' I replied, my heartiness too much even for me.

I wrung out the cloth and went on with the spongeing, gradually extending the range so that I could feel inside his undershirt and into his armpits. I hoped he would not guess what I was about but of course he did.

'Have I the buboes?' he whispered. There was terror in his tone.

'No,' I said.

I looked down at him, our eyes meeting. There was no need for either of us to feign our huge relief.

'Should they not have appeared by now, if it was the plague that so affects me?' Francis asked.

I don't know, would have been the honest answer.

Rapidly I reviewed all I knew of the plague. Infection was generally believed to be through the bite of a flea, and the sweats, the fever and the headache began a few days after the bite was received. Then the buboes would appear, initially in the vicinity of the bite: on the neck, in the armpit, in the groin. The delay between the onset of fever and the appearance of the first buboes was, to the best of my memory, around a full day and night.

'When did you first feel unwell?' I asked Francis, trying to keep my voice calm.

'Yesterday morning,' he replied promptly. 'I awoke very early, before it was light, and I had a terrible headache. I put it down to the ale I'd been served the previous evening, which tasted a little sharp. But then the shivers and the sweats grew worse as the day progressed.'

Yesterday morning.

'May I examine you? All of you?' I asked.

He probably knew why I wanted to. He nodded, fear in his face again, and swiftly I folded back the covers and, unfastening his garments, I felt the areas in the body where the swellings were known to break out.

I found none.

'It is too soon to say with certainty,' I said eventually, helping him to refasten his garments. 'But you are not showing the telltale symptom right now, which is promising.'

He looked at me, his anxiety written in the clearest of scripts across his haggard face. 'And will I?' he whispered.

I pulled up the covers and stood up. I managed a smile. 'Let us hope not,' I said.

He nodded, but the brief movement clearly hurt his head.

I poured water into the mug. 'Drink,' I said, holding it to his mouth, 'and then try to sleep.'

I could see the question in his eyes: If it is not the plague, why am I so very unwell?

I would very much have liked to have been able to provide the answer.

I left the Saracen's Head, having given strict instructions to Coxton to allow Francis Heron to sleep but not to leave him for too long at a stretch. 'And make him drink as much water as you can,' I added.

Coxton gave me a look that said, *You think I have time to be a nurse as well as everything else I have to do this day?* But all the same he gave me a grudging nod, muttering that he'd summon some of the Company to take over as soon as they appeared. 'He's one of them, isn't he?' he asked resentfully, and of course he was right.

I would rather have stayed with Francis and cared for him myself, but I had no choice but to leave him for a while. Others might even now be making their way to Rosewyke in search of the doctor, and in addition I desperately wanted to shut myself up in my study to consult my books and my notes.

The third urgent task – perhaps the most urgent of all – was to call in at St Luke's and say a fervent prayer that what ailed Francis Heron was anything but the plague.

I was on my knees in front of the altar when I heard soft footfalls.

Jonathan waited while I finished my prayer. Then he knelt down beside me and said quietly, 'Would you like us to pray together?'

I hesitated, then nodded.

A little while later we stood side by side by the church door.

'You've obviously heard,' I said. The nature of Jonathan's fervent prayers had just told me he already knew full well what had brought me to his church in such need.

'Yes,' Jonathan agreed. 'Well, such news travels as fast as fire.' He paused, his strange green eyes on mine, then added, 'How is the poor man?'

I didn't answer straight away. My instinct was to assure him that it wasn't the plague that ailed Francis Heron, but I could not be sure, and it would not be fair or right to give our parish priest false hope. 'He is very unwell,' I said eventually. 'But still no sign of the dreaded buboes, and it has now been a full day and night since first he took sick.'

'There is hope, then,' Jonathan said. 'I shall pray for him.'

'Pray for all of us, your reverence,' I replied. It seemed a moment to use Jonathan's proper title. 'If the man truly has the plague, many will catch it. Will have already caught it,' I amended, 'since he was in the close company of a great many people all day yesterday, and probably for many days before that.'

'Gabriel, there is hope,' Jonathan repeated, more firmly this time. 'Each hour that passes strengthens that hope.'

'Yes,' I said wearily. I rubbed my hands over my face. I was so tired, and there was so much I had to do.

Believing my purpose in coming to his church completed, Jonathan opened the heavy old oak door. But I closed it again.

He looked at me enquiringly. 'Something else?'

There was, but this matter was considerably harder to explain. Very aware of his full attention focused on me, I told my vicar about the weird experiences I had encountered in the Saracen's Head.

And when I had finished, he was looking as uneasy as I was feeling.

I rode on to Rosewyke.

Samuel came out into the yard to meet me, Tock just behind him as his permanent shadow, and I gave him Hal's reins. 'Tend him well,' I said – when had Samuel ever needed telling? – 'for I shall be off again presently.'

If he had noticed how carefully I kept my distance from him, he made no comment.

Then there was Sallie to deal with.

'Keep away, Sallie,' I said as I stepped over the doorstep into the kitchen, 'for I have been—'

Her face full of compassion, she interrupted me. 'No need for explanations, Doctor,' she said gently.

And looking behind her, I saw Celia standing in the door-way to the hall. My sister was home, and she had apparently already spread the news that there was a mysterious sickness within the Saracen's Head.

I indicated that Celia should go back into the hall, and went straight after her. 'What are you doing here?' I demanded, my voice made rough by my anxiety. I had believed her far away, a safe distance from me, in Plymouth with her fatuous friend.

I had thought that my unavoidable return to my house might put others in danger, but not my beloved sister.

She glanced over her shoulder towards the parlour. 'I went

to the inn early this morning.' She gave me a cold look. '*If* it's any of your business,' she added. She hadn't forgiven me for my verbal assault of the previous day, then. But, I thought, I hadn't asked for forgiveness. 'I wanted to find out what was happening,' she went on. 'I wanted to—'

'You fool!' I shouted. I wanted to shake her. 'To return to the very place where an unknown sickness has felled a man is utter madness!'

'Then it is a madness she and I share,' said a soft voice. Spinning round towards the parlour, I saw Judyth.

'You too!' I was still shouting.

'You were there,' my sister began, 'and I could not—'

'*I had to be there!*' I yelled. 'There was no choice!'

'No choice for me either!' Celia yelled back. 'You are my brother and I *love* you! Do you imagine I could calmly go about my day without knowing how you fared? I *had* to find out!' Briefly she glanced at Judyth. 'We both had to find out,' she said more calmly. 'We met in the inn yard, and someone told us you had gone home.'

I took a deep breath.

'I am sorry I shouted,' I said, looking at Judyth to include her in the apology. 'It's just that I'm frightened for you. For both of you. I have been tending Francis Heron all night, and it is still not certain that he does not have the plague.'

'Not certain?' Judyth asked sharply. I stared at her, unsure what she meant. With a tut of impatience, she said, 'Is there any sign of the dreaded swellings?'

'No.'

We went on staring at each other for a moment. I think we both knew this was a reason for deep relief, but neither of us said so. Like me, I surmised, she felt it was too soon to say or do anything that might encourage the abandoning of caution.

'What are you doing here?' Celia demanded. 'Shouldn't you be with Master Heron?'

'For one thing, I came to see if there were patients asking for me,' I said.

'There aren't,' she replied.

'Then I shall get on with the other matter, which is to consult my books, because—'

'Because if it's not plague, it must be something else,' she interrupted.

I smiled. I caught Judyth's glance, and she smiled too.

'Go on, then,' my sister said. 'I will bring food and drink up to your study. Quite a lot of both,' she added, 'since you look absolutely frightful – honestly, you need a wash and a change of linen before you go haring off again, Gabe – and I would wager a goodly sum that you have neither eaten nor drunk for hours.'

There was nothing to say but, 'Thank you.'

When I came downstairs some time later – washed, shaved, in a clean shirt, with my head full of possibilities and my belly full of Sallie's good cooking – it was to discover Celia sitting on the window seat of the little morning parlour, calmly embroidering. She was alone.

'Where's Judyth?'

Celia looked up. 'She too has patients who need her,' she replied.

Of course.

'I'm going back into town,' I said. 'I have some ideas as to what ails Master Heron, and most vitally I need to check him again to see if . . .' I didn't finish.

But Celia knew what I would be checking for. 'Be careful, Gabe,' she whispered.

I looked at her. Both of us were well aware of the impossibility of that.

On impulse I said, 'I called in at St Luke's on my way home. Jonathan will not, I think, stray far from his church today.'

She nodded. 'He knows we have need of him,' she said quietly. Then, after a pause, 'It's why I came home, Gabe. Just at the moment, being with Sidony, the prospect of seeing Fallon . . . Oh, I can't explain, but both of them are far too *trivial* for a time like this, when there is such a sense of threat.'

I knew exactly what she meant.

I wanted more than anything to go to her, hug her, drop a kiss on the top of her head. But I kept away.

'Don't go back to Plymouth,' I said. 'Please?'

She smiled very briefly. 'Very well. Not today, anyway.'
Then, after a moment: 'Come home when you can?'

'I will.'

Then I left her.

Before returning to the Saracen's Head and my patient, I
stopped at Theo's house. One of his stable lads came out to
take my horse, but I stayed where I was on the road, not
venturing into the yard.

'Would you please ask Master Davey to come out and
speak to me?' I said.

With a very nervous glance up at me, the lad did as he was
asked.

Only a short time later Theo opened the main door of his
house and began to move towards me.

'Stay there,' I commanded, and, paling a little, he stopped.

'Dear God, please tell me you're not sick?' he breathed,
the words barely audible.

'No,' I said. 'But let us not take any risks that we can
avoid.'

He nodded his understanding. 'Master Heron?'

I paused, still unwilling to put my conclusions into words.
But Theo was the coroner as well as my friend, and on both
counts had a right to know.

'When I left early this morning, there were still no signs
of the plague, and I am very much hoping I shall find him in
the same state when I get back to him,' I said. Theo muttered
words that were probably a prayer. 'Something very grave ails
him, however,' I went on. I paused, staring down at Theo. I
was almost reluctant to speak, for this was the first time
I would be putting my suspicion – and what it implied – into
words. 'I think,' I said quietly, 'that he may have been poisoned.'

'*Poisoned?*' Theo echoed.

'Yes. I have been looking through my books and my case
notes, and I believe whatever it is that is making the poor
man so unwell is one of two substances.'

'Well, go on!' Theo said testily as I paused to prepare my
words.

'You want me to tell you what these substances are?'

Theo rolled his eyes and muttered something that sounded like, *God help me, the man's a dolt!* 'Yes,' he said heavily.

'Oh! Well, it could be solanum,' I began, 'commonly called deadly nightshade. This occurred to me because I've observed that the Company have belladonna with them – which is made from the plant – in the form of drops for the eyes. The youth who played Desdemona had made his pupils hugely distended, so that his eyes acted like little mirrors, reflecting the light. I should warn him of the dangers of prolonged use of belladonna drops,' I said, recalling I had resolved to do just that before everything else drove it out of my head.

'Never mind that just now,' Theo said, clearly mastering his impatience only with difficulty. 'Deadly nightshade's a hedgerow plant, and widely available.'

'Yes. Small dark-blue flowers, then purplish-black berries. All parts are poisonous, as country children are told from the time they can walk, but especially the berries, roots and leaves. Symptoms of belladonna poisoning are hot, dry skin and mouth, dilated pupils, increased heart rate that is so powerful and loud that it can be heard by a bystander some distance off. Also the patient suffers convulsions, incoherence, confusion, and develops a high fever. Symptoms can take hours to develop and the patient may take days to die, and—'

'You're talking like a medical tome,' Theo interrupted drily.

'I'm not surprised. I've just been in my study, reading and memorizing every word I could find on the subject.'

Theo nodded. 'What's the other possibility?'

'Digitalis, which is derived from the foxglove. The leaves are the most toxic part. Digitalis strengthens the heartbeat, and it seems to have the effect – which is highly beneficial for patients with heart trouble – of increasing the time between beats.'

'So this stuff is used as a medicine?' Theo sounded incredulous.

'Not by conventional doctors, or I never heard tell of it. I—' I stopped.

It had been a strange, solitary woman known as Black Carlotta who had told me how to use digitalis. I had been treating a very old man who suffered great distress with a wildly erratic heartbeat and severe, cramping pains in his chest, and one day when I visited him there was an inexplicable improvement in his condition. He had been reluctant to talk to me; in fact he had closed his toothless mouth up tight and not said a word. His wife, however, had had more sense. As she showed me out of her immaculate little house, she leaned close and whispered. 'Speak to that Black Carlotta, Doctor T. *He*' – she jerked her head in her husband's direction – 'says it's secret and not to tell, but me, I reckon you medical folk ought to stick together and share your knowledge.' She nodded in confirmation. 'But don't you dare tell him I said!' she added in a hiss. I quite agreed with her about the pooling of knowledge, and, in a spirit of humble inquiry, I sought out Black Carlotta the moment I had a free afternoon.

'In small and very careful doses it's beneficial,' I said now to Theo, 'and I do in fact use it. But it is perilous, for too much makes the heartbeat more and more erratic, so that it starts to beat harder and harder and eventually stops.'

'And it acts as a toxin?' Theo prompted.

'It does. Other than the wild, powerful heartbeat, the symptoms are headache, nausea, vomiting, irritation of stomach and bowels and stomach pain. The breathing becomes laboured, there are convulsions and tremors. Sometimes the patient experiences a disturbance in the vision, so that everything is seen as if through a veil of yellow, and . . .'

Theo had started to move as I spoke, first diving back into the house, to emerge moments later wearing his dark robe and his cap, then to run into the yard yelling for his horse.

'What are you doing?' I asked as, his right foot still fumbling for the other stirrup, he urged his horse up beside me.

'You're going back to your patient to see what symptoms have developed,' he said. 'Aren't you?'

'Yes.'

'I'm coming with you.'

SEVEN

I could have predicted that Theo would want to come right inside the Saracen's Head with me and into Francis Heron's dark little room, and he did.

I stopped him in the doorway.

'I know you are His Majesty's coroner, and it is you who holds authority here,' I said firmly, 'but you can't come in, Theo.'

'Even overlooking the fact that you and I found what appeared to be a dead body that's since vanished,' he said in an angry hiss, 'you believe this man Heron has been poisoned! If you're right about that, then two crimes have been committed, one or both of which may well lead to a death, if one of them hasn't already done so!'

'I may not be right,' I countered. 'It could still be that Master Heron has the sickness, and you have a wife and family. The risk of catching it – even if he does have it – may be small if you keep your distance, but you are not free to take it.'

Theo stared at me for a moment, his expression hostile. '*You're* going in,' he said gruffly. '*You're* taking the risk.'

'I've already taken it,' I replied. 'I've been tending him since yesterday afternoon. And anyway I'm a doctor. Wait here, I'll come out and tell you if I find anything.'

Before he could think of any more objections, I turned away and strode off into the depths of the inn.

I performed a thorough examination of my patient. His lips were dry and cracked, he was burning with fever, and now and again his whole body tensed into a spasm. Very carefully I felt under his armpits, around his neck and down into his groin. Still no swellings. I said a silent and intense prayer of thanks, and momentarily had an image of Jonathan Carew, keeping his word and maintaining his prayers for us all.

Straightening up, rolling my stiff shoulders, I became aware that someone was standing just outside the open door, his deep eyes no more than dark pools under the heavy brows. It was Barnaby Abell. Like Thomas Lightbodie, he was one of the senior members of the Company; I wondered if the two of them, and the other older men, were particular friends of Francis Heron.

'Have you been looking after him?' I asked.

'Yes. Thomas and I both have, and Gerard sat with him for some time this morning. Reading to him,' he added, making a wry face.

'You have regularly given him water, as I instructed that innkeeper?' I demanded.

'When we've had the time,' Barnaby replied, stepping inside the room.

'Have you noticed any change in him?' I was thinking of the sudden rigidity I'd just observed. 'Convulsions, for example?'

'Doctor, we have much to do!' Barnaby's voice held a mild reproof. 'We have a Company of players to reassure, and if you can name a group of men more likely to gossip and fall to superstitious mutterings and believe the very worst of a situation than a band of actors, I'd like to hear it. In addition we have a performance to put on this afternoon.'

I had been thinking about that, wondering if I should tell Theo, or maybe our local Justice of the Peace, to cancel the performance. But in the end I'd decided there was little point, since for one thing most of the people who would make up the audience had been to at least one play already, and for another, I was now all but sure that what was making Francis so desperately unwell was poison.

'It doesn't *stop*, you know,' Barnaby added with sudden vehemence. 'The play may seem a trivial thing to you, Doctor, when a man lies so sick before you, but the theatre is our livelihood, and if we don't perform we don't eat.' He paused. 'However,' he went on more calmly, 'we've done our best, Gerard, Thomas and I, and for my part, I observed no convulsions. The boy's been in and out too, when Harry Perrot lets him out of his sight,' he added, and there was a tinge of spite in his voice.

'The boy?'

'Raphe. Raphe Wymer. Our leading lady.' Now the spite was unmistakable. 'Played Desdemona, Titania and the Noblewoman.'

'Ah.'

The young man who had so thoughtfully given me the strawberry spotted handkerchief to bind Francis's head.

And who – far more disturbingly – I'd seen have his head cut off in the mirror.

Barnaby cleared his throat. 'You've been examining him?' He nodded in Francis's direction.

'Yes,' I said shortly.

He leaned closer. 'Well?' he said. His face was rigid with tension.

I could have punched myself.

'I am so sorry,' I said, meaning it. 'I should have told you straight away. It's good news. There is still no sign of the pestilence.'

'Praise the Lord,' Barnaby whispered, and I saw him furtively cross himself.

I wanted to do the same thing myself.

By the time Theo was back in his office he knew Gabe had been absolutely right to stop him going into the sick man's room. All the way home, Theo had been trying to recall how close he'd got to Master Heron the previous afternoon, and he couldn't remember getting that near.

'Not close enough for him to breathe on me, or for an adventurous flea to jump into my garments and bury itself,' he muttered. 'Or so I fervently hope.'

He took off his long robe and sank down in the old oak chair behind his desk. Quite soon now, when the working day was over, he would be going upstairs to the family's living quarters. To Elaine, Carolus, Isabella and Benjamin. Would he be unknowingly taking a death sentence with him? Gabe had been as good as his word and come out again to report on Francis Heron's condition, and told him there were still no ominous swellings, but was that proof enough that this wasn't the plague? He groaned aloud, burying his face in his hands.

He was still sitting like that when there was a tap on the door and Jarman Hodge quietly entered the office.

'Trouble?' he said as Theo removed his hands and looked up at him.

'This *blasted accursed* sickness,' Theo replied furiously, quite surprising himself with his sudden vehemence.

Jarman nodded. 'Know how you feel,' he said. 'It's the uncertainty, isn't it? Has the poor sod got it or hasn't he? If he has, how far has it spread?'

'And Gabriel Taverner's no help!' Theo said resentfully. 'Won't come down on one side or the other, damn him.'

'I'm sure he will as soon as he can,' Jarman said reasonably.

Theo nodded, feeling a sharp stab of guilt. 'Course he will. He'll be back with Master Heron even now, watching him like a hawk, I've no doubt, for the first sign of – for anything,' he finished, reluctant to put the dreaded symptom into words. 'Sorry,' he added.

Jarman grinned briefly. 'Not to worry, chief, don't suppose he heard.'

'Sit down,' Theo said.

Jarman did so. 'I've been on the trail of the young man in rust-red velvet,' he said.

'Rust-red velvet . . .' It took a moment for Theo's memory to work. 'Yes.' He shot Jarman a rueful look. 'He'd been driven to the back of my mind, what with one thing and another. What have you found out?'

'Bugger all,' Jarman said. 'I thought I'd located him – I saw someone in the street dressed in that precise shade, and followed him on a winding, doubling-back trail through most of the streets of Plymouth, which I might say was no mean feat, given how crowded the town is just now.'

'You caught him?' Theo asked eagerly.

'No, chief. Well, I did, but it wasn't the man seemingly lying dead behind the stage who *you* saw in the velvet costume, it was that lad that takes the main female roles, the one with the huge eyes and the long neck.' He swore under his breath, lengthily, colourfully and without repetition. Then he said darkly, 'I reckon they're playing games with us.'

Theo frowned. 'So let me work this out . . . Gabe and I

were standing beside the stage and heard a scream, and we ran into the tiring room and saw a body dressed in rust-red velvet, and Gabe reckoned he might well be dead, but before he could make sure we were called away because the other man – this Master Heron – had collapsed, and when we got back the body had gone.'

Jarman started to speak but Theo had remembered something else. 'And Gabe noticed the rust-coloured costume didn't fit him very well – it was too small!'

Jarman nodded thoughtfully. 'So, what are we thinking? The costume properly belongs to this lad with the lustrous eyes, and for some reason he – or someone else – decided to dress another, bigger man in it and then kill him, only to sneak the corpse away when nobody was looking, strip the velvet costume off it and give it back to the pretty lad?'

'Well . . .' Theo had to admit it sounded unlikely.

Jarman shook his head in frustration. 'In God's holy name, *why*?'

'I cannot begin to fathom it,' Theo admitted, 'although I have a worrying suspicion that if you're right in saying they are playing games, then I very much fear something alarmingly dark may be going on beneath the surface.'

Jarman gave him a long look. Then he said, 'My thoughts exactly, chief.' Before Theo could react – for Jarman was a level-headed sort of man who did not allow his imagination to run away, and his instant endorsement of Theo's fears was in itself worrying – Jarman spoke again.

'I *can* tell you something about this mysterious fellow Daniel,' he said, his voice reassuringly matter-of-fact.

His mind on undercurrents and sinister plots and the faint but horrible possibility of a fatal sickness in their midst, Theo could not recall for the moment who Daniel was.

Jarman supplied the information.

'The man who had the conversation with Francis Heron that you overheard in the alleyway behind the inn,' he said. 'When you'd taken your youngest out for his piss.'

'Of course,' Theo said, trying to sound as if he'd known all along. 'I told you to locate him and you said you'd discovered he was a carter, or a baggage-haulier, and lodged with his

fellow carters somewhere on the edge of town. Go on, then!
What else can you tell me?'

'Don't get your hopes up,' Jarman said in response to his
eager tone. 'It's not much, and it's more a question of who
he isn't than who he is, if you take my meaning.'

'I don't,' Theo said bluntly.

Jarman grinned briefly. 'He's not one of the players in the
Company, and out among the carters and luggage-handlers,
nobody seems to know much about him. Not a few of them
said they hadn't known there was a Daniel among their number,
and I was beginning to think you must have misheard the
name, or else I'd misheard you when you told me. Then
someone said there *was* a Daniel, and told me what he knew
about him.'

'It wasn't much, I'll wager,' Theo said disconsolately,
'because if it had been you'd have sought me out and told
me by now.'

Jarman nodded. 'You're right, boss, and in truth, it's not
really anything to get fired up about, and, like you just said,
there have been other things happening that have driven all
that out of the mind.'

Gritting his teeth, Theo said, 'What *have* you to say on this
Daniel?'

Jarman paused. Then: 'He's newly joined the gang who
do the heavy work. They're a tight-knit bunch, and most of
them on this tour have been with the Company for some time.
Course, they need to take on new hands when someone dies
or gets too old for the job – it's hard work, anyone can see
that – but it seems that wasn't the reason why this Daniel
came asking for a job with them.'

He paused. Theo waited.

'The man I heard this from didn't really want to talk to
me,' he said thoughtfully. 'I had to buy him a second mug of
ale, and even then I reckon he only spoke up in order to get
rid of me.' Theo smiled to himself. Jarman was as dogged as
a terrier after a rat when he wanted to squeeze information
out of someone, and it took a rare resolve to resist him.

'For one thing, there seems to be a rumour that Daniel's
not his real name,' Jarman continued. 'Not that in itself that's

much to get excited about, since there's probably thousands of people skulking about the country who are no longer known by their baptismal name, the times being what they are.' There was no need for him to elaborate; Theo knew as well as he did how the land still trembled at the thought of the religious strife that had riven the populace apart, and that was still too vivid a memory in most people's minds. And now there was a new monarch on the throne, and even after a year and a half nobody really knew what the future held. His wife the Queen was said to favour Catholics, for one thing, and some went so far as to say she had converted to the faith. The King's mother, of course, had been utterly staunch in her devotion to Rome . . . Rumours of plots and counter-plots were everywhere. Nothing was sure, nothing was certain.

But Jarman was still speaking. Theo came out of his brief troubling reverie and listened.

'. . . confided in this man I talked to while they were on the road, seemingly, over a jar or two of ale one night,' he was saying. 'Probably more than two, given that it appears he let his guard down. Said that he'd needed to get out of London. Didn't we all, my new friend replied, but this Daniel, he said it wasn't the plague so much as the fact that someone was on his trail, and when my fellow laughed and said, "Owe someone money, do you?" he said it was far worse than that, only then he seemed to realize he'd said too much already and closed up tight as a fist.'

'And your man didn't learn any more?'

'Well, not directly, but there was something else. Now this is third-hand at least,' Jarman said warningly, 'and from what I can tell, this gang of carters and what have you gossip and mutter behind their hands as much as or possibly even more than any other group thrown into close proximity with each other for weeks on end.'

'Oh, for God's sake, Jarman!' Theo exploded. 'Never mind the caveats, just *tell* me!'

'Sorry, boss.' Jarman shot him a quick look. 'Well, seems our Daniel, or whatever his name is, has a troubled conscience or something, because it seems he suffers from nightmares, and one night on the road between Bath and Barnstaple he got so bad that the three men sleeping nearby had to shake him to wake him up.'

'Then what happened?' Theo demanded.

'He denied it all,' Jarman replied. 'Said they'd misheard – not likely, given that all three reported pretty much the same words – and then that he'd had too much cheese for supper and it had affected him, and that his belly was swelled and tight like a sheep with bloat. Seems his three bedfellows didn't believe that, either.'

'What had he said, then? When he was having the nightmare?'

'He didn't *say* it, seemingly, he yelled it, or maybe howled it,' Jarman said gravely. 'He was moaning and sobbing, said it wasn't any use asking him because he didn't know, had no knowledge of it, that they hadn't told him anything because he wasn't of their number and in any case he'd never had anything to do with them anyway.'

'Who was he referring to?' Theo asked. For some reason he found he was whispering.

There was quite a long pause. Then Jarman said – and Theo thought he heard a tremor of unease in his tough, reliable and self-sufficient agent – 'Ever heard of a group calling themselves the Scholars of the Numinous?'

EIGHT

I was standing on the quay, staring out at the sea crashing against the wooden piles of a jetty, taking what I told myself was a well-earned break from poor Francis Heron's increasingly malodorous little room. The day was cold but invigorating, and I filled my lungs again and again, imagining all the foul and very possibly dangerous miasmas being expelled from my body to be replaced with clean, fresh, salty and above all healthy sea air.

I was fooling myself, and I knew it. If there was infection lurking in that place, then breathing in the purest air in all the world wouldn't make any difference, and Plymouth harbour was nowhere near as clean as I'd just been trying to convince myself.

I was about to turn and go back to my patient when I heard someone call my name. As I spun round, Theo came hurrying up.

'What news?' I asked, hearing the tension in my voice. I don't know what I feared, specifically; but the times were worrying just then.

Theo shook his head. 'Nothing much,' he replied. 'Seems this Daniel had been raising a few suspicions even before the Company arrived in Plymouth.'

'He's been found?'

'No, Gabe, I'd have told you,' Theo said patiently. 'Jarman's been talking to the gang who work with him and share their sleeping quarters with him. He's clearly got an uneasy conscience, because there are reports of nightmares, of yelling and sobbing in his sleep, and it seems he was on the run from someone – or perhaps several someones – who wished him harm.' He paused, frowning. 'He mentioned some bunch known as the Scholars of the Numinous.'

I tried to remember what numinous meant. It made me think of matters of faith; of strange and arcane spiritual beliefs and practices. All of which was pretty vague and of no help at all. 'Never heard of them,' I said.

Theo looked exasperated. 'Then how are we to—'

But I knew someone who very likely would know of this group. 'I'm going to make one further check on Francis,' I said, interrupting, 'and then I'm going to Tavy St Luke to talk to Jonathan Carew.'

The tautness in Theo's expression eased. 'Of course,' he said softly. But then: 'Gabe, is it right to call on him?'

'I will be sure to stand apart from him,' I said. My conviction that what ailed Francis Heron was not the plague was growing with each hour that the buboes failed to appear, and besides I was absolutely sure that Jonathan would not wish to hold himself aloof from whatever was going to come to pass, but it made sense to be cautious where I could.

Theo nodded. 'Take care, Gabe,' he said. 'Report back to me, please.'

'I will.'

It was wonderful to be riding out of the town and into the clean, green countryside. The conjoined rivers were running high, hurrying to pour themselves into the sea, and the air was full of the smell of brine.

Jonathan was not in his church, where I looked for him first, but in the Priest's House next door. He kept the place neat and clean, and it was furnished only lightly with his possessions. I noted again, as I had observed before, that he was a man of frugal habits. Yet the few items he did have were of fine quality and, to judge from their disposition near at hand to the chair by the fireside where he habitually sat, in very regular use. There was a thick notebook, a leather-bound prayer book, a small but beautifully made silver mug.

I don't think he heard my knock, but he did hear the door open, and called out, 'Come in – I'm in the scullery.'

He cannot have known the identity of his visitor, but such was his open-heartedness that it did not matter.

'It's me,' I called, ducking my head to negotiate a low doorway.

'Gabriel!' He looked up with a smile of welcome. 'I am

preparing food. Since I am quite sure you will not have eaten today, please join me. Go and sit down by the hearth and warm yourself, and I will bring it through.'

I hadn't realized how hungry I was. My rapid, unthinking consumption of the food Celia had brought up to my study early that morning seemed like something that had happened yesterday, if not before. It was quite possible, I thought, that appetite had only returned once I had quit the port and begun to breathe the clean air of the countryside.

I was quite sure this was also Jonathan's first food since early this morning, so I held back my questioning until we had both cleared our platters. There was smoked ham, two different cheeses, a thick hunk of bread with butter, pickled onions and some chutney, with a mug of ale to drink. Every morsel was delicious.

'Now,' Jonathan said, topping up our mugs, 'what news?'

Briefly I told him. On hearing that Francis Heron still showed no plague symptoms, he closed his eyes for some moments.

'The poor man is still gravely ill,' I said when he opened them again.

'Yes, I was praying for him,' Jonathan replied. 'But first, I was giving thanks that my pleas have been answered and we do not have a case of the dreaded pestilence on our doorstep.'

'It may still develop in him,' I warned.

He looked at me, his eyes steady on mine. 'Will it?'

In the face of his cool stare, I found myself saying what I truly believed. 'I do not think so.' After a moment I added, 'I am not well versed personally in the sickness, having no first-hand experience of treating its victims, but all that I have learned from my brother physicians suggests that if Master Heron was infected while still in London, he would have been dead of it some time ago.'

Jonathan nodded. Then he said quietly, 'Of course, it is possible he was infected somewhere on the road.'

'It is,' I agreed heavily.

'I shall maintain my prayer vigil,' he said. 'Tonight I shall be joined by some of my parishioners.'

I was about to protest that in these worrying times we should do all we could to keep distant from one another, but as if he knew what I was thinking, he smiled gently and shook his head. 'People feel the need to do something,' he said.

'They know?' I said sharply. Then I thought, of course they know.

And, his face sombre, Jonathan said, 'They do.'

There was a brief pause. He leaned forward to put more logs on the fire, poking at those beneath and sending out showers of orange sparks. Resuming his seat, he said, 'I fear the plague, as do we all, but my ignorance of it – how it is caught, how it is spread, what proportion of infections prove fatal – leads me all too readily towards despair, for I find myself believing the very worst. You just said that you had no first-hand experience of treating its victims, but I am quite certain, Gabriel, that you know more than I do.' He stared at me, and I saw enquiry in his expression.

I returned his stare. I had a fair idea what he wanted of me: a firm answer to the question of whether or not Francis Heron had brought the plague to Plymouth, and if he had, were others – in particular, the many men, women and children for whose spiritual welfare Jonathan was responsible – now in danger?

I was on the point of saying no, they are safe from this peril at least, when slowly he shook his head.

He held my gaze a little longer, then abruptly turned his face away. 'I am sorry, Gabriel,' he said very softly. 'It is not fair to demand the reassurance from a mortal man that can only come from God.'

The silence extended for some time.

Then Jonathan came out of whatever reverie he had been in – perhaps he had been deep in communion with his Lord – and reached for the ale jug.

'Glad as I am to see you and to have tidings of your patient,' he said as once more he filled my mug, his voice so absolutely normal that our recent worrying exchange might not have taken place, 'I cannot think that it was your sole reason for coming to see me?'

'It wasn't.' I had forgotten how perceptive he was. I

explained about the missing man Daniel, and how I'd thought
he was dead, only to have the body apparently vanish. I told
him what Jarman Hodge had found out. 'This Daniel had
apparently been raving in his sleep, and those who overheard
said he was terrified of a group known as the Scholars of the
Numinous, and—'

But at the mention of the name, Jonathan had jerked his head
sharply to look at me and I thought he muttered something.

'You know of them,' I said.

Slowly he nodded. 'I am not – unfamiliar with them.'

I waited.

After quite some time he said, 'We live, Gabriel, in a time
of change. Men no longer hold the same certainties. The world
seems to grow smaller as brave and greedy men explore it and
uncover its secrets. Faith is not, I must regretfully admit, the
anchor and the bulwark of us all that once it was, and those
of an enquiring mind search for other truths.' He paused.
'There is a fascination with alchemy, with astronomy, with
philosophy, and men require the proof that they can see
with their own eyes in order to believe what they once
took on faith. To further this fervent pursuit of the new knowledge, some men amass vast private libraries, and collect
instruments of science to assist their studies.'

'I have heard tell of such men,' I said when once again he
paused for thought. I hesitated, then added, 'In a very modest
way, I am doing much the same. I am a member of a small
group of men – physicians like myself – who try to meet
from time to time to discuss ideas and developments in our
field, and to share each other's thoughts.' In truth, the
Symposium – our somewhat grandiose name for ourselves
– had not met for some time, and before we next did so I still
had much work to do on my lecture concerning the doctrine
of signatures.

'Many others similarly come together for mutual advantage,' Jonathan commented. 'Sir Walter Raleigh runs one
such group, although since December of last year its members
will have had to manage without him.'

It was last December, I recalled, that Raleigh had been
imprisoned in the Tower for allegedly plotting against the

King. From all accounts it was not an arduous imprisonment; it was said he was comfortably housed and well looked after, able to pursue his studies and his writing and even to entertain guests. Nevertheless, I'd always thought that imprisonment of any kind must be very hard on a man like Raleigh, who undoubtedly wanted more than anything to return to the Orinoco river and try once again to locate the fabled city of gold and the gold-covered, undoubtably mythical figure known as El Dorado . . .

'Sir Walter is not the only man of renown and position to pursue such studies,' Jonathan was saying. 'He is said to be close to Sir Henry Percy, the—'

'The Wizard Earl!' I interrupted.

'Indeed,' Jonathan said with a grin. 'So called, however, less for the unlikely possibility that he can perform magic and appear and disappear at will, than because of his deep interest in astronomy and alchemy. Others are said to be connected with Raleigh's Durham House group, such as Christopher Marlowe and Thomas Harriot.' He paused, shooting a quick, assessing glance at me. Then he said softly, 'John Dee.'

I knew the name, but for the moment I couldn't think why. I was already very tired, and the food had combined with the ale and the warmth of Jonathan's fire to make me dull-witted. 'John Dee . . .' I repeated. Then, suddenly remembering, 'The Queen's astronomer! Was it not him who told her the most auspicious date for her coronation?'

Jonathan smiled. 'I do not imagine a man as wise as Dee *told* the Queen anything,' he murmured, 'but, yes, that was him.'

Slowly I shook my head. 'I have not heard that name for years,' I said. 'I'd imagined he was dead.'

'Not dead, no, but in recent years he has been far away from his beloved house in Mortlake and warden of Christ's College in Manchester. Although he may be back by now,' he muttered, frowning. 'For a man who loves London and its glittering society as much as John Dee does,' he added with a rueful smile, 'perhaps it amounts to much the same thing.'

Belatedly I recalled the question that had led to this

outpouring of information. 'The Scholars of the Numinous?' I prompted.

'Yes,' Jonathan said. 'I hadn't forgotten, but what I have to tell you required a context.'

'So this society, school, or whatever they call it, is the same sort of thing as Raleigh's Durham House group?' I demanded.

He frowned. 'In its form, perhaps.' The frown deepened, and I thought a shadow fell across his face. Perhaps it was simply that night was falling. 'But the matters they explore are altogether darker. They go willingly into danger, for the very nature of their studies is perilous. Moreover, the focus of their intelligence and their fiercely pursued inquiry would, were proof of it to become known by those who wield power in our land, put them on the direct path to the Tower, and to imprisonment without the least semblance of a trial. They would, quite simply, disappear. Not be there. And, even as the servants, relatives, friends or casual acquaintances were beginning to scratch their heads and ask themselves, "Where's *he* got to, then?" would be suffering the most dreadful, agonizing and prolonged death.'

And like an echo in my head, I heard Theo telling me what he'd overheard in the alley outside the Saracen's Head: *I fear for my life, Daniel, and the death that stalks me is a particularly awful and long-drawn-out one that haunts me by night and day.*

Francis Heron had spoken those words. And the very next day he was lying desperately sick, and now – I admitted it to myself there in the tranquil privacy of Jonathan's little house – he would in all likelihood soon be dead. Even though I was now all but certain it was not the plague, nevertheless he was visibly sinking. I looked up and met Jonathan's eyes. I wanted to ask a dozen questions, to push him to tell me more, so much more. But it was brave of him, even in his own house, to tell me as much as he had done. Besides, thinking of Master Heron had reminded me that I ought to be heading back to him. I stood up, and, unsteady on my feet, staggered slightly.

'You are exhausted, Gabriel,' Jonathan said. 'I hope you are not planning to ride back to Plymouth?'

'I am,' I said shortly.

He sighed. 'In order to tend others efficiently, first tend yourself,' he said. I opened my mouth to protest, for all that it was precisely what I'd told myself, but he didn't let me. 'I know there is no hope that you will be sensible and return to Rosewyke and go to bed' – he was quite right, there wasn't – 'but I suggest instead you go upstairs to the tiny space that I refer to as my second bedroom, remove your boots, cover yourself with the warm blanket you'll find there and sleep for a few hours. I will wake you,' he added, 'at whatever time you specify.'

I closed my eyes. The room spun round a few times, and I think I may even have slept very briefly even as I stood there.

'No later than midnight,' I said. 'I have your word?'

'You do.'

I was on the small and not very comfortable bed, tucking the blanket around me, when I heard the door open and close quietly as Jonathan went back to St Luke's. I was already falling into deep sleep.

NINE

I t was in the deep darkness after midnight and before the first of the light that I made my way back to the Saracen's Head. Hal was resentful at being disturbed and removed from his warm stable, and it was a good half a mile until he developed any enthusiasm for the excursion.

The streets of Plymouth were deserted. The night was very cold, which was no doubt keeping even the most hardened of the nefariously minded indoors. Here and there a light showed in an upper room. I imagined a woman sitting with an elderly dying relative, or a mother with a restless infant.

I felt very alone.

The Saracen's Head was in darkness, and profoundly silent. I knew the way through the maze of passages and managed to negotiate it, and the occasional short flight of steps, without incident. Here and there soft light filtered through from some unknown source, and it sufficed.

I had fully expected that someone – Barnaby, or Gerard, or the young actor Raphe Wymer, even the innkeeper himself – might either be keeping watch on Master Heron, or else, hearing my approach, come out to see who it was. But there was nobody about. I was surprised, and then angry. Surely someone should have been looking after poor Francis?

Even as I'd crossed the inn yard and gone inside, I had begun to feel that something was amiss. Hurrying along the final little corridor leading to the sick man's room, my unease was rapidly increasing.

For some reason I kept wanting to look over my shoulder.

My mind filled with the absurd notion that there was something . . . unnatural, or even otherworldly, lurking.

But those were no thoughts for a man of science to entertain. Quite forcefully, I pushed open the door to Francis's room and stepped inside.

And as I drew close to my patient, every single sensation

that I had just been experiencing increased tenfold, so that, just for a moment, I felt myself quake under the onslaught.

'I have a patient to attend,' I muttered aloud.

I bent down over the bed. Used to the various stenches of sickness as I was, even for me it was a struggle to remain so close to him. But then I saw how he was fighting to breathe. How his wide-open eyes searching for mine were filled with panic and the fear of death.

He reached out and grabbed hold of my fingers. His hand was like a claw, the long nails yellowish and curved like talons. I could see from the blood vessel pumping in his temple how fast his heart was beating; releasing myself from his grip, I put my fingers on his wrist. The pulse of his heart was wildly erratic, speeding up to unsustainable levels one moment only to die away to a sluggish movement that I struggled to detect.

'My head aches so,' Francis moaned, his voice cracking and barely audible. 'I wish I could—'

But whatever he wished for I would never know, for just then his body arched up off the mean little bed and he began to twist and writhe in a violent convulsion. After a short time it ceased, and I was just wringing out a cloth in the bowl of water on the floor beside him when he had another one.

Looking down at him, pity squeezing my heart, I wondered how much more of this torment his exhausted body could bear.

Presently he lay quiet. He was so still that I thought for a moment the life had gone out of him. Then I perceived that he was still breathing, but so shallowly that it was all but undetectable. While he was seemingly unaware, I put my hand to his neck, and then felt down under the blanket and inside his garments to his groin.

There was not a sign of a swelling.

I said a brief, heartfelt prayer of thanks.

Then I sat down on the edge of the bed and took his hand.

His eyes were closed, but he was sufficiently aware to register my presence.

'I am dying, Doctor,' he said on a long sigh.

I did not answer, save to hold his hand more tightly. After a moment I said, 'Do you wish me to summon a priest?'

He made a sound that could have been a laugh. 'A priest!' he echoed. 'Oh, dear, I think not.' He paused, struggling to take a few breaths. 'I do not believe there is any use, thank you, Doctor,' he said, so courteously that he might have been declining the offer of an extra blanket. 'I fear I do not have long enough to confess all that I should, for long ago I took the path into darkness.'

'Redemption is there for us all,' I said. 'We have only to open our hearts to God and beg his forgiveness for our sins, and—'

Again with that exquisite courtesy, he said, 'No, thank you.'

We sat in silence. His breathing was faint now, sometimes ceasing altogether for what seemed like an impossibly long time. He felt very hot, his skin bone-dry and stretched over the bones of his skull.

I sensed his consciousness slipping further away.

Feeling all at once very alone, I thought back to what he had said about taking the path into darkness. And against my will I remembered what Jonathan had said about the Scholars of the Numinous concerning themselves with dark secrets . . .

What had he meant? Now, despite the fear that I could feel creeping through me, I found myself wishing he had either said more, or else nothing at all.

And what, exactly, had Francis Heron done?

As if he felt my mind questing towards his, suddenly he opened his eyes very wide. 'It was so very seductive, you see,' he said, his voice so faint that I strained to make out the words. 'We all felt that our awareness was newly opened. That it was us, with our superior intelligence, our enquiring minds and our highly developed intellects, who had been chosen to push back the boundaries of knowledge. To break apart the rigid bonds of the powers that once held sway and that still would have us kept in blind ignorance, unquestioning, helplessly floundering in the muck and the mire.' The long outpouring, with barely a breath, left him panting and gasping. Looking vaguely surprised – perhaps at hearing himself talking after so long a silence – he tried to sit up, emitting a whimper of pain. Gently I pushed him back onto the pillows.

After a while he spoke again.

'What men they were!' he breathed, his dry lips cracking as he tried to smile. 'Sir Walter, with his uncrushable spirit, his courage, his ruthless determination to find his golden city of Manõa, no matter the cost!' Dropping his voice, beckoning me closer, he murmured, 'He *will* find it, you know – this sojourn in the Tower will end, and our new monarch will fund an expedition, just as his predecessor did, for who could resist all that is promised in that wonderful book?'

I knew which book he meant: it was entitled *The Discovery of Guiana*. Raleigh had written it on his return from the Orinoco in the late 1590s, and even his best friends and most loyal supporters quietly admitted that it was full of the wildest exaggerations, in particular concerning the ease with which he was going to find enormous amounts of gold in the country. His aim, of course, had been to persuade Elizabeth to pay for another expedition, and the old Queen would have been all too readily persuaded, believing, as did the majority of the English, that the Spanish had no right at all to the vast wealth they had plundered from the Americas and that its rightful place was in the coffers of England. Raleigh in particular loathed the Spanish, and had once famously said that without their territories in South America, Spain's monarchs would be no more than kings of figs and oranges.

I dragged my mind away from Walter Raleigh and back to what Francis had just said. Hearing it again in my head, it sounded as if he was predicting the future. The thought gave me a shudder of dread. Weren't such practices regarded as heresy?

But he was still speaking, and his wide-roaming thoughts had moved on.

'And the Wizard Earl, down at Petworth!' he exclaimed. 'Wealthy as a king, and, in his diabolical triplicity with Raleigh and Henry Brooke, how very much greater the potential for power! Oh, you should have seen his library!' He paused, panting, his face alight with the power of his memories. 'The drawers full of maps to fire the imagination and the wanderlust!

And the alchemical experiments! Oh, what would I give to have that life again!' His eyes burned as he stared up at me. 'This is not me, you see.' He lifted his hand – the effort seemed monumental – and indicated his thin, twisted body. 'I am not the man you think I am, Doctor, and you would not believe what I have seen.'

The talking had exhausted him, and for some time he lay silent, inert, his eyes closed, his breathing a mere shallow, intermittent puff.

I waited, for I was sure the end was close now.

But then he murmured, 'They ransacked his library, you know. When he was far away in Poland. He returned to ruination and the heartache of knowing his vast treasury of learning had been broken up, sold for vulgar gain, trampled in the mud and hurled in the Thames.' Two tears rolled down the sunken cheeks. 'Poor, poor man. How did he stand such pain?'

I thought he was still speaking of this Wizard Earl, and I was about to comment, to attempt a question or two, but he hadn't finished. 'We searched everywhere. We all knew those precious objects were priceless, although their value was incomprehensible to the common man. I would not give up, even when the others did, and my perseverance was rewarded!' His eyes shone with a fervid light and he grabbed for my hand. 'You've seen it, haven't you? Full of magic, isn't it?' He made a sound that I realized was laughter, but it was horribly distorted. Then abruptly his voice dropped to a whisper and he hissed, 'They want it, they have followed me all this way because they are determined to have it, but I shall not give it up! I could have burnt it – *should* have burnt it, for it is perilous – but, you see, it was his.' More tears overflowed from his weary eyes. 'How could I destroy it, when there is so very little left?'

I had no idea what he was talking about. I suspected he was delirious, and I said soothingly. 'I'm sure you acted for the best, and—'

But with incredible suddenness, a profound change came over Francis Heron.

His face contorted into anguish, then into deep, violent

hatred. He flung out his clenched fists, aiming for my face, but I ducked out of the way. Screeching in frustration, he opened his mouth and let out streams of curses and blasphemies that were among the worst utterances I had ever heard.

It was horrifying.

Among the terrible outpourings there seemed to be some consistent threads – certain words repeated several times – but I was at a loss to extract a meaning. He ranted about devils, about spirits with the skill to pollute the innocent, about apparently innocuous objects turned into powerful instruments of destruction through the acquisition of secret and terrible knowledge.

In the end I covered my ears and waited for him to finish.

It seemed a very long time until dawn began to lighten the sky. My patient was quiet now, the wild ravings long finished. I did not think he had the energy for any more, for he was very close to death.

Some alteration in the darkness aroused my attention, and I raised my head and looked round the room.

Even as I turned away from him, Francis stirred – a tiny movement – and called out something that I could not make out. He sobbed, just once, and briefly his body clenched in a final convulsion. Then he fell back onto the bed and was still.

I leaned over him, and there was no longer even the faintest suggestion of breath. I put my fingers on his wrist, unable to detect a pulse. I sat for some time, still holding his arm. I had the strongest sense of his presence, but then abruptly it was gone.

Francis Heron was dead.

Some time later – I was not sure how much – I heard someone shuffling their feet in the passage outside. Getting up, my body stiff from sitting still so long, I went across and opened the door.

Barnaby Abell stood there.

'Is he . . .' He paused delicately.

'He's dead,' I said bluntly.

Barnaby nodded. 'Thought it was close, last night,' he said
in a whisper, as if the dead man could still hear.

'You did tend him, then?' I asked caustically. 'And don't
tell me you paid regular visits all through the night, because
I shall know it for a lie. I was here myself from not long after
midnight.'

Barnaby looked down. He muttered something.

'What was that?'

He seemed to be struggling with himself, but then abruptly
he burst out, 'I *did* tend him! Four times – well, three anyway
– I came along to wash his face and try to get him to drink,
but then' – his face was twisting as he tried to go on – 'then
I didn't come any more. *I couldn't!* Couldn't make myself,
even though I knew I should, and I was virtually the only one
of us that even *tried*! Dear merciful God, I've told myself to
ignore them, the players and the inn servants and that, when
they lurk in corners whispering of their ghastly experiences,
but . . .' He broke off, muttering a jumble of broken words
and phrases, and then, raising his head and meeting my eyes,
he whispered, 'There's something *so wrong* here.'

I could hear the terror in his voice, and even in the pale
light, I could see that his face was white and glistening with
sweat.

It seemed unlikely I would extract anything more from him
by yelling at him. I said quietly, 'What happened?'

And when he'd told me, I wished fervently that I hadn't
asked.

I staggered out into the clean, cold air of the inn yard.
Barnaby had melted away somewhere into the private regions
of the establishment, and I hoped very much there was a
warm bed waiting for him, and the comforting presence of
others of the Company. What he had seen, or thought he
had seen, last night had clearly shaken him badly. It had
shaken me too, and I was only hearing about it, not experiencing it. The trouble was that in those dark, ancient, secret
passages at the rear of the inn, I had already felt that something
was not right.

I looked up at the stars, fading now as the light waxed.

Then someone softly spoke my name.

I spun round so fast that my neck creaked. 'I am sorry, I believe I startled you,' said Jonathan.

Startled, I reflected, was quite an understatement.

'No matter,' I replied. I was about to ask him why he had come but then I knew.

'He is dead?' Jonathan asked.

'Yes. Not long since.'

'Did he ask for a priest?'

'Er – I suggested he might like one, but he said no.'

Jonathan nodded. 'If you will show me the way, Gabriel, I will offer up my prayers for him and sit with him a while.'

I would have said that returning to the dead man's room was the very last thing I wanted to do, and that I'd find it impossible not to show my dread. But I had underestimated the powerful effect of Jonathan Carew's presence. He had undoubtedly been in his church all night, and it seemed to me as I walked through the darkness at his side that he had brought with him something of the bright, benevolent, loving Lord he served so devotedly. At one point I actually thought I saw a halo of light hovering in front of me, encircling a strong face with a gentle smile, but admittedly I was very tired.

Jonathan looked into the room at Francis Heron's still body. Then he turned to me and said, 'Thank you, Gabriel. I will look after him now.'

And very shortly afterwards, I found myself back in the yard.

I had put the saddle and bridle on my horse, fastened my bag and was about to mount up when there was the clatter of hooves on the road outside and Jarman Hodge rode into the yard.

I led Hal forward so I could speak to Jarman without raising my voice.

'Master Heron died just after dawn,' I told him.

He stared at me, his eyes intent on mine. Almost imperceptibly he raised his eyebrows.

I knew what he was asking.

'His body shows not a sign of the plague,' I said quietly.

'Thank God,' Jarman muttered, and I saw him surreptitiously cross himself.

At times of high emotion, I've noticed, men tend to revert unthinkingly to the religious practices of their childhood.

'You look dreadful, Doctor T,' Jarman said bluntly.

'I'm tired,' I replied with a smile.

I could have given him a different answer. Could have passed on to him a condensed version of what Barnaby had just revealed to me. Told him that inexplicable and very frightening things had been happening in the Saracen's Head, that several people had seen mysterious dark-robed figures, that a serving girl had gone home weeping in terror because she'd seen 'something that ain't possible', although her pitiful state had made the other inn servants reluctant to force her to elucidate. That Coxton, when some of the younger Company men had challenged him, had shrugged indifferently and said the inn had stood there a very long time and seen its share of violence and unnatural death.

That quite a few of these inexplicable happenings involved the antique mirror. Which made me more than half inclined to believe these accounts were true, given that I had seen a woman in black have her head cut from her body in that very same glass.

I forced my attention back to Jarman Hodge.

'You are looking for me?' I asked.

He jumped slightly. His thoughts too had clearly been far from the inn yard. 'Aye, Doctor,' he replied. 'A lad's just called at the coroner's office to report there's a pair of corpses been found. On the moor edge on a track off the road out beyond Buckland, in a little-used old barn.'

'And Master Davey requires my presence.' I didn't need to ask, for I knew the drill.

'He's gone on ahead,' Jarman said. 'The farmer who found them has gone with him. Man insisted on showing him the way,' he added. 'As if a man born and bred right here didn't know every inch of the area as well as *he* did.'

I felt my shoulders slump. I'd been visualizing a quick ride

home, a bite to eat and then my bed, for as long as nobody
came knocking on my door demanding the services of a doctor.

It wasn't to be.

'Very well,' I said wearily.

The barn might have been old but it was reasonably sound.
Someone who knew what they were doing had repaired the
roof, and there was a water trough against the front wall and
straw stacked inside.

Theo and the farmer were standing some few paces from
the partly open door. They turned ashen faces as Jarman and
I rode up.

'What is it?' I demanded, sliding off Hal's back. I'd have
thought Theo was used to death in all its forms, and a man
who farmed surely would be too, but here they were, the pair
of them looking like spinsters faced with an unexpected
glimpse of two dogs coupling.

I handed Hal's reins to Jarman and went to go into the barn,
but Theo grabbed my arm and with surprising force stopped
me. '*No!*' he gasped.

'For God's sake, Theo!' I tried to throw him off, but
he wouldn't let me. I spun round to face him. '*What?*' I
demanded.

'Have a look from here, Doctor,' the farmer said in a hoarse
whisper. He had gone to stand beside a spot where two of
the planks that formed the barn's walls had warped, leaving
a narrow space. 'No closer than you must, mind!' he added
sharply.

His big moon face was pale and glistening, and I could
smell the sweat of fear on him.

I put my eye to the widest part of the gap and looked inside
the barn.

I spotted the first body straight away, for it was directly
opposite, leaning against the far wall. It was that of a man,
youngish, muscular and barrel-chested. He was roughly
dressed in clothes that had had a long and hard life and
seemed to be made primarily of sacking. His fair hair was
dirty and tangled. His face wore an expression of abject

horror, either from the pain of whatever had ended his life or, perhaps, from whatever had been the last sight he saw.

I leaned closer, pushing away the farmer's hand as he tried to hold me back. I had thought I recognized the dead body straight away, and now that I looked closer at the face, I knew I was right. It was the young man called Daniel who had been felled in the tiring room behind the performance area at the Saracen's Head. I'd wondered if he might have been dead then; I hadn't been able to feel his pulse, although I'd had only a very brief moment before being called away. Now, staring in at him, I reckoned death might have come a little later, although I wouldn't know for sure until I was closer. However, that incident had been in the late afternoon of the day before yesterday, and even from where I stood I could see that this poor young man wasn't freshly dead. I still couldn't tell what had killed him; I was too far away.

I shifted my position and let my eyes go round the barn until I spotted the second corpse.

Then immediately I wished I hadn't.

I wished I was nowhere near this accursed barn.

That I and all those I loved, my family, my friends, my acquaintances, all my patients, the entire population of south Devon, were far, far away.

Because the second man's face was viciously swollen and distorted, the skin mottling with dark purplish streaks which, even as I watched, seemed to spread out like the vigorous shoots of bramble.

I'd told Jonathan last night that I had no personal experience of treating a plague victim, but I had a fair idea of what the sickness did to the human body.

And in that first horrified look, it seemed to me that it had ravaged its foul way through the body of the second man as if it had a score to settle.

TEN

I strode back to where Jarman was holding my horse. Somehow I had to protect myself, and I thought – hoped – I had what I needed rolled up at the bottom of my bag. Dumping it on the ground, I rummaged inside. To my great relief, I felt the slightly tacky surface of the cloth, and I pulled it out.

It was a close-fitting, sleeved garment made of coarse linen, long enough to cover me from throat to feet, with a stiff collar and a hood with drawstrings. It fastened tightly, the two front edges overlapping generously and fastened with many ties, and the linen had been waxed. I was putting my faith in it because I had read papers by two different doctors who reported its efficacy, the theory being that the parasitic, blood-sucking insects that carried the plague could not penetrate the treated fabric.

As I did up the fastenings and tied the strings of the hood tightly under my chin, I prayed that my brother physicians had done their research thoroughly.

Theo, Jarman and the farmer were watching me anxiously.

'You surely do not think to . . . to *go in*?' Theo could only mouth the last two words, so horrified was he at the very suggestion.

'I do,' I replied curtly, drawing on the gauntlets attached to the sleeves of the garment. 'We have to find out how the younger man died, and for that I have to inspect his corpse.'

'But—' Theo's bright blue eyes were wide open.

'I know, Theo.' Briefly I put my hand on his arm. Jarman and the farmer, I noticed, had taken a few paces back, as if they were beginning to fear my proximity even *before* I'd gone inside the barn.

Theo met my eyes. 'Are you not risking your very life?' he whispered.

Was I? I really hoped not.

'Dear friend, I have no desire to die,' I said, trying to speak lightly. 'I believe this will help' – I indicated my waxed shroud – 'and also—'

'But what of the miasmas?' Theo hissed.

I reached behind my head and delved inside the high collar, unfastening the rolled-up piece of fabric that came up over the head and down to cover the face. The top section had a pair of eye holes, into each of which was inserted a circle of fine yellowish horn. When I was sure every part of me was covered, I walked on into the barn.

The pieces of horn meant I could see little, especially given the dim light of the interior, but I knew where the young man lay and went straight to him. I grabbed him under the arms and tried to lift him, but he was solid, and heavier than I'd reckoned. So instead I took hold of his shoulders and began to drag him backwards across the barn floor. It was a struggle, and I was finding it hard to draw breath beneath my protective mask. I paused briefly to rest – I was almost in the doorway now – when suddenly there was someone beside me, adding his strength to mine, and in no time we had the body out in the good clean air.

I turned. Jarman Hodge stood panting beside me.

'Coroner tried to push me out of the way and go in himself,' he said quietly. 'Hope he'll not hold it against me.'

'Hold what against you?'

'I just punched him.' I was about to ask when he went on, 'He's a family man, see. Three young children, that lovely wife.'

He didn't need to say any more. 'Thank you, Jarman,' I said. In the quick assessing look I gave him, I noted with relief that he had paused long enough to fasten his tunic tightly, pull down the brim of his cap and cover his face with his kerchief.

I turned and went back inside. Jarman tried to come with me but I told him very firmly there was no need: 'I shall be very quick,' I said. 'I have no intention of trying to bring the other body out.' There was no need: I'd already seen how he died.

Jarman began to say something, and I was aware of Theo

sitting up and rubbing his jaw – the farmer had retreated a good fifty paces down the track – but I ignored them.

I stopped a couple of paces away from the terrible corpse, remaining only long enough to verify that life was extinct. It was quite obvious that it was; rats had begun on him, and I could smell putrefaction. Then, crouching down, careful to keep the body at arm's length, I felt the ground all around, letting my fingertips do the work instead of my eyes, half blinded as I was by the horn lenses. I found what I thought was probably a pack, and kicked it away in the direction of the barn doorway.

Then I straightened up, took three big steps backwards and took a steady, assessing look at the body.

The man was dressed in dark-coloured garments of very good quality: a beautiful black velvet doublet, an expensive-looking black cloak with a very stylish high collar. His long legs in fine wool hose were stretched out in front of him, the right crossed over the left at the ankle, and the knee-length leather boots were the finest and would have cost half a year's wages for a working man. He had been armed: beside him, close by his left hand, lay a high-quality, wide-bladed dagger and what I thought was a Toledo sword. It was a rapier, in fact, the blade graceful and very fine, the hilt richly decorated.

At last, with vast reluctance, I raised my eyes to the head, tilted towards his right shoulder, and the dreadful face.

It was, as my first swift glance had told me, a mass of swellings. Trying to see beyond the blood, the bruising, the puffy, blackened eyelids and the nose smashed against the face, I made out a man of early middle age who would have been very good-looking before the fatal sickness ravaged him. He was dark-haired, the face strongly featured, the long, pointed chin accentuated by the close-trimmed spade-shaped beard. He had a sophisticated air about him; a *London* air, perhaps; the fine, well-shaped eyebrows would have lifted so readily into a sarcastically quizzical sneer as the wide mouth turned down in mockery. I would have taken him for a man of learning, of intellectual curiosity, of refinement, even had he been barefoot and dressed in a peasant's smock.

Blackened eyelids.

Smashed nose.

I was so busy fighting down my terror and my revulsion that it took some time – far too long – for my brain to receive and understand the message that my senses were urgently sending. I'm sure it was that first glimpse through the gap in the planks that led to my mistake, for even then I believe I took in more than I realized; even then I had noticed the *look* of him, and a part of me had seen him as a cultivated, intelligent man of London, a frequenter of its highest circles.

And London, of course, was where the plague raged.

But this man hadn't had the pestilence. He'd had a severe beating.

I shot a rapid glance at his right hand, lying gently curled in his lap. The knuckles were dark with bruises and it looked as if he'd dislocated his thumb. I heard my father's voice in an echo from childhood: *Always make sure you keep your thumb out of your palm when you bunch up your fist to punch someone.*

The dead man had fought back.

I leaned in closer. It was hard to see in the dim light and through the horn lenses, but I thought I could make out the line of small bruises that indicate where an assailant's knuckles make contact. Eager now, I put my hand on the man's neck, under the point of his jaw, then delved inside his garments to his armpits and down into his groin. I checked every part of him.

He was as innocent of buboes – of any sort of swelling, save for the ones on his face – as Francis Heron.

It was time to go.

I turned and walked back towards the door, kicking the pack before me. It was, I noted, of the same high quality as his clothing and kit: beautifully crafted and made of fine, supple leather.

Then I was outside.

My three companions were waiting for me. Seeing their anguished faces, shame flooding through me because I had not shouted out my discovery as soon as I'd made it. I glanced at each of them. Theo was on his feet, looking furious as well as very worried. The farmer, perhaps in some belated attempt to make himself useful, was holding the now-restless horses, although still some distance away. Jarman was looking alternately at me and Theo, and he seemed very uneasy. I hoped this reflected his apprehension at his superior officer's reaction to being punched rather than anxiety over me . . .

I stood a little away from them and peeled off my waxed linen shroud. It was good to have my face uncovered, and I took several deep breaths of the cold air. I was postponing the moment, and mentally I kicked myself into action.

'I have led you astray,' I said, waving my arms to include them all. 'I'm very sorry to have caused you unnecessary worry. When I saw the second corpse, I made too hasty a judgement. I was wrong, and he—'

'What the *fuck* do you mean?' Theo burst out. From his expression, I reckoned he was some way beyond furious now, and I was quite sure he knew full well what I meant.

'The man did not die of the plague,' I said. 'He's been beaten severely, and probably that's what killed him. From the state of his hands I'd say he fought back.'

Theo fixed me with the coldest glare I'd ever received from his bright blue eyes. After a brief but very uncomfortable silence, he said icily, 'And you couldn't have told us that straight away, the instant you got a proper look at him?'

Stung, I snapped back, 'I didn't *know*, then!'

'You're a doctor, aren't you?' Theo shouted angrily. 'Can't you even recognize plague when you see it?' He frowned briefly and added in a mutter, 'When you *don't* see it.'

'I'm very sorry,' I said again, trying to sound calm and reasonable. 'I've been watching out for the signs in Master Heron, and it seems obvious the man had come from London. I believe I saw what I expected to see, not what was really there.'

'You panicked,' Theo said bluntly. 'You saw a face covered in swellings and you leapt to the conclusion that the man had died of—' But he couldn't make himself say it. 'You leapt to the wrong conclusion.'

'Better too cautious than not cautious enough,' offered

Jarman Hodge. Unwisely, for Theo turned on him an even more devastating scowl than he'd given me.

It would take rather more than one or two pacifying remarks, I reflected, for Theo to forget that his subordinate had just punched him.

'What about this here dead body lying right outside my barn?' piped up the farmer. 'What about my barn, come to that,' he added, 'with another dead body propped up inside?'

Theo looked at me. 'You're quite sure you have it right this time?' he said, the sarcasm sharpening his tone. 'You're not going to change your mind again and tell me it was the pestilence after all?'

'No.' I decided brevity served me best.

He was still staring angrily at me. He muttered something that I reckoned it was as well I didn't hear, then he squared his broad shoulders, hitched up his robe and said decisively, 'Put the body back inside the barn with the second one. *You* can do that, Doctor. *You*' – he spun round to face the farmer – 'close the door, bar it, make sure nobody goes in. I will—'

'How am I meant to do that?' protested the farmer. 'I've got better things to do with my time than stand outside my own barn all day turning away the curious, I can tell you!'

Theo took a very audible deep breath. 'I'm not asking you to stand here all day, only for as long as it takes me to ride back to my office and dispatch men and a cart to collect the bodies.'

'I'll watch the barn, master,' Jarman Hodge said quietly.

Theo eyed him for a few moments. 'You will,' he agreed. Then he murmured, 'And if you think thus to make amends for your attack on me, you are wrong.'

He turned, strode over to where the farmer still held his horse, mounted and, slamming his heels into the startled animal's sides, cantered away.

The farmer was staring after him. 'Jesu, is he always like that?' he asked.

Jarman and I met each other's eyes. Neither of us replied.

The farmer handed us our horses' reins, then with a muttered farewell, stumped away. I picked up the dead man's pack.

Then I clambered up onto Hal's back and turned his head down the track.

I looked down at Jarman.

I knew I should have said something reassuring about Theo's anger, made some remark to the effect that I was sure the men and the cart wouldn't be too long. But all at once I was so tired that it was all I could do to sit in the saddle, and my mind seemed to have gone blank.

'I'm going to . . .' I tried to think what I had to do next, and for a frightening moment, I couldn't.

Jarman flashed me a smile of understanding. 'Go home, Doctor T,' he said kindly.

So I did.

I woke up in my own bed, clean and in fresh linen. For a few moments I simply lay there, relishing the comfort and the security of my own four walls. Then simultaneously I remembered everything that had just happened and I noticed that my pillow was damp.

Fever! I'd been sweating, I must have been, and so profusely as to soak the linen case and the feather-filled pad within, and—

Then, already ashamed of my panic, I also recalled that I had thoroughly washed my hair and my scalp when I got home, and fallen into bed with my hair still damp.

There was a tap on the door. 'Come in,' I called out.

Celia opened the door and peered round it, responding to my beckoning gesture and coming to sit down on my bed.

Before she could say anything, I reached out for her hand. 'I'm sorry.'

She studied me. 'Sorry?'

'The other day. When I burst in on you and the actor in your room. I said things I shouldn't have said. I said you had no sense of decency.'

She nodded slowly. 'You did.'

'I was wrong. I know you better than that.' I'd been on the point of explaining that I'd been shocked to find the two of them standing so close, already concerned because I feared history was going to be repeated and she'd make the same mistake with the actor as she had with Jeromy Palfrey, but just in time some ancient, wise voice in my head told me not to.

So I just smiled at her and, smiling back, she said quietly, 'Apology accepted, but don't do it again.'

Into the rather awkward silence I began to tell her all that had happened.

'Gabe, I know,' she interrupted gently. 'Jonathan and Theo are here and between them they seem to have told me everything that's happened today. They're in the library, and we've just finished eating. There's plenty for you,' she added.

I was glad to hear it. I was famished. 'What time is it?' I asked.

'Late afternoon.'

I nodded. I hadn't been asleep as long as I'd thought. Then I realized what Celia had said. 'Why are they here? Theo and Jonathan?' I felt I ought to know, but I was having trouble organizing my thoughts.

She hesitated. Looked away, looked back at me.

'Events have moved quickly while you have been asleep,' she said eventually. I sensed her gathering herself. Before I could ask what had happened, she said, 'Theo's officers have collected the bodies from the barn and they are now in the cellar of that house that he uses. But he thinks we should keep the deaths a secret, because if word gets out there may be panic, and—'

'Neither man died of plague, and nor did Francis Heron!' I cried, sitting up so fast that I made myself briefly dizzy.

'Nobody is saying they did,' my sister said calmly. 'Yet nevertheless we have three men dead, and a sizeable company of outsiders in the town.'

'You're saying—' I began, but then I found I didn't know how to continue. 'What *are* you saying?'

Celia grinned. 'Goodness, you really must have been exhausted when you stumbled in,' she remarked. 'It's not like you to be quite so dim.' I was about to protest at the implication that I was always dim but not usually to such an extent, but she was still speaking. 'Who always gets the blame when something bad happens? The stranger! And at the Saracen's Head we have any number of strangers, and a population already excited and thrilled by the plays the Company have put on. It was *Titus Andronicus* this afternoon.' She sighed. 'I was looking forward to seeing how the Company performed it.'

Something in my memory was snapping for my attention, but I ignored it. I was concentrating on what Celia had just said. She was right; the Company probably would indeed be suspected of being involved in the three deaths, and this was reasonable considering I was pretty sure that somehow they were, even if they hadn't actually carried out the killings. And when a close-packed population such as the townsfolk of Plymouth took it upon themselves to take their own sort of retribution, it wasn't pretty.

I shook my head in a vain attempt to shake my wits into some sort of order. What must I do? Find out the truth. How?

I hoped it was no more than a symptom of fatigue and hunger, but in that moment I couldn't even think how to begin going about the task.

Celia was watching me, her face soft with gentle sympathy. 'You don't have to do it all by yourself, Gabe,' she said softly.

'How did you know what I was thinking?' I demanded, my tone far too rough. But the accuracy with which she'd read my mind was uncanny.

She smiled, getting up off the bed and straightening her skirts. 'I usually do,' she replied. Then she added, 'Get up and come down to the library and we can all talk together.'

I started to push back the bedclothes, then stopped.

'If you're really insisting I get out of bed,' I said lightly, 'you'd better leave the room, or at least turn your back, since I'm not wearing anything.'

She glided gracefully over to the door. 'Then I'm definitely going,' she said.

But in the doorway she turned.

'Be quick, because I do not think Jonathan will be staying,' she said very quietly.

'He has said so?'

She shook her head. Then she whispered enigmatically, 'I just know.'

She closed the door and left me alone.

She was quite right.

I found Jonathan in the yard, holding his cob's reins.

'You're heading back?' I asked. 'You won't stay and eat?'

He smiled. 'I've eaten, and very well.' Then, his face turning solemn, 'I cannot abandon my church, Gabe,' he went on softly. It was, I noticed irrelevantly, the first time he'd called me by the diminutive. 'You have been tending a man who you believed might have the pestilence, and I have learned from Master Davey that at first you thought the dead man in the barn might also be a victim. In both cases your fear was unfounded, and I thank the merciful Lord for it.' He paused, his face briefly creased in anguish. 'But there is a mood of unease, of dismay, abroad. Those at the Saracen's Head suffer worse than dismay, for they are deeply afraid. Something is profoundly amiss within its maze of rooms and dark corridors.' He stopped, staring down at the ground, brows drawn together in a frown.

'But your own parishioners at Tavy St Luke's surely cannot be affected by this spreading fear?' I said. 'Is it not a phenomenon of the town?'

He raised his head and met my eyes. 'But many of my parishioners have business in Plymouth,' he replied. 'Besides, not a few have been to one of the Company's plays; some have seen more.'

'But—'

'I sense strongly that I must be present in St Luke's or in the Priest's House,' he interrupted, giving me a very brief smile. 'I cannot say why. I am sorry.'

I shook my head. 'You have no need to be.' I grinned. 'If you're going to be praying, will you pray for me? I have three dead bodies to examine first thing tomorrow, and I must not only determine precisely how they met their deaths but in addition come up with some idea as to why they were killed, and just now I'm very much doubting that I can.'

He reached out and laid his hand on my arm. 'Of course I

will pray for you,' he said. 'You didn't have to ask. Go inside
now,' he urged. 'Eat, drink, talk to your sister and your friend
– and in case you're worried, he's forgiven you for not reassuring him immediately about the second dead man. If he's
still out of sorts now it's because Jarman Hodge hit him, but
it was with good reason, which of course makes it far worse
since Theo has no justification for being so cross with him.'
He paused. 'Then *rest*, Gabriel. Go to bed, clear your mind,
sleep. You will be your usual capable, perceptive, decisive self
again in the morning, and we *need* you to be.' Eyes fixed on
me, he added quietly, 'God works through us, and our actions
need to help and not hinder him as he holds us up.' Then,
somewhat to my surprise, a genuine smile spread across his
face. 'Have faith, dear Doctor,' he murmured.

He turned away and mounted his horse. Then, his expression solemn, he raised his right hand and blessed me.

I watched him ride away. Then I went back inside the house
to where Theo and my sister were waiting for me.

Celia had lit the candles and the library fire was going well.
I hadn't realized how late it was, for now afternoon was
merging into evening and I was in dire need of the promised
food and drink. I nodded to Theo, pulled out my chair and
sat down at the table, and as if she'd been waiting for that
moment, Sallie came in with a laden tray and spread the
contents before me, nodding an acknowledgement of my
thanks and hurrying out again.

'The bodies from the barn are waiting for you,' Theo said
as I threw in the first mouthful of buttered soft white bread,
cheese and a slice of onion, 'and I've had my men fetch Francis
Heron's corpse from the Saracen's Head.'

I chewed, swallowed and said, 'They can wait till morning.'

He looked momentarily disgruntled, then muttered,
'Suppose so.'

I glanced at him, decided not to answer and went on eating.

After some moments, when I'd assuaged the worst of my
hunger and drunk half a tankard of ale, I said solemnly, 'I
should have called out straight away that the second body in
the barn hadn't died from plague. I realize I caused you, Jarman

Hodge and the farmer more anxiety than necessary, and my only defence is that I was too busy with my own huge relief to think about anyone or anything else.'

He grunted. Then he said, the indignation still clearly hot, 'Hodge hit me!'

Hodge, I noted.

'Because he believed you were proposing to approach a plague victim totally unprotected,' I said as calmly as I could. 'There was no time for carefully reasoned argument.'

Theo tried and failed to suppress a grin. 'You're probably right,' he said. He rubbed his jaw. 'For a lean fellow who's not very tall, who'd have thought he'd have punched with such force?'

Deciding that was best treated as a rhetorical question, I returned to my supper.

Presently Celia said, 'Jonathan believes something's going to happen. He thinks he should be with his parishioners.'

'Yes, he told me.'

I looked up, first at Celia, then at Theo. Both faces wore the same expression, which I interpreted as a courageous attempt to pretend they thought everything was all right when secretly they were very much afraid it wasn't.

It was exactly how I felt too.

ELEVEN

I sat alone by the library fire, finishing my ale. Theo had left some time ago, Celia had retired to her own quarters and, although it was not late, I was looking forward to going to bed and getting a proper night's sleep. The house was so quiet, so peaceful and warm, that I kept dozing off.

But then there was a knock on the door.

I swore silently, and very briefly considered pretending I hadn't heard. But I got to my feet and, stiff from too long in my chair, staggered out into the hall to the door, flinging it open to reveal Judyth, warmly wrapped in her heavy cloak, its deep hood covering her thick black hair.

'It's not too late, is it?' she demanded. 'You hadn't gone to bed?'

'No, and no,' I replied.

'I was not minded to come in,' she added, still lingering on the step, 'but Samuel heard my arrival and hurried out to take charge of my horse, and so I thought I might as well . . .'

I liked it that such was our familiarity with each other that she knew the name of my servant.

'I'm glad you changed your mind,' I said, ushering her in. 'Go through to the library. I'll feed the fire, and there's some ale in the jug. I'll fetch another mug.'

When I joined her in the library, she'd already built up the fire and was kneeling in front of it warming her hands.

'I believe you just implied an untruth,' she remarked as I poured out ale for her. 'You *were* about to go to bed, weren't you? You'd let the fire die right down.'

'Perhaps,' I agreed. 'But I'm happy that you're here.'

She turned, the new flames making her fine pale skin glow pink. 'Truly?'

'Truly.'

I sat down in my chair, and after a moment she took the one opposite.

I knew she would say what was on her mind in her own time, so I waited. She was frowning, as if unsure how to begin, but then abruptly she said, 'Something's wrong.'

'You too!' I exclaimed.

She shot me a glance. 'But you weren't there, so how—' She stopped. 'Explain,' she said simply.

So I did, telling her about Francis Heron, about the young man known as Daniel, about the well-dressed sophisticate who'd tried to fight off his killer and failed.

'And since there are no obvious means by which you could know of those three deaths, and the way in which they have made my sister, Theo, Jonathan Carew and no doubt many others too so very uneasy,' I finished, 'what were *you* referring to when you said something was wrong?'

She looked slightly embarrassed, then grinned briefly and said, 'Please don't think I'm cross, or complaining, both of which would be totally unreasonable given all that you've been dealing with in the last couple of days, but I believe you and I arranged to see a performance of *Romeo and Juliet*, which in your absence I attended alone, and it's that which—'

Then, of course and far too late, I understood what had been niggling at the edge of my mind.

'Judyth, I am so sorry!' I blurted out. It seemed to be my day for apologies, and this was the most abject of all. 'Yes we did, and I can't tell you how much I was looking forward to it, but . . . but . . .' Wildly I tried to remember what I'd been doing that had so totally distracted me. 'Was it today?' I asked, frowning.

'Yesterday,' she replied. She was smiling at my discomfiture. 'And very good it was. The thin young man who played Emilia in *Othello* was a heartbreaking Juliet, and Romeo was the redhead we saw playing Cassio, who I now know to be called Quentyn Barre, and apparently he was a magical Puck. He was most touching as Romeo, and the vulnerability he conveyed as his love for Juliet undermined him made you overlook the fact that he was a little too old for the role.' She took a sip of ale. 'The day before it was a very violent revenge tragedy entitled *The Demon's Glass*, and today's performance was *Titus Andronicus*, which if possible was even more bloodthirsty.'

Yes. I'd known which three plays were to be performed. I'd planned to see the first, watched part of the second with Theo just before we found and lost the man called Daniel, and only this afternoon Celia had expressed regret that she hadn't gone to see the third.

I met her eyes. 'I forgot,' I said. 'I was tending Francis Heron, and then I got involved in trying to find a missing body, and at the time it all seemed so very important and—'

'It *was* important,' she said calmly. 'It *is*. It's what you do, dear Gabe. Since it's what I do too – the tending of people who need me, anyway, if not the hunting for missing bodies – there is no need to explain.'

'But—'

She held up her hand, and I stopped.

'I didn't come to make you feel guilty.' She smiled very sweetly at me. Then, her expression growing grave, she said, 'I said just now something was wrong, and I was referring to the plays. I—'

'You saw all three?'

She nodded. 'I did. I should not have, and I shall be working late into the night to finish the tasks I ought to have attended to these past afternoons, but something was troubling me after we all saw the Company perform *Othello*, and when the same thing happened at their production of *Romeo and Juliet*, I felt compelled to attend the next two plays to see if what was troubling me was really there or if I'd imagined it.' She paused. 'I hadn't.'

'What was it?' Was it, I could have demanded, the weird way in which the Company seemed to twist meanings, to shift emphases, to confuse and misdirect their audience by pushing some aspects into such total dominance that every other element was ignored?

She was staring into the fire, and the frown was back. 'I love the theatre,' she said dreamily. 'Possibly because I spend my day with the hard facts of people's tough and often painful lives, I find it a joy to be – to be *taken away*, transported to a magical realm where things aren't quite real, removed to a world of the imagination, with wonderful scenery, costly objects, gorgeous costumes, handsome and beautiful actors.' She paused, then added softly, 'I went to Exeter, a while ago, to see a travelling company. You and Celia had recently been to London, and Celia told me about the theatre beside the river. I should not have given in to the temptation, for there were worthier things on which to spend my savings, and it meant others taking on my work for the days I was away, but, truth to tell, I wouldn't have missed it for the world!'

Her eyes sparkled at the memory, and as I looked at her, I felt several strong emotions flow through me. I was moved that she had confided in me. I was full of admiration, because there had been something she'd really wanted to do and she'd done it. I was ashamed, because Celia and I had thought little of the much greater expense of our London trip, taking for granted something that had meant so much to Judyth. I was filled with profound liking for her, sitting there across the hearth in my library and looking so beautiful.

And I could have kicked myself for my cowardice in only admitting, even inside my own head, *profound liking* when what I really meant was love.

'—no need to be telling you this,' she was saying now, 'but I'm doing so because you have to know that I'm not ignorant when it comes to plays and how they are performed, and I've seen two of the plays before, which means I have something with which to compare them.'

I leaned forward, elbows on my knees. 'I think, Judyth, that I would have believed you – no, *trusted* you, and your judgement – even if that were not the case.'

She bowed her head. 'Thank you.'

'Tell me?'

She paused, drew a breath and began to speak. 'In each case I felt I was being manipulated,' she said. 'Persuaded, and quite forcefully, to step into another world that lies alongside our own, and that is full of . . . magic, I suppose, and possibilities. I am familiar with *Romeo and Juliet*' – yes, I recalled that she'd known full well it was a tragedy – 'and I had not thought that any great importance was placed on Friar Laurence and his potion, save in that it was the means by which Juliet was able to feign death. Yet in the Company's version, the matter of potentially harmful potions was such an ever-present theme that I came to believe they must have altered the dialogue. I had not seen *The Demon's Glass* before, but today's ghastly offering of *Titus Andronicus* was similarly . . . *weighted*, is the best way to describe it.'

'And what,' I asked after quite a lengthy pause, 'are we to make of these weightings?'

She stared into my eyes. 'I think somebody is trying to tell us something. If it is not too fanciful, I believe that with each play we are being presented with a surface impression, and that perhaps someone who only saw one performance would be content to accept it and not see anything amiss. Perhaps the impression of wrongness only comes when someone sees *more* than one of the plays.'

'Wrongness?'

'There are layers of darkness beneath this surface, Gabe, I'm sure of it. And they are hiding something very potent. There's a secret, and some or all of the Company know it, and some of them are afraid, and can only call for help in the most subtle ways, and—' She shook her head, making a loud *aaaah!* of frustration. 'I am sorry, I cannot explain, but—'

'You *have* explained,' I said. 'It's odd, because I only saw *Othello* and the last part of *The Demon's Glass*, and like you I'd never seen that one before, but nevertheless I understand what you mean. And—'

'The glass!' she said suddenly. 'That looking glass! It just keeps on turning up. They twist the plots somehow so as to introduce it into *every* play and I – I've grown to be quite fearful of it!'

She tried to laugh, as if to indicate she didn't really mean what she'd just said.

But I was absolutely sure she did.

The mirror.

As I'd stood in the dark and silent tiring room the first night I'd tended Francis, I'd sensed a presence of such malevolence that even the memory of it shook me. I'd truly believed the mirror had crept up on me. I'd seen horrific images in it.

I'd seen a woman lose her head in a bloody spurt of crimson. Even before that night, I'd been suspicious of it. Now I knew I was right to fear it.

After a pause, I said very softly, 'What are we to do?'

Her face softened. 'Are you asking *me* for advice, Doctor Taverner?'

'Yes.'

'We could adopt the sensible path, which is to agree that there is something dark, dangerous even, then quickly turn our backs, wait till the Company depart and put the matter behind us.'

'How long till they go?'

'Today's play, *Titus Andronicus*, was the penultimate performance. Tomorrow they are putting on a light and frivolous comedy, which I imagine will be a relief to both players and audience after such a bloody and violent *Titus Andronicus*.' She paused, her expression grave. 'But I think that is not the real reason. They are afraid, lodged there in the inn with the whisperings, the rumours of sightings, things seen in the shadows, and they're convinced now that it's haunted. And, of course, a man has died. Those players *need* a comedy.' She glanced at me. 'But, to answer your question, I imagine they'll begin the long process of packing up the following day. Then presumably they'll set out for the next destination on their itinerary.'

'Two, perhaps three days left,' I murmured.

She laughed softly. 'So we're not going to turn our backs, then.'

I met her eyes. 'Did you think we would?'

'Not for a moment.'

We went on looking at each other for several moments too long, then I lowered my eyes. 'My first task tomorrow is the inspection of Francis Heron, a young man known as Daniel and a wealthy-looking man found with him in a barn near—'

'I know,' Judyth said.

'*How* do you know?'

'I was in Plymouth today. I told you, I was at the Saracen's Head for the performance. You forget, I think, how fast gossip spreads.'

She was quite right. 'There was a costly leather pack in the barn,' I went on. 'I'm hoping that both the bodies and the pack will have something to tell me.'

She nodded. 'Theo Davey puts much store in you, Gabe. If there are mysteries to be uncovered, I'm sure you will.'

She was getting to her feet, already moving towards the door. 'You're going?' I asked, thinking even as I spoke what a stupid remark it was.

'I am,' she agreed, her quick smile indicating she thought so too.

'Will you not stay a while? Another mug of ale?'

'No, Gabe,' she said. 'I told you, I have much to do before I sleep, and by the look of you, a good night's rest will not go amiss.'

We walked across the hall and I opened the door, going with her round to the yard. Samuel appeared, tightening the chestnut's girth and running the stirrups down the leathers with practised speed, then nodding a farewell and melting away again. I gave Judyth a leg-up and looked up at her.

'Sleep well, Gabe,' she said. Then she put her heels to the gelding and hastened away.

I'd thought I would lie awake for a long time, sleep driven back by images of Judyth and what she'd told me, but I was worn out. When I woke, early light was colouring the chamber pale grey and I knew it was time I was up and on my way.

I washed and dressed while the sun was climbing up over the moors in the east. Sallie heard me coming down the stairs and, sensing my haste, flew round the kitchen selecting foods that could be swiftly prepared and even more swiftly consumed. 'Somebody in dire need, I have no doubt,' she said, nodding sagely. 'I didn't hear the door?' She turned it into a question.

'Not that dire, Sallie,' I replied through the generously buttered soft bread roll, split and filled with a chunk of ham. 'They're all dead. Not newly dead,' I added, already regretting the levity and anxious to take the shocked expression off her face, 'and nobody came to summon me, for my attendance was arranged yesterday.'

She gave me one of her looks and went to put the side of ham back on the pantry shelf.

Finishing my food, I said to her rigidly disapproving back, 'Please will you tell Mistress Celia when she comes down that I have gone to work in Master Davey's crypt?'

'Very well, Doctor,' she said. Then, relenting, she added a soft, 'God go with you.'

I went straight to the house with the cellar where Theo stores dead bodies. He had fitted a strong lock, as well as a heavy padlock on the door to the cellar, but I had my own keys. I lit a couple of lanterns from the hooks in the hall, opened the cellar door and went down the stone steps. I could smell death even before I'd got the door open.

The bodies were laid out on three trestles set in a row, each covered in a sheet of clean linen. There were more lanterns on a board beneath the one high window, as well as torches set all round the walls. I lit every one.

The first body I uncovered was that of Francis Heron. This would be the hardest to examine, for I had known him in life. I'd tended him, sat beside him, talked to him. Hoped he would live while all along had expected him to die.

'But you did not die of the pestilence, my friend,' I said quietly to him, 'for which all of us give fervent thanks.'

Then I took off my leather jerkin and my doublet, rolled up my sleeves and began.

Purely to give myself one last reassurance, I drew up his nightshirt and checked every inch of his lean body for swellings or buboes. I didn't find any.

Even as I was muttering my prayer of thanks, already my hands and my eyes were busy on my late patient as I tried to make up my mind what had killed him. My initial thought was that someone had given him deadly nightshade; given it and perhaps gone on giving it, for it had taken him some days to die. When I'd checked my reference books, I'd found a list of symptoms, and among them – although I'd forgotten till this moment – was the presence of a rash. Now, looking down at the bony arch of Francis Heron's ribcage, I thought I could just make out the echo of a pattern of tiny, fading pinkish spots.

I straightened up.

Had I guessed right? Had the killer helped himself –
herself – to some of the wide-eyed young Raphe Wymer's
belladonna drops, or perhaps even gone out and dug out the
source of those drops: the deadly black berries, the roots
and the leaves?

Then, in the cold darkness of that stone cellar, another image
crept across my vision. There were the players again, costumed,
on stage . . . Puck and his love potion that confounded the
Faerie Queen and the foolish lovers; Juliet and the sleeping
draught that made poor tragic Romeo believe she was dead;
Romeo himself, in the storm of grief swallowing the apothecary's deadly preparation and dying almost instantly. Othello
and the magic-impregnated handkerchief made of silk from
holy worms. And, in the ghastly *Demon's Glass*, something
in a small blue glass bottle that had been dribbled into a man's
eyes and made them smoulder as it threw him into savage
death convulsions . . .

The Company knew all about poisons. The deadly potions
disguised in their elegant and costly receptacles might be
make-believe, employed by them only for the purposes of
the drama, but their effects were entirely based in the real
world: they worked.

It slowly dawned on me that my feet were cold.

My limbs were stiff as well, and I could feel the pain at
the base of my spine that I get when I've been standing still
for too long. Apprehensive – although I didn't straight away
understand why – I spun round and looked at the lanterns I'd
lit when I came into the cellar.

The candles inside their glass had burned a good third
of the way down.

Fear raged through me, a superstitious chill as if someone
had thrown icy water over me. Because I had been standing
there, deep in my visions of poisons and deadly potions, for
so long that the sun had moved round and was now shining
in through the high cellar window.

I paced several times round the chilly room, stamping my
feet, berating myself. I was a doctor, a man of science, I told
myself. If someone was trying to draw down a veil of mystery

and confusion to conceal what they were about, then they'd chosen the wrong man in me.

But, no matter how I tried to convince myself, there was no escaping the fact: that was precisely what they *had* done.

I went back to Francis Heron. I drew up the linen sheet and made sure he was covered. I paused a moment to say a few quiet words to him, then I turned away and began on the next body.

This one was that of the fair-haired, sturdy young man who we had found in the tiring room towards the end of the Company's performance of *The Demon's Glass*. Then he'd been clad in the rust-red laced doublet that had been too small for him. When I'd found his body in the barn he'd worn old, dirty and torn sackcloth. Now he was naked.

Holding a light right in front of his face, the first thing I noticed was that he was younger than I'd thought: sixteen, perhaps even younger. It was his short, stocky, well-developed body that had made me think him more mature. As I ran my hands down his arms and legs, feeling the powerful muscles, I wondered if he really had been the carter, or scenery-bearer, people had believed him to be. He was certainly strong enough, but then if you were going to adopt a disguise, you'd hardly pretend to be a man whose job required physical power if you were built like a mild and timid scholar.

A thought occurred to me and I examined his hands, the backs, the nails, then turning them over to look at the pads of the fingers and the mounts and ridges of the palms. He'd certainly been engaged in tough, hard work, but he hadn't been doing it for very long; not long enough for his flesh to have built up the protective calluses in the areas that take the most punishment. And, peering closer, I could see in several places the tender red skin that marks a recently healed blister.

I stepped back, thinking. There could well be an innocent reason for Daniel, or whatever his name was, to have taken on a new job. Perhaps, like so many, he'd seen plague tear through London and sought any employment that would get him away from the city, even one that was far removed from his usual occupation. Perhaps he had really been a scholar;

learning wasn't the preserve of fine-boned, ascetic-looking men.

Still wondering, I returned to the body.

And, when I looked in the right place, it was perfectly clear what had killed him. Back in the tiring room, I'd only got as far as a quick check to the neck and throat before I was called away. If I'd gone on to pull open the lacings struggling to hold the doublet closed, I'd have found it. Not immediately, for it was well concealed. But wouldn't have taken me long; I had come across such fatal but delicately inflicted wounds before.

He had been pierced in his side in the manner of the spear thrust into Christ on the cross, upwards and between the ribs, except that this wound was on the left and we are told that Christ's was on the right. And it had been no centurion's spear that had done this, but a very fine, very keen blade. Which, as far as I could make out – again I bent close, holding a light right over the wound, narrowing my eyes to tighten their focus – had had two sharpened edges rather than the single one of a domestic knife.

Daniel would have died almost immediately, for if I was any judge of anatomy and the arrangement of the interior organs, this blade must have pierced his heart.

But my close inspection of the wound told me something I wasn't expecting: it couldn't have been inflicted there in the tiring room. It was now three days ago that we had found and then mislaid Daniel's inert body, and the fatal piercing was no more than a day old.

I covered him up. I had found out how he'd died, and also that he'd still been alive when he'd been spirited out of the inn; when, perhaps, he'd left of his own volition, pausing to take off the rust-red velvet costume that hadn't fitted and replace it with the dirty old sacking.

As to why he'd subsequently been killed, and why such lengths had been taken to confound us – I remembered how Jarman Hodge had followed a figure in rust red, only to discover it wasn't Daniel but Raphe Wymer – I had not the least idea.

Already cast down at the thought of Theo's reaction when

I reported back to him – he still seems to expect me to uncover all the deepest secrets of how a man died the moment I look at their dead body – reluctantly I returned to my task and drew back the sheet on the last corpse.

He too was naked.

His body had not been touched; the blood and the bruises were only on his face. Studying them more closely now, I could see how unlikely it was that the battering had caused his death. Swiftly I went over the rest of him, and I found two injuries I hadn't previously noticed. His right ankle was broken, and I recalled how he'd crossed it over the left as he lay slumped in the barn, as if perhaps it eased the pain to raise it off the ground. There was a deep red weal on the back of the ankle, as if he'd backed very swiftly into some object that tripped him up and the trip broke the bone. But that hadn't killed him, either.

Someone had broken his neck.

Images flashed through my mind, and I saw him facing his assailant, backing hurriedly away, feeing the bone in his ankle snap as he fell over some object behind him, falling, backing away until he reached the wall of the barn and could go no further. Crossing the right ankle over the left, knowing he couldn't move, staring up into the face of the man who was about to kill him. The one small mercy was that death would have been as fast as blinking.

I smoothed the long, dark hair back from the forehead. The brows were dark too, and, raising one of the eyelids, I saw an eye that looked black in the lamplight. He had been vain of the small spade-shaped beard and the moustache, for the flesh of his cheeks was close-shaved to accentuate their careful outlines. Once again, I had the strong impression of a man who had been very handsome; a man who frequented the highest circles; a man who loved the finest clothes and the most expensive leather; a man who knew how to conduct himself.

Only he hadn't known how to defend himself. He'd seen his death coming for him, and he'd been unable to turn it aside.

I checked his hands again. Bruised knuckles and dislocated

thumb. Yes. He'd done his best, poor man. A sudden thought struck me, and, returning to Daniel's body, I uncovered his hands. I'd checked them just now, but I'd been looking for something else. Now I studied the knuckles.

But there was no sign that he'd hit anybody recently, either as part of an attack or of a defence.

I finished my inspection of the dark-haired man. Again, there was very little new information for Theo. I'd just have to—

But then I remembered the leather pack, and I thought perhaps I'd have something for my friend after all.

TWELVE

I slipped away from the empty house without first going down the road to knock on Theo's door. There were discoveries concerning the three bodies that I ought to have reported to him straight away, but I decided to wait until I had begun to resolve the mysteries that had just been stirred up. Or that was how I reasoned; it would have been more honest to admit that I was burning with impatience to get home and examine the spade-bearded man's pack, in the privacy of my study with the door firmly closed.

Samuel came out to take care of Hal as I rode into the yard, with Tock his ever-present shadow. He greeted me with the news that Mistress Palfrey had but recently gone out and Sallie had left with a basket over her arm to hunt for late mushrooms in the woods above the river.

So I had my house to myself.

The pack was in the corner of my bedchamber, where I'd thrown it yesterday shortly before collapsing onto my bed for a much-needed sleep. I fetched it and took it along to my study, where I cleared my wide desk of everything else so that the pack stood in solitary state. Slowly I sat down, simply staring at it. It was almost as if it held me in a spell, and—

Angry with myself, just as I had been after standing in the cold crypt while time passed by outside my knowledge, I reached for the pack and, my hands rough and impatient, unfastened the buckled straps.

It was made of as fine a piece of leather as I'd ever seen, let alone handled. It was a rich, glowing shade of chestnut, buffed to a rich sheen, and so supple that it moved like cloth. Yet it was sturdy and strong, and although clearly well used, showed not a scratch or a stain. I folded back the flap and looked inside. There were two compartments separated by a partition of a darker shade of leather. The front compartment held papers and a book, the rear one held a pewter inkhorn, several quills, one or two objects wrapped in velvet and a small wooden box.

I drew out the papers first. Some had writing on them; the work of several different hands. Place names, one or two dates. I ran my eyes over the pages and, with a powerful sense of disappointment, realized I was wasting my time. The small amount of writing on them meant absolutely nothing to me.

Then I reached inside the pack again and drew out the book. It was small, very well used, bound in leather worn and grubby from handling. Its thin pages were covered in dense blocks of incomprehensible writing. On the flyleaf was that familiar symbol.

Either I was dreaming again, or this was Francis's notebook.

I'd put it back in his bag, I was sure of it. I would go and check to make absolutely sure, but—

Half out of my chair, I stopped. I heard myself say aloud, 'Where is it? What did I do with Francis's bag?'

And, frightened now, I realized I couldn't remember.

I couldn't remember *anything*.

I sank back into my chair. For several long moments I sat perfectly still, my hands resting on my desk. I don't think I have ever felt more terrified.

I'm sure we all fear madness. We see old men and women in their final years, trotting out a trite and familiar little fact and totally forgetting they've just told you the same thing, several times over. We see the loss of memory, the failure to recognize a familiar and much-loved face. We see the fading of all reasoning power, the gradual and horribly inevitable slide into non-thinking and the collapse of all reason, all mental facility and flexibility. And we dread it, of course we do, because while we are still in our right minds, we recognize that it is a one-way journey, and nobody ever comes back.

As I sat there in my study, surrounded by my books, my notes, the long shelf of journals that record my life as a healer, my medical impedimenta, my rows of potions and preparations in their little jars, pots, phials and bottles, I wanted to reach out and grasp the lot, hug it to me, shout out that I was still young, still able, still a rational man, and please do not take away all that makes me *me*, not yet!

It seemed that some part of my battling soul remained my own. For slowly, as if I was wading through soft, wet, sucking sand, I began to fight back. I threw myself against the fear, forcing it into submission. And as a small amount of daylight cleared amid the blackness, I recognized this for what it was.

I'd just been attacked.

And instantly reason returned. I *had* put the notebook back in Francis's bag, but straight afterwards I'd gone wandering through the ancient passages of the Saracen's Head and experienced my waking nightmare. While I was absent, someone had crept into Francis's room and taken the notebook. I'd been pushed, violently, into that accursed mirror, hadn't I? What was more likely than that someone had made sure I was out of the way for that very purpose?

As if that first breach swiftly brought about the fall of the whole edifice, now I realized I'd been fighting a phantom; and, moreover, one conjured by the same skilled power that had had me in thrall down in the crypt. Angry now, I shouted aloud, '*I do not believe in conjurings!*'

So, what had they done? Who were *they*? And how had they done it? Moving aside the spade-bearded man's pack and its contents – in my fury, shoving it so hard that everything except Francis's notebook fell on the floor – I reached for my own notebook, inkhorn and quill and began to write.

Why does anybody attack? Because someone else is threatening them. Somebody had undoubtedly just attacked me, which led to the conclusion that they feared whatever threat I posed.

As I wrote, other thoughts crowded into my head. Judyth, yesterday evening, saying that the Company were concealing a deep secret: *there are layers of darkness beneath this surface*, she'd said. The Saracen's Head, its secret little rooms and its dark, twisting passages imbued with a sense of dread that, despite its reputation for being haunted, had not been present before. A man dying of poison, a youth feigning death even as a play of particularly repellent violence was enacted only yards away from him, later to be stabbed through the heart.

A spade-bearded sophisticate from London, dead in a barn with his neck broken. A *weighting* – Judyth's word again – of every play they had put on, as if a hidden message was being cried out to those who watched and heard. Some of whom felt, or sensed, whatever it was the Company was silently suffering.

And I was delving into the heart of the business. It had been I who tended Francis Heron, I who examined the bodies of Daniel and the spade-bearded man, I who only a few moments ago had been going through the contents of that man's pack. Somebody knew what I was doing, and didn't like it. And – my thoughts were racing now, my mind responding to my need with its habitual flexibility so that all dread fears of losing my reason had fled – this same somebody had tried to halt my probing, just as I'd been halted on the spot and held out of time, down in the crypt earlier this morning. As, the night after Francis Heron fell sick, I'd been assaulted by a horrific vision of beheading in a mirror that I was convinced had just crept up on me.

I put down my quill. I realized I was sweating, and I felt, I actually *felt* like a physical presence, the moment of fear that demanded, *Is it the pestilence?*

'It is not,' I said, my voice quite calm.

It was a very clever person playing with my mind. But this was where they would stop.

I sat still for several long moments. Then I stood up, walking over to the window to look out at the late autumn sunshine on the familiar landscape and the river winding its way to the sea. And as I stood there, quietly, with no effort whatsoever, I remembered exactly what I'd done with Francis Heron's bag.

I raised a clenched fist and punched the air.

Celia had woken with the strong need to talk to Gabe. Hurrying through the morning rituals, selecting one of her less flamboyant gowns and dressing her hair in a modest style of braids wound at the nape of her neck, she flew down the stairs, early enough – or so she'd thought – to find him just beginning his breakfast. And so it was with some dismay that she learned from Sallie that he had already gone out.

The bodies, Celia thought, consuming with scant attention the bowl of porridge sweetened with honey that Sallie put before her. Of course. He was going to examine the three bodies in Theo's mortuary first thing today. She was angry with herself for having forgotten; for having allowed her own preoccupations to blank from her mind all thought of anyone else's.

It was a flaw of which she was well aware.

She had thought, when Jonathan Carew had made mention of the dangers of self-absorption in his sermon a few weeks ago, that he was addressing her. But, even as she'd listened, head bent and eyes cast down, she had realized that this too was a demonstration of self-absorption, for undoubtedly she was not the only person among the parishioners of Tavy St Luke who was overly focused on her own thoughts and actions, overly determined to make her own path through life smooth and pleasant . . .

She finished her porridge, got up and took the empty bowl into the kitchen, where Sallie greeted her presence with some surprise. 'No need to have brought it through, Miss Celia!' she exclaimed. 'I was just about to come and ask you if you wanted more!'

'I've finished, thank you, Sallie,' Celia said. 'It was delicious,' she added, causing Sallie's eyebrows to rise even higher.

'Same as it always is,' she muttered, eyeing Celia warily as if worried that she was sickening for something.

Is it that extraordinary for me to be courteous and considerate? Celia wondered. 'I'm going out, Sallie,' she said. Before Sallie could ask where she was off to, she added, 'I'm riding into Tavy St Luke first, but I'll be out all day.'

She collected her heavy cloak and her velvet cap, then hurried out into the yard and called to Samuel to saddle her mare.

'I shouldn't be bothering you,' she said to Jonathan a short time later. 'You have far more important matters calling for your attention, I ought to have waited until Gabe comes back from examining the bodies in Theo's crypt and not—'

'Celia, I'm glad you came,' he interrupted gently.

'But you're *here*, in the church, so you must be praying. Or thinking. Or something.' She made herself stop, embarrassed.

She had knocked on the door of the Priest's House, opened it and peered inside when there was no answer, and he wasn't there. She had hurried over to the church, where he had been on his knees before the altar. She closed the heavy old door as quietly as she could, but it was pretty pointless because she'd already made too much noise throwing it open.

'Just now I'm in the church whenever I have nothing more pressing to attend to,' he said. He paused. 'We spoke briefly yesterday, you and Theo and I, agreeing that there was some grave disturbance in the air.'

'Yes.' It had been a worrying conversation, for she had felt the disquiet so powerfully; she knew it was real, and no invention of people avid for something alarming to gossip about.

'The mood is darkening,' he went on. 'Nobody wants to put a name to it, but people are afraid. When they are afraid, they seek the old comfort.'

Even as he spoke, the heavy door creaked and opened to admit two women and a child, who nodded to their priest and slipped away beneath the low arch into St Luke's Little Chapel.

'There are two men and three old women in there already,' Jonathan remarked. He smiled wryly. 'They appear to think the main altar here is my preserve, and so out of consideration they go into the side chapel.'

'Whereas in fact you'd far rather be in there,' she said softly, knowing without having thought about it that she was right.

'I would,' he agreed. He glanced at her, his strange green eyes shining in the light of the altar candles, and she could not read his expression. *If I hadn't known it to be highly unlikely*, she thought, *I'd have said he was briefly filled with joy . . .*

Abruptly aware that she should not waste any more of his time, especially with eight people in the side chapel, she gathered her courage and said, 'Gabe went out early and I've no idea when he'll be back, but I really do need to talk to someone I trust, so I hope you don't mind.'

'I don't,' he murmured. The strange look was fleetingly back, then his expression was sombre again.

'As I believe you know, I was staying with my friend Sidony in Plymouth in order to save travelling to and fro each day to watch the performances,' she began, aware that she was speaking too fast. 'But then poor Francis Heron fell sick, and Gabe thought it could be – well, it wasn't, so no need to say what it could have been. With Gabe being so preoccupied, and then that young man disappearing, it seemed wrong to be giggling with Sidony and going to the plays because one of the handsome young actors had asked me to alter a cloak for him and . . .' *And I'd been flattered by his attentions, bewitched by his good looks, found my heart beating fast when I was with him*, she had been about to say. But she held back the words. 'So I went home,' she said instead. 'Only now I regret it, because I abandoned Sidony without adequate explanation and, which is nearly as bad, I was running away. And I want to go back, call on Sidony and her father to apologize, and ask her if the two of us can attend the final production this afternoon. Which I am really keen to see,' she added, 'so perhaps the regret and the urge to apologize are just excuses so that I can have what I want?'

The rush of words stopped, and she found she was slightly breathless.

After some moments Jonathan said quietly, 'It sounds quite reasonable to me not to want to miss the final play. It's not as if a travelling company comes to town every week. And you don't need my permission, Celia.'

'I don't need *anyone's* permission,' she replied. Far too curtly: 'Sorry,' she muttered. 'I don't really know what I'm asking you, Jonathan. Don't know why I'm *here*,' she added.

'Perhaps simply to talk to a friend?' he suggested. 'We are all out of our usual humour, I think. Just now you said you felt you had run away from whatever so darkens the air at the Saracen's Head, and I well understand how you might.' He paused, frowning. 'I was there, very early yesterday. Your brother had called on me late the previous night, and, knowing poor Master Heron was near death, I rode down soon after dawn.' He stopped again. Then he said, his voice so soft that she strained to hear, 'I sat with his cooling body, as I have sat with so many. I prayed for his soul, I spoke to the man he had been. I told myself God was with us both in that isolated little room, I tried again and again to convince myself that what I was sensing so powerfully was only in my imagination; the result of a lonely little room, a dark and twisting passage, an ancient, creaking inn, the echoes and shades of those days of thrills, violence, romance and drama as the Company put on their plays and made their audience believe that fiction was fact.' He stopped suddenly. Then he said, 'But it did not relent. As I sat there, I had the dreadful feeling I was being overcome. I thought I was losing myself.'

Celia gasped, quickly suppressing it. Unthinkingly she reached for his hand, and he took hers in a tight grasp.

Amid the turmoil in her head, the thought briefly struck her that she had come to him for comfort, and here he was seeking the same from her.

As if he had all at once realized what they were doing, he disengaged his hand and leaned away from her a little. Gave her an awkward smile. She thought that her impetuousness must have offended him, and she was heartily glad he could not have picked up what she was thinking.

But then, once again leaning close to her, he said quietly, 'I believe my parishioners can do without me for a spell. May I ride into Plymouth with you?'

'You're certain this was in Francis Heron's bag?' Theo said.

I was in his office. I'd given my report on the three dead men, and now the spade-bearded man's pack lay unfastened on his desk. He was holding up Francis's battered old notebook.

Francis's bag, as I'd remembered as soon as that frightening mental mist had cleared, had been fetched from the Saracen's Head when they went for his body and left for safe keeping in the coroner's office. And the notebook wasn't in it.

'Quite sure,' I said. 'The spade-bearded man, or someone acting on his behalf, took it from Francis's bag. And if you compare what's inscribed on the flyleaf with this' – I flipped through the papers from the pack to the one with the series of drawings – 'you'll see someone's been copying that symbol.'

Theo grunted an agreement.

'I wondered if it's astrological,' I added. 'I thought the cross might be a Christian symbol, but the equal-armed cross is older than Christ, I believe.'

Theo looked up, his expression suggesting that there were more important matters for our attention than a scholarly discussion of symbols and their meaning. Then he went back to the notebook.

'Code,' he muttered. 'Pages of it, in the front.' He flipped through the pages. 'And here at the back, what look like lists of words, mostly the same length, five letters long . . . are they names?'

He held it out to me in his fingertips as if he feared it was about to burst into flames. I fought the strong reluctance to take it – it was a *book*, for the good Lord's sake, a much-used, dog-eared, cheap and dirty one, so what harm could it do me? – and opened it.

But just then there came the sound of the outer door opening and one – no, two – people came along the passage to Theo's inner office. Before whoever it was could knock on the door, he moved out from behind his desk and flung it open. Jonathan stood there, with Celia beside him.

I stared at her. 'What are *you* doing here?' I demanded.

My sister looked taken aback, not to say offended, at my tone, but before she could protest, Jonathan spoke. 'Celia said she was coming into the town to ask her friend to accompany her to the Company's final performance this afternoon, and—'

'I am, Gabe,' Celia put in, her jaw set. 'I owe Sidony an apology for leaving so abruptly, Francis Heron didn't have what we all feared he had, and there's no reason whatsoever why I shouldn't see today's play!'

The echoes of her words rang in the room. Into the brief ensuing silence, Jonathan said quietly, 'No danger, at least, from the plague.'

I spun round to look at him, noticing that Celia and Theo did the same. He nodded, and it seemed to me he paused for a moment, as if in preparation.

Then he said, 'But all of us know there *is* danger.' Glancing at Celia, he added, 'It's why I suggested Celia and I came here to join you, so that we could speak together, share what we know.' He paused. 'What we fear,' he murmured.

Theo had returned to his own side of his desk, almost as if he was making it clear that this was his office, reminding us that he was the coroner and dead bodies were his responsibility. He waved a hand to a couple of chairs set against the wall and Jonathan drew them forward, offering one to Celia. He stood with his hands resting on the back of the second, I stayed where I was.

Theo had actually started to speak but, with a brief glance of apology, Jonathan forestalled him.

'Three men are dead,' he began, 'one by unknown means and—'

'Francis Heron was poisoned,' I said. 'Daniel was stabbed,' I added, 'and the other man in the barn had his neck broken.'

Jonathan was silent for a moment. Then he continued. 'All three deaths have occurred within days of the arrival of a London theatre company, who have been attracting large audiences daily with their captivating, not to say enchanting or even bewitching, performances.'

'There is the sense that this Company have their own very distinctive way of portraying the plays,' I said. I thought of Judyth, and her conviction that the productions had been weighted so that a message could be transmitted, or a truth obscured. 'Which may have a definite purpose behind it.'

'Yes,' Jonathan agreed. 'In addition, those of us who have spent time at the Saracen's Head other than during one of the plays' – he glanced at me – 'have noticed that there is an unwholesome air within the inn. This – this *disturbance* has spread, and for the last couple of days St Luke's Church has received a steady flow of people who seem to want nothing more than to sit quietly in the peaceful silence.' He paused, then added, 'Most of these people have been to see at least one of the Company's plays. It is as if they have brought something away with them, and that whatever it is has spread to others in the village.'

'As if it were a sickness,' Theo said very quietly.

'It is not the plague,' I said, not quietly at all. Somebody needed to make that fact absolutely plain, and I was the doctor.

'Not the plague,' Jonathan repeated. 'And, I would suggest, not a physical ailment at all.' He paused, once again looking round at each of us. 'Instead, something of the mind.'

Celia drew a sharp breath. Theo looked as if he wanted to throw himself out of his office and start banging heads together. Jonathan met my eyes. 'Gabe?' he said. 'Could this really be happening? Is it possible?'

'I would say no to both questions,' I replied, 'but I can't because I've experienced it myself. I have spent the greater part of two nights in the Saracen's Head, and what I saw and felt there – what I *thought* or was *made to believe* I saw and felt there, I should say – was horrible. And I was not the only person to be affected.' I turned to Jonathan. '*Something is profoundly amiss* is what you said, and one of the players, a man called Barnaby Abell, said, *There's something so wrong here.* Now, if we are not to let ourselves believe in a sudden outbreak of ghosts and gruesome hauntings in an old inn that has stood there for centuries with no such horrors, then it's too much of a coincidence to suggest this wrongness just happens to have materialized precisely when a London theatre company came to stay.'

'You're accusing the Company of having brought it?' Celia demanded. 'But,' she went on angrily, not giving me a chance to respond, 'why in heaven's name *would* they?'

'I have no idea,' I said. 'Theo? Jonathan? Do you think I'm right?'

'It seems a little unlikely for the whole Company to be involved,' Jonathan said thoughtfully, 'but yes, I think it's entirely possible that someone among them may be perpetuating this, er, this illusion.'

'There's something else,' I said. 'They – he – whoever it is has a long reach.' Suddenly I felt as if I couldn't go on; as if a strong hand was on my throat, stopping the words. *It's an illusion*, I told myself very firmly. *That's what Jonathan just said – whoever it is is perpetrating an illusion. There's nobody here except my sister and my friends.* 'This morning I was in my study at Rosewyke' – the words seemed to explode out of me, causing Celia to look at me in alarm – 'and all at once

I couldn't think. I couldn't remember anything. Oh, you may laugh' – nobody was even smiling – 'but at the time I truly believed my mind was going. And it wasn't the first time, because earlier when I was examining the three bodies in the crypt I suddenly found I'd lost quite a lot of time, and—'

'What do you mean, lost time?' Theo demanded. He too was looking at me worriedly.

'Exactly that,' I said. 'I'd been studying a rash on Francis Heron's chest and concluding it had been caused by the deadly nightshade, which is the poison that I believe killed him. The Company use belladonna drops, or at least some of the players do. The young lad who plays female roles has abnormally wide pupils, and that's what the drops do. Then it occurred to me that there have been many references to potions and poisons in the plays that have been performed over the last few days, and that this might suggest someone within the Company knew rather a lot about the subject. But all at once I realized that my feet were cold.' I paused, for the alarming power of that moment was still uncomfortable, even in memory. 'I looked at the candles in their lanterns, and the top third had burned away. Somebody, somehow, seemed to have put me into a trance.'

There was a stunned silence. Then Theo said a little too loudly, 'You were concentrating on what you were thinking about! And you're *tired*, Gabe! Exhausted! When did you last have a proper night's sleep?'

I shrugged.

Theo glared at Celia, then at Jonathan, as if trying to force them to agree with him, but neither said anything. 'Jonathan?' he demanded angrily. 'You're a man of the church, surely you don't believe in this rubbish? In this absurd suggestion that a person not even present – not visible, audible or tangible – can affect another's mind?'

Jonathan smiled slightly. 'I think, Theo, that you are looking to the wrong man for support,' he said gently. And Theo, frowning briefly as he worked it out, looked away, abashed.

It did not take him long, however, to recover.

'What, then, are we to do?' he demanded. 'If we agree that

someone, or more than one person, in the Company is trying to confuse our investigation into these three deaths, what is our next step?'

'As I told you all, I'm going to call on my friend Sidony and we will go to see the Company's final performance,' Celia said.

I turned to her. 'Are you?'

'Yes,' she said, with a touch of defiance. 'I know you're going to say *Is that wise?* or something equally crushing, but I've made my mind up.'

'I wasn't.' I smiled at her. 'I was going to say, keep alert, but then I'm sure you will anyway.'

Theo, who had been frowning in thought, said, 'Jarman Hodge reports that this Daniel was new to the Company, and—'

New to the Company.

Out of memory, I remembered something that Francis Heron had said, shortly before he entered into his final convulsions. He had been recalling his past, the life he had once lived, the person he had been . . . and he said, *I am not the man you think I am. And you would not believe what I have seen.*

Which did not sound, I now thought, as if he was talking about his life as an actor.

Theo was still speaking, but I could not wait.

'I don't believe Francis Heron had been with them very long either,' I said.

Theo stared at me, drumming his fingers impatiently on his desk. Jonathan had a watchful air, Celia looked as if she wanted to be gone.

And after a short pause, Theo said, 'Three men have died, as Jonathan said at the start of this extraordinary conversation. I am His Majesty's coroner, and it is my job to ascertain how, and why, they died. We know how; Gabe just told us. You three can go haring off after ghosts and fanciful notions of dark horrors and disembodied spirits with the power to confuse men's minds and stop them dead, and men who for their own reasons choose to obscure their own past, and I wish you all success. My task is clear and straightforward, and I'm going to get on with it.' Abruptly standing up, reaching for his long black robe, he yelled, '*Jarman!*' and strode out of the room.

THIRTEEN

'I'm going too,' Celia said as the swirls of disturbed air set off by Theo's departure settled.

I saw Jonathan shoot a swift look at her. I thought perhaps I could read what it said.

'I must return to St Luke's,' he said. 'What about you, Gabriel?'

I was following a line of thought of my own, and Theo's desk and grand wooden chair stood invitingly before me. 'I shall stay here for a while,' I said. 'One or two things I wish to check.'

I waited until I heard the outer door close behind them, then dived straight back into the spade-bearded man's pack and took out the contents.

I perched on the edge of Theo's desk turning the pages of the tattered little notebook, staring at the closely covered pages as if sheer concentration would provide the key to their meaning, which of course it didn't. I turned to the lists. They might have been names, as Theo suggested, and some of them might be ones I knew, but I had no way of knowing because they were all written in that code of random letters and little pictures.

Frustrated, I got up off the desk and sank down in Theo's chair.

My mind turned back to the bodies I'd examined first thing that morning. Francis Heron, Daniel, the spade-bearded London man. What, if anything, I wondered, linked them? Francis and Daniel had both been of the Company, both had been newcomers, and – I sat up straighter, remembering the conversation overheard by Theo – they knew a secret. They had carried it out of London, disguising themselves as members of an acting company, one of them a player, the other one a manual worker, and their flight had been hidden among that of the others who were escaping the fatal dangers of the capital on the Plague Tour. A very good explanation for a swift departure . . .

Except that their true purpose was something quite different; as Theo had overheard the young man Daniel say, there were reasons other than the plague for a man to flee the capital.

What was theirs? What had flung them out of whatever life they lived in London and sent them on the road, forced them to take on unfamiliar roles in a sort of work that was novel and tough? I remembered the dead Daniel's hands, so very evidently new to hard and constant heavy work. I remembered Francis Heron on stage as Graziano in *Othello*, his performance adequate at best, and Theo said he'd been noticeably unfunny as Flute the Bellows-Mender in *A Midsummer Night's Dream*. I knew now why that was: Daniel hadn't been a carter and Francis wasn't an actor.

What *had* they done to earn their living? I wished I could ask then, but they were both dead. And the fact that they'd been killed – that Francis had been poisoned and Daniel stabbed in the heart – strongly suggested someone not only knew which circles they had moved in and the work they had done but also the deadly secret they had uncovered there.

I sat in Theo's chair, gently tipping it back and letting it fall again. My mind seemed to be detached; I felt . . . I felt relaxed. As if nothing mattered.

But it did. I shook my head, then slapped my own cheek, hard.

I sat up straight, wondering suddenly why it seemed so hard to move forward; to work out where to go to find out the answers to my questions, to begin to speculate who might have poisoned Francis Heron, and who had slain Daniel and the bearded man. What was this odd mood that I seemed to be fighting? And then it struck me with the force of certainty that I wasn't the only one of us to be affected this way: that Theo was feeling it too, and this was why he was so cross. And Jonathan? Was he too infected with this deadly inertia?

And where was it coming from?

The walls of Theo's office were closing in on me, and I knew I had to leave. I still had the small, tatty notebook in my hand, and unthinkingly I tucked it into a pocket inside my jerkin. I flung myself out into the passage and into the yard, where to my relief Theo's stable boy had my horse saddled ready. Mounting, I kicked Hal to a canter and headed down into Plymouth.

The yard doors of the Saracen's Head were just closing as I hurried up, but I shoved the right-hand one open again and pushed my way inside. Nobody accosted me to ask for payment, so I edged along behind the back row of the audience and found a spot where, sheltered beneath the overhanging gallery above, I could see out without my presence being too obvious.

I glanced around to see if I could spot my sister, but I couldn't find her on the balcony opposite where I was. When we had all come together to see *Othello* we had stood almost exactly above my present position, so I guessed that was where she now was.

Then the play began.

Perhaps it had always been the Company's plan to end with a comedy. Perhaps they had decided that, after the death of an actor and a carter and too many days spent in a dark old inn where far too many frightening things were happening, something frivolous and light was in order. Whichever it was, the crowd were in a mood to be amused and they were laughing already, as one of the actors, dressed up as a fat old woman with red cheeks and a vivid yellow wig under a huge hat, took the stage to explain who she was and what was happening.

The play promised to be bawdy and full of sexual innuendo, for the story dealt with a haughty young noblewoman who was betrothed to a very wealthy young lord but, knowing that she would not pass the test of virginity he insisted on before the wedding, was planning to persuade, coerce or pay her serving maid to disguise herself as her mistress and suffer the examination in her stead. Unbeknownst to the young noblewoman, however, the serving maid and the wealthy lord were already lovers; the fat old woman's lewd and hugely exaggerated winks as she hinted at how that scene might play out had the crowd roaring with laughter and stamping their approval. As the old woman told the audience about the characters, each one in turn appeared on the stage. The young noblewoman was the boy who had played Emilia in *Othello*, in a gorgeous gown and a wig of glossy auburn curls, and I recognized Thomas Lightbodie, whose sneer of distaste might have been part of the character of the young woman's father or, alternatively, Thomas's opinion of the whole cheap, trashy play.

The performance got into its stride. Scene followed scene smoothly and quickly, and regular breaks were included for raucous songs with easily learned choruses in which the audience were encouraged to join. The crude, filthy lyrics, concentrating almost exclusively on highly unlikely sexual practices and extreme bodily functions, got the crowd baying along. Sensing their audience's delight and loud, vociferous approval, the cast threw themselves into the debauchery, and, letting my gaze move round from the stage to encompass the inn yard, it seemed to me that everyone in the uproariously laughing crowd was wholeheartedly appreciating the afternoon's entertainment.

But then I spotted the man in the far corner.

It was as if he had deliberately taken up a position and a pose that mirrored my own. I was on the far right of the yard, a few paces short of where the tiring room opened off it. The man was on the far left. I stood with my right shoulder leaning into the wall that separated the inn yard from the street; he with his left shoulder to the wall of the main inn building. Both of us had our arms folded.

And we were looking straight at each other.

I had noticed him because, in all that throng of hard-working, sweaty players and red-faced, happy, exuberant audience, he was the only person who was not laughing; not even smiling, but leaning there in his corner with a face entirely devoid of expression.

He was tall and lean, with a long, thin face. He wore a high-collared cloak, expertly cut and made of black wool of so fine a quality that it had a slight sheen. His greying dark hair was beautifully styled, smooth and sleek to his shoulders, and there was a frill of fine white linen at his throat above the black velvet of his doublet. He was the essence of elegance and sophistication, and as soon as I'd spotted him, I'd been put in mind of the man we'd found dead in the barn.

He held my gaze, his face hard and cold. He seemed to look me up and down, and as if in silent comment on what he saw, his thin lips turned down in a sneer. There was something compelling about him; even across the width of the crowded, heaving inn yard, his intensely dark eyes under dead-straight brows stood out clearly in his pale face.

I'd had enough. Pushing myself away from the wall, I was on the point of elbowing my way through the throng to accost him, demand what he thought he was about, staring at a stranger in so hostile a manner, but then something happened.

At first I didn't believe I'd actually seen it, for it seemed impossible. But I blinked, looked again, and it had. I hadn't seen any movement – nothing at all – but the man in the cloak was no longer alone in his corner; someone was standing close beside him.

I'd been watching him intently, every single instant. And I hadn't seen *anybody* come striding, or creeping, or hurrying, or dawdling to join him: one second the newcomer wasn't there, the next he was. It was as if somebody had been holding up a black curtain in front of him and had suddenly let it fall.

I stared at the second figure. He was shorter than his elegant companion and much broader. He wore a soft wool cap over what I suspected was a bald head, and his brows were so light as to give the impression that his face was also hairless. He too stood with his arms folded, his right hand clasped to his bulging left bicep. The knuckles of the hand were dark with bruising. He too wore the dark cloak, but it had taken me a moment to recognize it since his was rumpled, mud-stained and draped carelessly across his stocky body as if it was a sack.

The audience were in high good humour by now, many crying with laughter and hastening their descent into total incoherence with mug after mug of Master Coxton's ale. Their amiability was to my advantage, for few of them objected to, or even seemed to notice, the rough way I pushed through them as I crossed the inn yard to the opposite corner.

I burst out into the small patch of open ground to find it
empty. The elegant man and his stocky companion had
vanished.

I ran into the inn.

After only a few paces I stopped. The echo of my boots on
the flagstones rang out, then ceased as suddenly as if somebody
had shut a door on it. I realized, standing there in the deserted,
eerie emptiness, that the inn was utterly silent and still. Yet,
only a short distance away down the passage, was the open
yard where a band of actors were throwing themselves lustily
into a vulgar comedy and a whole crowd of happy townspeople
were roaring and stamping their noisy appreciation. I had the
weird sensation that I had stepped through a veil, and passed
unwittingly from one realm into another . . .

Oh, God, what was going on in this place?

I knew I should be racing on in pursuit of the cloaked men,
but I could not make myself do it. I turned back, under an
arch, round a corner and along a short corridor until I could
see across into the taproom. Coxton and his staff were standing
in the open doorway, backs to the interior, totally taken up
with the play and enjoying it as much as the crowd outside.

The other world hadn't gone away, then.

Berating myself with a few choice expressions from my
years at sea, I went back into the inn's dark and increasingly
disturbing interior.

I reached the spot where I had stopped and went on, further
into the maze of passages and odd little flights of stairs towards
the rear of the building. I paused at a corner where passages
dived off in two different directions, listening. But there was no
sound of running feet, no slam or even click of a closing door,
no murmur of hushed voices. There was nothing at all.

Then, as if some watchful power had responded to my
straining ears, there came a low, sort of *huuuaaaah* sound; the
noise you make when you breathe out a warm, open-mouthed
breath over a shiny surface in order to buff it. And I swear I
felt the soft breeze of it, as if a window had been opened on
a sweet day of spring.

Once again, I had to give myself a few hard words before
I could go on.

I was about to take the right-hand fork when I became aware of a new sound. It was tiny, and I waited, absolutely still, for some moments before it came again. It was coming from somewhere down the left-hand fork, which was the passage leading to the part of the inn where the accommodation was, and, beyond, the dark little room where Francis Heron died.

I turned round and, slowly and apprehensively, set off to investigate.

There was no light at all in those rear corridors and I stumbled a couple of times, feeling my way along towards the source of the sound. Rounding a corner, the utter darkness was alleviated by a faint patch of light coming through a partly opened door. The door was, I realized as I hurried towards it, the one to Francis's room.

I slowed right down, making barely a sound as I drew level with the doorway. Peering inside, it seemed at first glance that, apart from the absence of the body, nothing had changed. But then the small sound came again, and my eyes were drawn to the slim figure standing right in the far corner, all but invisible in the deep shadow.

He moved slightly, and a small amount of light fell on his face. The large eyes were enormous now, the head twisting to and fro in anguish on the long neck, and Raphe Wymer said, his voice breaking in distress, 'I had to come! It is awful, and I feel his presence and the shock of his death, but I *had* to!'

He was crying.

I moved towards him, my hand out to comfort him, but in a sudden violent movement he backed away from me.

'He was lapsing in and out of unconsciousness at the end,' I said gently. 'I do not think death was a shock, exactly, and—'

'How can it not be?' Raphe asked, his eyes so wide now that I could see a rim of white all round the irises. 'It is the instant when we leave one existence and enter the next. Of *course* it is a shock, a profound and terrible shock!'

His face was fixed in a rictus; the face of a fanatic, who believes against all argument that what he believes – what strange, unlikely, outlandish facts he has taken to be his own truth – cannot, will not, be denied.

I wondered, in that moment, if Raphe Wymer was entirely sane.

He was clutching something in his left hand, holding it tight against his breast. Against his heart.

I forced a smile. 'What have you got there?' I asked, trying to sound cheery and interested and succeeding only in sounding patronizing, as if Raphe were a distressed seven-year-old.

He held the object closer for a moment, then, with extreme reluctance, held it out.

It was white and quite small.

It was the silk handkerchief embroidered with strawberries. And I had last seen it when this poor, trembling, weeping lad in front of me had given it to me for Francis's headache.

'You thought to bind Master Heron's head with it to ease his pain,' I said gently. 'That was a compassionate gesture.'

He nodded vigorously. 'Yes! Yes, I liked him very much. I wanted to help him.'

'You did, I'm sure you did.' The poor boy needed a kindly word. I hesitated, then said, 'Perhaps you ought to keep it, as something to remember Master Heron by?' Celia, I was sure, would happily make another one.

But Raphe was looking horrified, shaking his head now as violently as he'd just been nodding it. 'No, no, *no!*' he said in a suppressed shout. 'I cannot keep it, *nobody* can keep it! It must be destroyed, burned, thrown into the heart of a fire, before – before—' He was swallowing convulsively, his throat working as he tried to speak, only the words wouldn't come out.

I felt a touch like a cold finger on my spine. 'Why must it be burned?' I asked. My voice didn't sound like mine.

And eventually, his face contorted with fear, he managed to say, as I had known he would, 'Because it has magic in it.'

In horror I followed the trail of the silk handkerchief backwards in time from this moment. Raphe gave it to Francis Heron, and he must have taken it from wherever Fallon Adderbury had put it away ready for the next time the Company performed *Othello*.

And before that Celia had given it to Fallon.

My sister had *made* it.

My mind racing, filling with awful possibilities and images I didn't want to even think about but somehow couldn't keep at bay, I wondered just who it was that believed in this magic, and how many people – especially people of power and influence – accepted it as the truth.

Then suddenly I wasn't standing frozen in some dim and dank room hidden away at the back of an inn, I was thundering back along the twisting passages, Raphe Wymer forgotten, Francis Heron forgotten, magic mirrors, supernatural apparitions and strange, alarming visions forgotten, driven out by the one imperative thought forcing me on: find Celia and get her to safety.

FOURTEEN

Celia was aching with laughter, and even Sidony's constant little shrieks of outrage at the worst excesses of vulgarity going on down in the inn yard couldn't spoil her delight. Anyway, Sidony was only pretending to be offended, and in truth she was loving the play, so helpless with giggling that she kept leaning weakly against Celia. You couldn't help yourself, Celia thought, the players were *so* rude, and they just didn't seem to care about poking out their bare bottoms to be smacked and being discovered in the most intimate of personal moments, such as when the man who had been Bianca and Helena, this time playing the maid of Oliver Dauncey's wealthy noblewoman, had to be inspected to see if she was pure or not, and when Gerard Cuddon in the role of a fat old woman in a huge hat and a bright yellow wig had bent over to pick up her basket and farted loudly in someone's face.

And, as if being made to laugh so uncontrollably wasn't enough, her enjoyment was augmented by the fact that Fallon had a role, although only a minor one. Much to Celia's relief, it was a part that allowed him to maintain most of his dignity. He kept his clothes on, anyway, and wasn't called upon to wear a ridiculous hat or a stupid wig, and he delivered his few lines cleverly enough to make the crowd laugh and hoot. Not that this was any great feat by this time, Celia had to admit . . .

To her relief, neither Sidony nor her father had held her abrupt departure earlier in the week against her. Gilbert Baynton had said graciously that there was no need to apologize, and Sidony's initial petulance had rapidly faded when Celia slyly said that if they were quick, they'd get to the Saracen's Head for the start of the performance. Now the play was nearing its end, the ludicrous story winding to its unlikely conclusion.

The crowd down in the inn yard were rowdy and boisterous, one or two skirmishes had broken out and many people were drunk. There was an air of lively celebration, Celia thought, looking down, but it was threatening to turn imminently into something darker. As some of the audience up on the balcony started to push their way past on the way to the steps, perhaps with the idea of getting out before everyone else clogged the exits, she glanced round for Phillips and edged closer to Sidony; it wasn't the time to become separated.

Then someone approaching the steps cried out in protest, and said loudly, 'You can't come *up* this way, us up here are trying to go *down!*' Lots of people all began pushing, someone shouted an oath, a woman squealed, Celia grabbed Sidony's hand. Phillips was standing protectively right behind them, his face rigid with disapproval.

Whoever was trying to push their way through was making headway, thrusting people aside as if they were children. The crush cleared, the big newcomer broke out into the open and Celia saw that it was Gabe.

He came right up to her, taking hold of her arm. 'We have to go!' he said urgently, starting to pull her away. Just then some new piece of comic foolery reached its climax down in the yard, and the audience howled with laughter.

'I'm not going *now!*' Celia had to shout over the racket, wriggling and struggling to pull her arm out of Gabe's iron grip. 'Don't be absurd, Gabe, it's nearly over and I have no intention whatsoever of missing the cast's final bow!'

He would not let go. He shook her impatiently and, also raising his voice, said, 'You *have* to, Celia! It's imperative that you find a place of sanctuary. You *must* believe me!'

'But I'm with Sidony! What about her?'

Gabe's face darkened in irritation. He glared at Sidony, spotted Phillips and said curtly, 'You're with them? Miss Sidony and Mistress Palfrey?'

'I am,' the manservant replied. 'And you are—'

'Get her out of here,' Gabe commanded. 'Don't ask questions, just *do* it.'

Phillips stared at him for a moment, then did as he was told.

'Gabe, what on *earth* do you think you're doing?' Celia demanded as he dragged her to the steps and down into the yard, forging a path through the ranks of the audience, out onto the road and along to the stables where he always left his horse. '*Answer me!*' she cried as he pushed her inside. 'I won't stand for this, even if you *are* my brother!'

He turned to her, his face rigid with tension. 'Where's your horse?' he demanded.

'In Master Baynton's stable! Where do you *think*?' She was furious, spitting the words out, so angry with him that she wanted to hit him, and would have done but for the fact that he was holding her right arm – her punching arm – too tightly for her to wrest it free.

'No time to go there now,' he muttered. '*Ouch!* Don't *do* that!' She'd just bunched up her left fist and thumped it hard into his right bicep. 'Celia, I know you think I'm being high-handed and bossy—'

'That doesn't even *begin* to describe what I think!' she yelled.

'—and I'll explain as soon as we're on our way, then you'll understand. Or at least I hope you will,' he added in a mutter. 'But now we must go, as quickly as we can.'

The ostler had appeared, and, after a glance at Gabe's expression, swiftly had Hal ready. Celia gave a cry of surprise as Gabe lifted her up into the saddle, trying to arrange her skirts to protect her legs from the ostler's interested eyes.

'Sit astride,' Gabe ordered, and before she could protest, he had mounted up behind her, his feet already in the stirrups, and then he was kicking Hal into a smart trot up the road, shouting to people milling about to get out of the way.

Sitting so close to him, she could feel the tension in him. It was more than tension; at one point a drunk staggered out into their path and Hal shied away, almost unseating her, and Gabe's reaction was so angry, so violent, that she hastened to hold him back before he could do the man severe harm.

Then they were out of the town, on the road that led out along the river estuary, and Gabe kicked the big black horse to a canter and then, as the traffic cleared, a gallop.

Celia felt a brief stab of fear, for she was sitting in front of the saddle and without stirrups, without reins, her hands wound tight in Hal's long, thick mane. But then Gabe put an arm round her waist, and she knew he wouldn't let her fall.

Then the ride was exhilarating, and she felt her blood run hot with the excitement of it. She and Gabe had ridden like this when they were children, each egging the other on until they tested their courage right up to the limit. As the memory of those thrilling days was revived, for several miles she almost forgot she was angry with him.

They went thundering down the long slope into Tavy St Luke's, and Gabe drew Hal to a steaming halt outside the Priest's House. He jumped down, held out his arms to her, and as she landed beside him, said, 'Into the church. *Quick!*'

'But Hal! He's really hot, aren't you going to—'

'*Get into the church!*'

And finally his extreme anxiety penetrated her resentment and her anger. He's afraid! she thought, staring at him, and suddenly she was no longer flustered and far too warm but felt as if icy water was running down her back.

She picked up her voluminous skirts and ran to the church, heaving at the heavy door. Then Gabe was with her, pushing it open as if it was made of tin, and they tumbled inside.

'Sssh!' Gabe hissed, staring round the interior. There didn't seem to be anybody there, and the smell of extinguished candles and melted wax suggested that a service might just have ended. He took a couple of steps forward. 'Jonathan?' he called softly. 'Are you there?'

There was the sound of quiet footfalls, and Jonathan appeared in the low arch that led through to St Luke's Little Chapel.

Celia was close enough to Gabe to feel the relief flowing through him. He grabbed her hand, and together they strode around to the entrance to the side chapel, where Jonathan was waiting. Leaning down to speak very quietly – but not so quietly that Celia couldn't hear – he said, 'Jonathan, what are the rules of sanctuary and do they still apply?'

Jonathan's eyebrows went up in surprise. 'Sanctuary,' he repeated softly. Then he led them into the little chapel, over to a pew standing alone at the back next to the entrance, indicating for them to sit down. Celia thought Gabe was going to protest, was going to yell out, *I have no time for sitting down, this is desperate!* and the same thought must have struck Jonathan, because he frowned slightly and nodded towards the main church, where two old men, a middle-aged woman and a child knelt in prayer. A family group of perhaps half a dozen sat nearer to the altar.

'Oh. Didn't notice them,' Gabe muttered.

Jonathan sat down next to Celia, with Gabe on her other side. 'Sanctuary was largely abolished under Henry VIII,' he said, just loudly enough for them to hear. 'Law-abiding citizens didn't like the presence of the lawless disturbing the peace and interrupting trade, and a statute was passed in 1540 that withdrew the right in the case of murder, rape, arson and burglary, and one or two other crimes as well, as I recall, and—'

'But is it still law?' Gabe demanded.

Jonathan frowned. 'Well, I can't speak for the present, but at the time when I was a scholar of canon law, there had not actually been a statute that *specifically* denied it, so—'

'Then we need you!'

Briefly Celia met Jonathan's eyes. He seemed to be as mystified as she was. 'Why?' he asked simply.

Gabe reached for Celia's hand, squeezing it hard. 'I've just come from the Saracen's Head. The inn was horribly quiet – unnaturally so, and I – never mind.' His jaw tightened. 'I went to the room where Francis Heron died, and the boy who played Desdemona was there, the one with the big eyes and the elegant bearing, and—'

'Raphe Wymer,' Celia put in.

'Yes, him,' Gabe snapped. 'Sorry,' he muttered. 'He was – oh, Lord, there was something very seriously wrong with him,' he hurried on. 'He was in deep distress, weeping uncontrollably, and the things he said didn't make any sense because he was talking about magic, and an object that had been imbued with magic and become very dangerous, fatally dangerous, and I thought he was losing his reason. But what was really awful was that—' he paused, and briefly glanced at her, and in his eyes she read some deep emotion that troubled her to her depths – 'was that I saw that he was clutching that silk handkerchief with the strawberries, and *you* made it, Celia.'

Now she was full of fear. 'Yes, I did.' Her voice sounded tiny.

Gabe dropped her hand and put his arm round her, drawing her close. 'It's all right, the lad's going to burn it, he was going to go and do so straight away,' he said, the words tumbling out, 'so even if there are people in high places who believe in such rubbish and come looking, there won't be a problem because the handkerchief will have been destroyed!'

Celia thought the artificial brightness in his voice would not have convinced a child. It certainly didn't convince her, and she could see that Jonathan was equally dubious.

There was a very difficult silence. Then she cleared her throat and said, 'If there isn't a problem, and no danger for anyone involved in the *bewitching* of the handkerchief' – she hissed the perilous word, but both men flinched as if she'd shouted it – 'then why, Gabe, did you come bursting up onto the gallery, haul me away and come galloping up here as if hell hounds were after us to demand that Jonathan gives me sanctuary?'

Gabe didn't appear to be able to reply. After a few moments, Jonathan said, 'It is, perhaps, as well to take the precaution, even if it proves totally unnecessary, as I am quite sure it will.'

But he, Celia thought with a quaking heart, didn't sound any more convincing than Gabe had done.

I wanted to stay. I wanted to set up a defensive position in St Luke's Little Chapel, to find a place somewhere up under the roof from which to watch out so that I'd see them coming. I wanted to question Jonathan about every detail of the privilege of sanctuary, demand that he search through his memory until he came up with the answer I was so desperate for.

He had told me very firmly that he was sure Celia was safe inside the church. 'Look at it rationally,' he had said, with a coolness I much admired. 'First, we only have the word of this poor mad boy that anyone is even searching for the hand-kerchief and the person who made it. Second, only a few people know that it is Celia's work, and third, it will have been destroyed by now anyway. Fourth, even if the unthinkable happens and someone does set out to hunt for her, nobody except the three of us knows she's here, and *I'm* certainly going to keep it to myself.'

I met his calm eyes. 'Yes, you're right,' I muttered.

He smiled. Then, leaning close to me, he said softly, 'The privilege of sanctuary may not be an undeniable right any more. But there is another protection for those who come in supplication, and even those who are guilty are not rejected if they are penitent. Celia has done nothing wrong, Gabe. She *will* be safe here.'

And so, with Jonathan's reassurance ringing in my head, I was acting against my every instinct and leaving them there in the side chapel, my beloved sister and the man I had learned to trust like a brother. While I was still there to stay beside her, Jonathan had gone to the Priest's House for food, water, blankets and pillows, as well as a bottle of brandy and two small mugs. As he set them out in a corner, I took Celia's hand.

'I'm going back to the town,' I said, 'but I shall call in at Theo's house first, where I hope to find him and, with any luck, Jarman too.'

'But you—'

'Celia, something very dangerous is happening,' I said, not letting her speak. 'It's concentrated on the Saracen's Head, on the Company, or perhaps certain members of it, and somehow they have spread such fear and dread in that place that it is permeating outwards through the town and beyond, for those with the eyes and ears and sensitivity to feel it, and people have died because of it.'

She looked up at me, her eyes clear and very bright. 'And you're going to get to the bottom of it, and sort it out all by yourself?'

'No, I just said, I'm going to get Theo and Jarman to help.'

She was still staring at me, and I now realized her eyes were so bright because they were full of tears.

It was time to go.

Jonathan came to the door with me. The main body of the church, I noticed, was empty now. 'Thank you,' I said.

He shook his head. 'No need for gratitude. Celia is innocent in this matter. Of course I will protect her, and I will not be alone.'

I stared at my boots, not knowing quite how to reply.

After a moment, I said, thinking to lighten the mood, 'It's going to be a long night. Have you plenty of candles?'

'Yes. And we shall—' But he stopped, and I sensed he too felt awkward, but for a different reason.

I opened the door, fastening my jerkin against the cold. I felt something in my pocket, and, remembering, took out Francis's little notebook.

'If time hangs heavily,' I said, handing it to Jonathan, 'the pair of you might amuse yourselves with the contents of this. They're in code,' I added. Then, with a wave, I strode over to my horse, mounted and hurried away.

It was now late in the day, and the sun was about to dip below the horizon. Darkness would soon be coming, and for once I really did not welcome it. Hal was eager to move, and we covered the ground between Tavy St Luke's and Theo's house quickly. Even as I approached, however, I sensed Theo wasn't there.

I dismounted and banged on the outer door, then opened it and called out, 'Theo?'

One of his agents came out of the front office, chewing. 'Not here, Doctor Taverner,' he said. He wiped his mouth. 'Sorry, just grabbing a bite to eat.'

'Do you know where he is?'

'Said he was going down into the town. Jarman Hodge is there, following up some enquiry, but I can't tell you more than that, and—'

I heard a door opening along the passage and Theo's wife Elaine looked out. She looked anxious, which was not like her, and she beckoned to me. 'I heard voices and recognized one as yours,' she said quietly.

'What's happening, Elaine?' I muttered.

'You feel it, then?'

'Oh, yes.'

'It isn't everybody,' she whispered. 'Many people I've spoken to today are quite oblivious. But . . .'

'Are your children affected?'

She shivered, wrapping her arms round herself, although it was not cold in the hall. 'Very much so, I'm afraid. Benjamin slept cuddled up with Isabella the night before last, and last night Carolus joined the huddle. Which was not a good idea' – she tried and failed to smile – 'because the poor boy had an awful dream – well, a very intense and *powerful* dream best describes it, from what he managed to tell us – and woke not only his sister and brother, but Theo and me too. Tonight they're all coming in with us.' She glanced along the passage at the door. 'Assuming Theo returns . . .'

'I'm sure he will.' I tried to sound convincing. But she was far too astute to be comforted by a remark based on nothing more than optimism. 'Where is he?'

'The Saracen's Head,' she murmured, glancing round as if looking for eavesdroppers. 'He sent Jarman there earlier, and now he's gone too. It's where it's all coming from, isn't it? Those strange players?'

'I think so, yes. Thank you, Elaine' – I touched her hand – 'I'll go and find him.'

She nodded, already turning to go back up the stairs to the family's quarters. But then she looked at me over her shoulder. 'They – they make ideas in your head,' she said, her voice a mere whisper that I only just heard. 'That play we took the children to see, the dreamers in the magic forest, the fairies, Puck, people being made to see life *differently* . . .' She broke off. 'It's what produced my son's dream, I think. He wasn't very coherent, poor boy, but he said he could see *underneath* everything, and it was full of brilliant colour and vivid with life, and then suddenly a huge black shape came, and it was alive but not human, just a faceless, limbless body, and *evil*, malignant, and it fell on the bright vividness and crushed it.'

For a moment we just stared at each other. Then she added softly, 'Make of *that* what you will. Go well, Gabe,' and started up the stairs, quietly closing the door onto the passage behind her.

The Plymouth streets were quiet in the lull between people going home after the day's work and emerging again to enjoy the various diversions of the evening. I put my horse into the capable hands of the usual ostler. 'I've worked him hard,' I said.

'I can see that,' the ostler muttered. He gave me a narrow-eyed look. 'Not like you, Doctor.'

'No.' I'd had my reasons, but I wasn't going to use valuable time in explaining them. 'Look after him, please.'

'When do I ever do otherwise?' said the ostler.

But I was already hurrying away.

The crowd in the taproom of the Saracen's Head was overflowing into the yard, and the mood of febrile excitement was almost tangible. It dawned on me that not long could have passed since the afternoon's performance had ended; probably not much over an hour, for all that to me it seemed far longer, and people who had already downed several mugs of ale to assist their enjoyment of the play were now consuming more. A big sweaty man with an overflowing mug in his hand waved it in my face and said, 'Have a drink, my friend! It's their last night, so let's make the most of it!'

I shoved him aside, but he was an amiable drunk and not a vicious one, and he only laughed.

I was trying to look in every direction at once, searching for Theo and for Jarman, but I could see neither of them. Many members of the Company were in the room, mixing with the crowd, accepting congratulations on a highly entertaining week of plays, no doubt, and the dark-skinned man who had played Othello had just finished telling an anecdote to a mixed group of players and townspeople, making them all laugh. A young woman was gazing at him adoringly, trying to get close to him, but he was staring at Raphe Wymer, a look of unmistakable yearning on his handsome face which I realized I'd seen before: no wonder he and the lad had been so convincing as Othello and Desdemona, I thought in a flash of understanding, for they loved each other. Raphe was deathly white, and I thought I could see him trembling as he sidled up to the dark-skinned man, whispered something and then crept away. Undercurrents seemed to flow all through the room, as if the reality that was visible on the surface hid something far deeper and more mysterious.

Someone elbowed me very hard in the back, and there was a deafening burst of laughter. I spun round, my hand already in a tight fist, but then a thin young man standing right behind me said, 'Sorry, sorry! I slipped,' and I realized it had been an accident and not an assault.

I stood still, taking a couple of steadying breaths. Then I resumed my perusal of the taproom.

I spotted Thomas Lightbodie. He saw me too, and his eyes seemed to stare right into me. He was in a corner with the other senior players, their heads close together. There were four of them, one of whom was Barnaby Abell, another a tubby, balding man. There was a younger player with them, his back to me, the vivid red hair identifying him as Quentyn Barre. The four older men looked as if something serious was on their minds.

No – that did not begin to describe it. As I stared, unable to look away, the tubby man turned to face me. He had the residue of bright red make-up on the edge of one cheek, and I recognized the actor who had played the fat and jolly old woman in the yellow wig in today's comedy.

But he wasn't jolly now. His face had fallen into lines of despair, of deep distress, and his eyes were puffy and red as if he had recently been weeping. I wondered what was making him so sad, and as if a separate part of my mind was providing the answer, I thought, *Francis Heron's death.*

Without stopping to think, to wonder if I was right to stay with these players and should not instead be doing what I came here for, which was to hunt for Theo and find out why three men had died and who had killed them, I shouldered a way through the hot, sweaty throng and advanced on their corner.

FIFTEEN

Thomas Lightbodie saw me approaching; indeed, he hadn't taken his eyes off me, and it briefly occurred to me that he'd known I would go over to talk to them but had been trying to stop me.

Then the little thought vanished, and I forgot about it.

Quentyn Barre had disappeared.

'Doctor!' Thomas said loudly, and even before he hurried on, to tell his three companions that I was the physician who had tended poor Francis, I picked up that he was issuing a warning to them: *This man is overly inquisitive, be careful.*

The plump man struggled to smile. 'You did your best for him, I am sure, Doctor . . .?'

'Taverner, Gabriel Taverner.'

He dipped his head in a courteous little bow, a hand to his breast. 'Gerard Cuddon.'

'You know Barnaby, I believe?' Thomas Lightbodie asked. I nodded. 'And this is Humphrey Brewiss.' The fourth man muttered a greeting. 'Today was our last performance here in Plymouth!' Thomas hurried on, and I had the impression he was filling the pause before I could speak. 'Six days of plays, and all, I believe I may say, have gone down rather well.'

'You have had good audiences,' I said.

'Yes indeed, and our coffers are comfortably full!' He laughed pleasantly.

'You move on tomorrow?'

'Not tomorrow, for it is a day of rest,' Thomas said, a note of mild disapproval in his voice. 'However, we have already begun dismantling the temporary home we have made for ourselves here, and one or two wagons bearing the heavy crates and properties will get on the road later this evening. For ourselves, we shall not set off until the day after tomorrow.'

I held his gaze. I was probably imagining it, but I thought

I saw a brief flash of light in his eyes as he spoke of setting off. 'And where do you go next?'

He hesitated, and, with the strange new perception I seemed to have acquired, I thought, *It doesn't matter what he answers, because he'll be lying.*

And so, when, after a swift glance at Barnaby he said 'Exeter,' I merely nodded.

I was watching Gerard Cuddon out of the corner of my eye. He was struggling hard not to let his distress overcome him; I sensed he longed to go off by himself so that, at last at the end of this long day, he could stop pretending, stop keeping up a smiling face, stop *acting* and at last give way.

I should have been kind. I was a doctor, after all, and I had taken an oath to do no harm.

But I was tired of it all; worn by this constant sense that so much was going on and I only had the vaguest idea of what it was all about. So I turned to him and said, 'I am sorry for your sadness, Master Cuddon. Francis Heron was a close friend, I gather, and you mourn him profoundly.'

His swollen eyes filled with tears and his mouth quivered. 'Yes, indeed, and for him to have died here, so far from all that he held dear, all that mattered to him, is just too . . .'

Much too late, he became aware that his three companions were all staring at him, so shocked by what he had blurted out that they forgot to mask their dismay.

Into the silence I said, 'It was my understanding that he had but lately joined the Company.'

And then they all spoke up at once.

'Yes, that is true, and of course we barely knew him,' Barnaby Abell said smoothy.

'He was just one of those men with whom friendship develops very swiftly!' Thomas Lightbodie added.

'A man of great charm,' said Humphrey Brewiss.

But, 'How did you know?' whispered poor Gerard Cuddon. 'It was meant to be a *secret!*'

They all stood staring at me, fixing me with identical expressions of such intensity that I felt an almost physical onslaught. So much mattered on how I answered: I knew that even as I knew my own name.

I did not know if it was the right response; it was, however, the only one. This creeping around the edges of whatever was happening here was not in my nature and I'd had enough of it.

So I set them alight.

'Oh,' I said disinterestedly, 'men talk in delirium. And when they enter their final moments of life, there is often a compulsion to unburden themselves of their secrets. Of their sins,' I added, 'and, if a priest is not present, frequently a doctor has to do.'

Then, smiling, I stared at each of them in turn.

Gerard Cuddon was, predictably, the first to break. Grabbing at Thomas's sleeve, he said, 'I *knew* it would not work! I *told* you, and—'

'Enough.' The single word was icy, and Gerard seemed to crumple. I heard him emit a little whimper.

Humphrey Brewiss put an arm round him, but it was hard to tell if it was to comfort him, to hold him up or to clutch him so that he could not move away. 'This has all been too much for Gerard,' he said smoothly, turning to us all in turn. 'I shall escort him to his room and help him get to bed. You'd like that, wouldn't you, Gerard?'

'Yes,' he whispered. He shot me an anguished look as Humphrey led him away, and I thought he muttered something to Thomas; it sounded like, 'I'm sorry.'

He had made a bad mistake, that was plain. He'd let someone outside their inner group find out something that should have been kept hidden; he'd allowed me to see his distress, he'd fallen right into my trap when I'd said he and Francis had been old friends, and then, as if that was not enough, he'd uttered the giveaway *How did you know?* and compounded it by saying to Thomas, *I knew it wouldn't work!*

His companions were furious with him, and I was in absolutely no doubt that he was terrified.

But, looking at the two men who remained, I realized that they were too.

Their two set faces wore the same closed-up expression. Very pointedly, Barnaby Abell turned his shoulder to me. And Thomas said under his breath, 'We shall soon be gone far

away from here, Doctor Taverner. Give it up.' Then he too
turned away.

Stomping out of the taproom, remembering that my purpose
here was to find Theo and Jarman, it struck me that Thomas
Lightbodie might in fact have said *give* us *up* . . .

I was not going to put myself at the mercy of whatever power
held sway here by stumbling round in the dark. The corridor
behind the tiring room was crammed with big hampers and
packing cases, already half-full of costumes and properties,
and on the wall behind a stack of boxes I spotted a row of
lanterns hung on hooks. I took one down, and lit its candle
from a sconce on the wall. Telling myself it would all be quite
different in the light, I hurried on.

In the inn's accommodation area, room after room showed
signs that the Company were packing up. Here and there
men and boys were within their rooms, and once I caught a
muttered remark, the speaker hastily shushed. In contrast
with the rowdy, raucous taproom, it was unnaturally quiet.

I went on.

Now the passage had narrowed, the ceiling was low, the
walls too close. I took a turn, another, another . . . and surely
by now I should have reached the tiny little corridor where
Francis had died . . .?

I stopped, holding up my lantern. I was standing before an
opening where I would have sworn there had not been one
before. I put out a hand, felt around it, and, putting the light
right up to it, saw that there was a door frame made of very
old oak, so cleverly concealed that you had to detect it by
touch and not by sight. And the door – I put my head and
shoulders through the opening – was pushed right back
against the passage wall on the other side.

I stood very still, for I thought I had heard someone breathing
softly, somewhere very near.

I swung the lantern round in wide sweeps, once banging
it against the wall, trying to see everywhere at once, fighting
the memory of every horror, every phantom, every malign
spirit I'd encountered since the Company came to lodge at the
Saracen's Head . . .

There was nobody there. And the sound of quiet, steady breathing had gone.

I made myself go on.

Ahead of me the passage led to a flight of narrow stone steps, steeply descending. To my left was an opening. Peering into it, I thought I saw a very faint light. I did not know this place. Somewhere I'd taken a wrong turning, and I was lost.

I could retrace my steps, which would be the sensible thing to do. Or I could go through the opening and investigate the source of the light.

Bending down – because it was both narrow and low – I went through the opening.

There were arched doorways on either side, quite widely spaced, and I thought they might be storerooms; I had the sense I had been descending as I followed my rambling route, and I could well be far underground now, deep in the old inn's cellars. It was not a comfortable thought. To stop my imagination flying away, I squeezed through the next opening I came to and once again held up my lantern.

I was in a room about four paces square. Much of the space was taken up by three very thick columns supporting the vaulted ceiling, which was so low that I couldn't stand upright. I swung my light around in a quick inspection; it really wasn't a place in which to linger. I thought at first the crypt-like space was empty, but as I turned to leave I saw what looked like a bedroll against the wall to the right of the entrance. Crouching down, I found folded blankets, a tallow candle in an earthenware bowl and a cheap fabric satchel half-packed with dirty clothes. Spinning round, holding the lantern low to the ground, I made out three more bedrolls.

Was this no more than overspill accommodation, perhaps for the lowliest members of the Company who had no choice but to make do with a dark cellar where there was no natural light and the air smelt stale and musty? Whoever had been sleeping here had started to pack up, so it looked as if it was.

Increasingly uneasy, I went back out to the passage and walked on.

More of the low, arched openings on either side. Then nothing, save that ahead that soft, flickering light beckoned.

The passage was still descending – it made me very uneasy
– and abruptly it made a sharp turn to the right, the light
suddenly increased and I fell heavily across a broad body
blocking the way.

In the first shock I thought it was another victim.

But then I realized it was warm, it was shoving me off and
it – he – was muttering angrily.

It was Theo, and Jarman Hodge's face loomed up, pale in
the light of my lamp, just behind him.

'What do you think you're doing?' Theo demanded. 'You
could have killed me, a man as heavy as you falling on top
of me!'

He was rubbing hard at his left shoulder, which had taken
the main force of my weight, and I guessed I really had hurt
him. I'd hurt myself, too; a narrow stone passage is no place
for a tumble. 'I'm sorry, Theo,' I said. 'Do you think you've
broken a bone?'

'I'll let you know,' he growled.

I handed the lantern to Jarman and made Theo extend his
arm and move his hand and each of his fingers. He swore, a
lot, but it looked as if he was only bruised.

'Well?' he said when I was done. 'What are you doing down
here?'

'Looking for you,' I said. 'What are *you* doing?'

Theo turned to look at Jarman, and then said heavily, 'You'd
better come and see what we've just found.'

There was something in the way he'd spoken, something,
even, in the way he and Jarman walked ahead of me, heads
down, that warned me. We went on for a short way, rounded
a corner and then a high-ceilinged, gracefully vaulted space
opened up before us. It was circular, and there were niches
around its walls. In them were old-fashioned cresset lamps
made of earthenware, at least half of them lit. There were
spirals of smoke in the air; I caught a faint smell of incense.
Right in the middle of the stone-slabbed floor there was a
trestle – three narrow boards on two supports – and over it
was draped a dark-coloured cloth. Lying on the cloth was a
slim body.

I pushed Theo aside and hurried to the trestle.

The eyes were wide open, huge, and they held a faintly accusing expression. The long neck rose up from the white linen frill of the shirt, still graceful even in death.

Except that there was a cord wound tightly and efficiently around his throat.

Raphe Wymer, although still warm, was undoubtedly dead. His face was suffused with dark blood and his black tongue protruded through his swollen lips. From long habit I put my fingers to the spot beneath the jaw where the heartbeat pulses, but there was nothing. I waited for far longer than necessary before saying quietly, 'Only recently killed.'

'You're sure?' Theo asked.

I looked at him. 'He was in the taproom a short time ago. I saw him.' And he had been dressed in black.

And Theo, not a man usually given to sympathetic gestures, must have seen my distress, for he put a warm hand on my shoulder.

I turned back to Raphe.

The cloth on which he was lying swept down to the floor on one side of the trestle. I gathered it up and draped it over him, closing the lids over those wide, expressive, soulful eyes before covering his face.

'Why were you crouching back there in the passage?' I asked Theo.

'We were waiting,' he replied tersely.

'What for?'

'Whoever lit the candles and the incense and was going to return for the ceremony.' He pointed over to the far side of the vault, and I saw an opening. Then, glaring at me ferociously, he added, 'We could *hear* them, Jarman and me! They were on their way, we were about to be rewarded for bending double in a damp, dark passage deep under the ground, but then *you* have to come along, crashing into me, waving your blasted lantern, crying out in alarm like some old grandmother frightened of a mouse, *and now the buggers will be miles away*!'

His anger and frustration boiling up and overflowing, he shouted the last words in a bellow that made the walls ring.

As the echoes finally died away – much to Jarman's and my relief – I said quietly, 'Theo, I didn't know.'

'He didn't know,' he mimicked. 'Dear God above, Gabe, now I have *four* dead bodies, and no more of an idea what is happening here than I had at the start!' He shook his head, his despair palpable. 'What am I going to do?' he muttered.

'I came across him earlier,' I said, nodding towards the still body on the trestle. 'In Francis Heron's room. He was deeply distressed, and when he told me why, I was too.' Briefly I explained. 'Celia's safe. She's with Jonathan Carew in his church. Now we – I – have to make sure he's done what he said he'd do, and burned the handkerchief.'

Before I could stop him, Jarman folded back the cloth and swiftly and efficiently went through Raphe's garments. 'Not on the body,' he said.

I nodded. 'Then let's hope it's destroyed.' I was thinking – trying to think – but my head felt full of mist. 'We must get out of here,' I said suddenly. 'It's as if—' I stopped, not wanting to put it into words.

So Theo did. 'As if someone's controlling us,' he said, his voice barely audible. 'As if, whenever we think we're on the brink of a discovery, somehow they know and they muddle our thoughts until it's gone away.'

'I couldn't have put it better,' I murmured. I moved round the trestle to the entrance on the far side of the vault. 'If you heard people approaching this way, it must go somewhere, and I have no wish to go back through the maze behind us. Come on, we'll see where it leads us.'

In the small room off St Luke's Little Chapel that served as a vestry, Jonathan and Celia had made themselves comfortable. 'If we're going to talk,' Jonathan had said, 'and eat our supper, and share a little of my rather fine brandy, then I'd prefer we did it in a secular place rather than the chapel or the main church.'

Celia had understood and immediately agreed, especially since there was a tiny hearth in the vestry, and Jonathan had lit a fire. They had arranged a semicircle of candles and lanterns around their corner, and placed two short pews at right angles to each other. 'Waiting for repair,' Jonathan explained, 'but they will serve us well enough.'

Now they had eaten the food, and Celia was clasping a little pewter mug with a couple of fingers of brandy in it, sipping it slowly, appreciating the fiery warmth. With the excitement of the wild ride long faded, and supper eaten, she was beginning to feel very awkward. She had never been alone with Jonathan before. She was afraid that, despite his courtesy and his welcome, he was already thinking what a nuisance it was going to be, having to be shut up here in his vestry because Gabriel Taverner feared for his sister's safety, probably with no foundation whatsoever, and wondering how on earth they were going to break the embarrassing silence and pass the long hours of the night . . .

'I'm sure Gabe was worrying about nothing,' she heard herself say.

Jonathan looked up at her, smiling. 'Let's hope so,' he replied.

'I'm really sorry you're having to do this,' she plunged on, 'Gabe can be so forceful, and people find it very difficult to say no to him when he's made up his mind he has to do something, although I usually manage better than I did this evening and I can often point out an alternative course of action that he hasn't even thought of, and . . .'

I'm gabbling, she thought. *Oh, Lord, what must he think?*

He didn't speak for a moment, and she realized he was waiting politely to see if she'd finished. Then he said, 'There can be no doubt that strange things have been happening at the Saracen's Head; all of us have felt the – the *oddness*, and we are not alone. And three people are dead. The Company have a purpose, Celia, and I fear there is danger in it.'

She felt cold suddenly, and drew her cloak more tightly round her.

He noticed. 'I'm sorry to speak of this,' he said. 'I do so because I want you to be quite sure that this – having come here to be within the walls of this ancient church, this hallowed place of comfort, of solace, of safety, that has been the refuge of the troubled and the desperate for so many centuries – is not something for which you should feel the need to apologize.' He paused, looking steadily at her. And, so quietly that she wasn't sure she heard aright, he added, 'Quite the contrary, in fact.' Then, as if he wanted to blot out what he'd just said, he added in a very different tone, 'There is something we could usefully be doing. Gabe left me this as he left' – he drew out a small, battered notebook from his cassock – 'and suggested you and I might pass the time by trying to work out the meaning of the contents.'

Immediately brightening – *Thank you, Gabe*, she said silently to him – Celia asked, 'What is it? What did he mean, work out the contents?'

Jonathan had moved to one end of his pew, making room for her, and he opened the book. 'It's written in code, apparently,' he said thoughtfully.

She settled down beside him, peering over his shoulder. 'Gabe and I used to make up codes when we were children,' she said. 'Very simple ones, such as writing out the alphabet and then writing it again underneath with each letter moved along several places. If you see what I mean.'

He smiled. 'Indeed I do.' He turned a few more pages. 'I fear this is going to present rather more of a challenge. Look' – he pointed to a tiny, delicately drawn image of a bird with a big, solid beak – 'that's a pictograph.'

'You mean a picture? A word that's being represented by a drawing?'

'Yes. Pictographs were among the very earliest forms of writing, and they are, roughly speaking, signs that represent ideas, as well as more definite concepts such as numbers and the names of places. They date back thousands of years.'

'*Thousands* of years . . .' She felt her mind stretch as she thought about that. Then she thought, *How does he know this?* and then remembered that Gabe had said Jonathan had been a scholar at a Cambridge college.

But he was talking, and she realized she was missing what he was saying.

'—and in a very simple example, a drawing of a bee could be—'

'B,' she supplied. 'Or a bee could mean what a bee does, which might be work, maybe working together in a group?'

'Hmmm,' he said. Then he handed her the book, got to his feet and, striding over to a large chest standing against the wall, took out a wooden board, an inkhorn, two quills, a small penknife and some sheets of paper. Returning, he put the board across their laps and placed the objects on it. 'I think,' he said, turning to give her a grin like an excited boy who has been promised a treat, 'we're going to need to write this down.'

As delighted as him – although she had no idea why and didn't stop to wonder at it – Celia pushed back her sleeves, took a piece of paper and copied out the first few symbols on the book's opening page.

SIXTEEN

The passage on the far side of the crypt seemed much like the one leading down from the rear quarters of the Saracen's Head, and here too there were hollowed-out chambers opening off it, although a quick glance indicated they were empty. We went on for perhaps twenty or thirty paces, I in the lead with my lantern, Theo behind me and Jarman in the rear. They had each picked up one of the cresset lamps, Theo remarking that he hadn't seen one of those since his old great-grandmother died.

We went on for what felt like a long time. At first I counted my paces, but after a hundred it became too disturbing; I was already fighting the fear that this was all for nothing. The tunnel had been continuing straight and featureless for a long stretch when abruptly I was facing a dead end: there was a wall of stone right in front of me. I held up a hand. Theo and Jarman's footsteps stopped.

'What?' growled Theo.

I was moving the lantern from side to side, trying to make out whether there was a way through. I saw, with considerable relief, that in fact there were three ways: there was an impossibly low opening like the mouth of a badger's sett down to the right, a straight way that kinked round the stone wall and then went on beyond it in much the same direction, and on the left, a short length of passage terminating in a rock fall.

'Straight on,' said Theo.

'Left?' said Jarman at the same time. 'Maybe that rock fall's a blind, and we'll get over it if we try.'

I couldn't make up my mind. My thoughts started to run wild, and I could see arguments and counter-arguments for both options. But Theo and Jarman were both staring at me, and I guessed they were waiting for my casting vote.

With a great effort, I stilled my thoughts. Just for a moment, I felt calm. And I *knew* – I would have said somebody told me, except that was impossible – that we must take the right-hand tunnel.

'It's this way.' I was already on my hands and knees, pushing at the sandy earth lying in a long, sloping heap. I thrust my head and shoulders through the opening, forcing a way, pushing on and trying not to breathe because the air was full of dust and soil and the roof was going to collapse and I would be buried under thousands of tons of rock and I'd never see Judyth again and . . .

And then I was through.

I turned, edged back the way I'd just come until I could see Theo's anxious face. 'This is the way,' I said. 'Pass me the lantern and come on through. It's all right,' I added with a smile, 'I've opened the gap enough even for you.'

I went back into the smooth-floored, low-roofed tunnel that unwound beyond the obstruction. While I waited, I leaned against the wall, trying to breathe calmly. I wasn't going to admit it to my companions, but pushing my way through had all but done for me.

We went on.

I was moving cautiously, warned by a change in the air – it was cooler, and I thought I sensed moisture on my face – when abruptly the ground dropped away in front of me. If I hadn't slowed right down I'd have fallen badly, smashed my lantern and probably done myself serious damage, because the drop turned out to be an incredibly steep set of steps. Theo had bumped hard into me and, to judge by the cursing, Jarman had bumped into him, and the three of us jamming up together would have been comical if it hadn't been so perilous.

'*Back!*' I yelled, as Theo, trying to dislodge Jarman, gave a violent lurch that almost had me over the edge. '*Steps!*'

We steadied ourselves, and, clutching each other, held out our lights and peered down into the darkness.

'That's not steps,' Jarman said softly, 'that's a bloody ladder.'

He wasn't far wrong. The steps went down what appeared to be a rock face, and the pitch was so steep that in places the descent was pretty near vertical. The only way to go down with any hope of a safe landing was backwards. I turned round and, my lantern in one hand, set off.

Theo waited until I was two body lengths down, then he followed. I heard a brief curse-laden muttering from Jarman, then he too started to clamber down.

The pitch began to increase when we were fifty steps down – I was keeping count, longing for the descent to be over – and after counting another fifty, I jumped off the final step and stood on level ground.

'Where are we?' Jarman whispered.

We held up our lamps and looked around. We were in a low tunnel, its roof a rough semicircle, its stone floor jagged and uneven. It went straight ahead for maybe ten paces, then began a slow curve away to the right.

'No idea,' I said. Without another word, I walked on.

The tunnel stayed roughly level, apart from one shortish stretch where we went down and then almost immediately up again, but the inclines were not severe enough for more than a few shallow steps at the steepest places. I'd been aware for a while of a different smell to the air, and presently I stopped – Theo and Jarman managed not to barge into me this time – and said, 'I can smell the sea.'

Neither man spoke for a moment. Then Jarman said, with the satisfied air of a man who has just been proved right, 'I *thought* so.'

We waited for him to explain but he didn't. '*What?*' Theo demanded tetchily. I didn't blame him for his ill humour; the passage, the perilously steep descent and now this low tunnel were hard enough on me – I couldn't stand upright – but even harder on him. He was a big man, and I knew that bending over for any length of time gave him backache. And not very long ago I'd fallen over him and done considerable damage to his left shoulder.

'Sorry, chief,' Jarman said. He probably knew about the back-ache too. 'I've been reckoning in my head since we left that underground room with the lad's body, trying to keep an idea of where we're going.' Jarman was famous for his acute sense of direction; his colleagues said of him that you could dump him in a sack out in the wilds of the moor on a pitch-black night and he'd find his way home without even opening the bag, but I didn't think anyone had ever put it to the test.

'And?' Theo sounded slightly less cross.

Jarman paused, then said, 'The Saracen's Head faces the inner harbour, and it's on the eastern end of the quayside. To begin with we went to the rear of the old inn, that's to say, roughly north. Then we turned to the right – east – down that bloody rabbit-hole, and then straight, maybe rightish a bit, and then after we came down that blasted ladder, we turned right again, so now we're going south-east, maybe a tad more south. Then back there a way we went down and up again, and now we can smell the sea.' He looked from one to the other of us, his eyes bright with expectation.

'Er—' Theo said.

'Go on, Jarman, tell us,' I said.

'We've come under the River Plym, I reckon, and now we're heading towards some inlet on the headland the far side,' he said. 'And although I'm not even going to guess what these here actors are up to right now, I know full well what these tunnels used to be for.'

'So do I,' Theo said.

As did I. As did anyone who was born and raised in the area. There were rumoured to be tunnels like this all around Plymouth, and no doubt everywhere else along the rocky, difficult, often unfrequented coastline of the long, thin peninsula that Devon shares with her neighbour Cornwall. It was said they went right back into antiquity, as long ago as man first had the desire to bring cargos ashore – food, drink, luxury goods, people – without making it widely known. And, of course, this long tunnel we had just traversed terminated beneath the Saracen's Head, an inn which had stood there on the Plymouth water-front for centuries. Coxton the innkeeper's predecessors undoubtedly would have had access to a clandestine supply of French brandy and Spanish wine, and he probably did too.

'Do either of you know the headland?' Theo asked.

And, predictably, Jarman said, 'Yes, chief.'

I stepped back to let him take the lead, and, squaring his shoulders, he set off on the last stretch of the tunnel.

*   *   *

It was so good to be in the open air again.

Theo was standing stretching his back, rubbing his left shoulder, groaning gently. Jarman was looking round, muttering to himself, frowning as he took his bearings. I was content just to stand on the shore, with the darkening sky above me glittering as the stars began to appear, and the lights of Plymouth shining out away to the north-west.

We were on a small beach, deserted, with not a habitation in sight. I was starting to wonder what whoever had been using the tunnel had wanted with this undistinguished stretch of shoreline when Jarman gave an exclamation and headed off towards where the land rose up gently to the south. Theo and I trudged after him, and as we scrambled up the slope, a small inlet came into view on the far side. There was a stone quay, and behind it, where a small stream wound its way down to the sea, a few hovels clung to the hillside. They looked deserted, and not one showed a light.

'Well,' Theo said after a moment or two, 'those damned players must come here for *something*.'

And he strode off towards the little settlement, Jarman and I following.

It was not as far as it looked; the twilight was deceptive. We walked along the quay – it was in good repair, I noticed, and the water looked deep – and on to the track leading up the slope. The hovels were in poor condition, some with roofs half-off, some with doors hanging on hinges, revealing interiors bare but for sticks of crude and broken furniture and the general depressing detritus of the very poor.

But the fourth house along was different.

The door was not only intact but closed and, as we discovered when Theo tried it, locked. The single window was shuttered, and, although the wood of the shutters was warped and the paint long gone, they were sound. But the warping had made a gap between the two sides, and Theo leaned down to peer through it.

He stood staring in for some time. Then, once more with a hand to his lower back, he said, 'Have a look.'

Jarman stood aside, and I went first.

The room was small, and a doorway in the far wall seemed

to lead to a scullery. No stairs – the hovels were single-storey – and little in the way of furnishings.

But the floor space was packed tight with packs, bags, bedrolls and blankets.

I stepped away from the window and Jarman took his turn. He whistled softly, and, as he too straightened up, he said, 'Either someone's just arrived, or else they're planning an imminent departure.'

Theo looked at me. 'Is that little harbour behind us big enough for a ship?'

'It depends on how big the ship is,' I said automatically.

'A coaster? A sea-going vessel?' he demanded.

'A coaster, yes. And the water looked to be deep, although I can't say for sure in this light.'

'Where are the Company going next?' Jarman asked.

'Exeter,' I said.

'Any advantage in sailing round the coast to Exmouth and shortening your overland journey?' Theo mused.

'They arrived from Barnstaple,' I said. 'Maybe they felt like a change from travelling by road?'

But Theo was shaking his head. 'No, no, I don't believe that's it,' he said. He looked at me, frowning. 'Something very worrying has been happening here,' he said softly, 'and we've all felt it, that sense back there in the Saracen's Head that they . . . that we . . . dear God, I don't know how to begin to describe it!' he exclaimed in frustration.

'Don't try,' I said. 'Take it that we understand.'

He nodded. 'Thanks. And that's even without the discovery of three – no, four – dead bodies,' he went on. 'These players have another, hidden reason for being here. Or, if not every last one of them, then a secret few.'

'You're thinking of that conversation you overheard,' I said. '*I fear for my life*, poor dead Francis Heron said, and the death that stalked him was a particularly awful one.'

'Yes, yes, and the other man – Daniel – said, he actually *said*, there were other reasons than the plague for a man to flee the capital!' Theo sounded jubilant.

'So?' Jarman's one, laconic syllable broke across the excitement. 'We still have not the first idea what this other reason

is, why it's led to four men's deaths and why some of the
Company have stored their packed belongings in there – if
the stuff in fact belongs to them and not someone else entirely
– and what's more, who's to say there isn't a perfectly good
reason for them storing some of their baggage here, all ready
for sailing along the coast to their next stop? The way I see
it,' he went on, almost crossly, 'we're grabbing at a very thin
straw and putting two and two together to make six.'

'Five,' I muttered. Jarman gave me a look.

But while he'd been lecturing us, I'd been thinking. And I
could see a very good answer to why the *perfectly good reason*
theory wasn't convincing.

'I don't agree,' I said.

'With which particular element?' Theo asked, the sarcasm
very evident.

'If it's all perfectly reasonable and above board, and they're
not working like fury to keep some dark secret they've fled
with from London, why in heaven's name are they acting so
mysteriously? And why,' I added, hoping very much it would
be the final convincing factor, 'why are four men dead?'

Jarman made a *humph* noise, but he didn't come up with
any argument against what I'd just said. Theo moved a few
paces back down the track, staring out over the moonlit water.

'What are you thinking?' I asked him, going to stand beside
him.

'I'm thinking that Jarman and I heard people approaching
that underground chamber, just before you came crashing along
and scared them off. They must have come out of the tunnel
just where we did, but they didn't come on to this little house,
if we're even right about it being where they were bound, so
maybe they guessed we'd come after them and had the sense
to go somewhere else, where they'll lie low till we've gone.'
He paused, glancing up into the sky. 'I'm thinking it's getting
late, and there isn't much more we can do tonight, so we may
as well head for home. And finally, I'm thinking that the one
thing I'm *not* prepared to do is return to the Saracen's Head
the way we came out, particularly as it means climbing up a
near-vertical set of steps, and the only alternative is to walk
up this side of the estuary till we reach the crossing and return

to Plymouth on the far side, and that's got to be four miles or more, and I'm tired out and ravenously hungry already.' He was glaring at me, but, just man that he was, he must have realized it wasn't my fault. His face relaxed into a smile, and he reached out and thumped my shoulder. 'Come on. The sooner we set out, the sooner we'll all be home.'

He beckoned to Jarman, and the three of us fell into step and set off along the track.

In the little vestry of St Luke's Church, Celia and Jonathan had covered several sheets of old scrap paper with notes and experimental solutions to the code. They had given up on the pages of writing at the front of the book and now were concentrating on the lists of short words at the back. Jonathan kept saying he knew they were near, and Celia, picking up his certainty, was restless with tension, constantly making yet another attempt, trying one more variation.

'There has to be one element which, once we've found what it is, reveals the solution to the whole thing,' she said, by no means for the first time.

Jonathan had stood up and was walking round the tiny space afforded by the small room, stretching his back, rolling his shoulders. She watched him, sensing the energy flowing through him. He was still vibrant and fresh, even though they had been working for hours and it was getting very late. As if he sensed her eyes on him, he turned to look at her. 'Let's have another go at one of the repeated series of symbols,' he suggested. 'But first,' he added, 'I'm going to make us a hot drink.'

'I'm not cold!' Celia said. 'You've kept the fire going well, and it's lovely and warm in here.'

He smiled. 'Actually, I was thinking more of stimulating our brains than warming us,' he admitted. 'I'm going to prepare a couple of mugs of my special mulled ale.'

'Oh, good,' she said brightly.

Then she returned to the code.

'Look at this series,' she said to him when he was back beside her and they had raised their mugs and drunk a toast to success.

'It's all in groups of five with odd ones, twos, threes or fours
following, and here the two fives are followed by a two, and
this same series of twelve symbols appears . . .' – she counted
under her breath – 'four, no, five times in the first three pages.
The second symbol of the first word and the last one of the
second are the same, and there's one other repeat, the fourth
letter of the first words and the last letter of all, at the end of
the odd pair.'

'The first repeat looks like a bird with a big pointed beak,'
Jonathan said. 'What does that suggest?'

'Beaks . . . stabbing, picking worms out of the ground – no,
that would be an open beak not a closed one – fighting other
birds, pecking, drilling—'

'Drilling?'

'Like a woodpecker does! That *drrrrr* sound you hear when
they're boring into a tree.'

And, as one, they turned to stare at each other. '*Drrrrr*,'
he repeated. '*D*, then – no, it's *r*. Try *r*.'

Carefully she drew twelve dashes, five, five, two, and entered
r in the relevant places. Then she nudged him, and said
excitedly, 'Come on, then! What does this other repeat symbol
suggest?'

Jonathan stared hard at it, as if the intensity of his gaze
might make it reveal itself. 'It looks like an eye,' he said after
a moment. 'An oval eye shape, and the two rows of lashes
along the bottom lid mean it's a closed eye.'

'Winking?' she suggested. She wrote the letter *w* over the
two dashes, but very lightly. 'I'm not convinced. What else?'

'Your eyes are closed when you're dead,' he said. She
frowned at him and he smiled. 'Sorry. I do see quite a lot of
dead people, it's what occurred to me first.'

After a moment she said softly, 'Sleep. You close your eyes
when you're asleep.'

'*A*, then? *S*?'

'Nodding off,' she said firmly. 'You say people nod off, and
a row of little *n*s in a sketch means someone's asleep.' Now
she wrote *n* on the two dashes.

There was only one other symbol among the twelve that
was a little picture and not a letter, and it was a stylized

drawing of a snake. 'That must be *s*,' Jonathan said. Celia wrote it in.

The remaining seven symbols were all letters. Three of them appeared frequently throughout the pages of text, two more than the third.

'The most common letter in written English is *e*,' Jonathan said, 'followed by *a*. The other vowels, *i*, *o* and *u*, are progressively less common, in that order.'

Yes. He had told her as they began that he knew quite a lot about codes. Swiftly Celia tried the letters in the appropriate places, changing them around so often that she filled yet another sheet of paper. It took a long time.

Then, breaking a long silence heavy with their joint concentration, Jonathan said slowly, 'Supposing it's someone's name?'

She raised her head, staring at him. '*Yes*,' she whispered. 'It's a long word – twelve letters. How many twelve-letter words crop up so regularly?'

And he said, 'We don't know the name of the man who died in the barn, in whose pack this book was found. But we know the name of the man who died with him.'

'Daniel only has six letters,' she pointed out.

'The other six could be his surname.'

They tried, but either the coded name wasn't Daniel or their hypothesis was wrong.

Then suddenly, making Jonathan jump, Celia grabbed at the paper, filled her nib and began writing so fast that the letters blurred and smudged. But she didn't stop, she didn't care, because suddenly she *knew* she was right.

She threw down the quill and turned to Jonathan, the thrill of discovery racing through her and making her heart beat fast. 'There's another name!' she cried. 'Think, Jonathan! Whose bag did this book come from?'

And, peering down at the scrawl of her writing, running a finger beneath the smudges and the blots, Jonathan stared down at the letters now filling in each of the twelve spaces, properly laid out at last.

Francis Heron.

He turned to stare at her.

She felt the impulse in him, recognized it because it was in her too: the urge to fling her arms round him, shout for joy because together they had taken this puzzle apart, worked on it without giving up and now they had a solution.

They sat very still, and neither looked away.

In that long, slow, deep look, something changed. She wasn't sure, couldn't swear to it, but she thought that, just before he lowered his eyes, almost imperceptibly he nodded.

And Jonathan, staring down at his boots but with the after-image of her excited, happy expression still vivid in his mind, had also felt the change.

'Of course,' he said, aware of how crushing he sounded, 'it actually tells us very little, since we already have our link between the man in the barn and Francis Heron, since the barn man had one of Francis's books in his pack, and—'

She grabbed at his sleeve and shook it. 'But it *does!*' she protested hotly. 'Don't you see? Oh, of course you do, you must, you know all about codes! Decoding Francis Heron's name is immaterial. It didn't matter which word or name we revealed, we just needed something, *anything*, to give us a way in, because now that we have ten translated letters – or symbols, it doesn't matter – we can decode the rest!'

As he looked into her lovely face, he thought, *I did know that. And, as she just said, as I told her at the start of this wonderful evening, I do indeed know all about codes, because spies are taught to code and decode and I was once part of the Queen's spy network.*

He knew, too, why it was that such an unforgettable, deep-seated element of his past[1] – for it had been terrible – had momentarily slipped his mind.

It was because of her.

'Celia,' he began, 'you're quite right, and—'

He wasn't sure what he was going to say; the words were still forming. But just then they heard the sound of the church's heavy outer door opening, and, as they sat stone-still, absolutely silent, straining to hear, stealthily being closed again.

---

[1] See *The Angel in the Glass.*

SEVENTEEN

We were back in Plymouth at last. Approaching the Saracen's Head from the eastern side and the rear, I could see a handful of lights in the windows of the upper storeys, although as we drew near it became apparent that the ground-floor doors and windows were shuttered and dark. We came to the corner where we would emerge into the street that ran in front of the inn, and, slightly ahead of Theo and Jarman, I saw three figures standing quite still in front of the inn and the big double doors into the inn yard.

Hastily I stepped back, flinging out a hand to hold back my companions, a finger to my lips urgently signalling silence. They edged back so that they were right against the wall in the shadow of the overhanging roof. I returned to the corner, very cautiously leaning forward until I could see into the street.

I studied the immobile men outside the Saracen's Head. They looked as if they were guarding the inn, positioned as they were at equal intervals along the street. They all wore the same distinctive, high-collared black cloak that I'd seen on the spade-bearded man in the barn. Straining my eyes, I saw that the figure posted right outside the yard gates was the tall, long-faced man who had stood opposite me at the play, and the stocky, dishevelled figure closest to me was his younger companion.

There was a sense of menace about them. I couldn't see if they carried swords, but I'd have put money on it. Whatever their purpose was in standing there so still, so watchful, I reckoned it boded ill for somebody.

I sensed a slight movement behind me. Stepping back to my companions, I held up my hands and, spreading my fingers, indicated three. Then I mimed drawing a sword. Theo nodded. Jarman put his hand on the hilt of the knife in its sheath on his belt, raising his eyebrows, but Theo shook his head and said very quietly, 'Not here.'

When I looked out into the street again, the men had disappeared.

I went on staring for a while, in case they had sensed someone watching and slipped back to check. But there was no sign of them.

'They've gone,' I said, turning back to Theo and Jarman.

'Who are they?' Theo asked.

'I don't know. I saw two of them this afternoon. They were in the inn yard, watching the play. Watching me, in fact.'

'Did you challenge them?' Jarman asked.

'I tried, but when I made my way over to where they were standing, they'd gone. They were dressed like the dead man in the barn,' I went on, 'same black cloak with that high collar.'

'What are they here for?' Theo murmured. 'Four men, if you count the dead body in the barn, undoubtedly well armed and clad in quality garments. And careful to keep themselves concealed.'

We all thought about that.

We were of an age, the three of us, to have lived through the days when Queen Elizabeth's spies had held maximum power. Like everyone, we'd known enough about what they did to fear the network of agents, counter-agents, assassins and informers which had been set up by the great spymaster Francis Walsingham, his life's long work relentlessly driven by his perpetual fear that someone would evade his vigilance, creep into the country and kill his beloved Queen, and in all likelihood this killer would be a Catholic and originate in Spain.

'Does the new King also send his spies to watch us like cats at a mouse hole, then?' Theo demanded angrily. 'Waiting to pounce when – no, probably before – we have the temerity to take a step out of line?'

'Dangerous talk, chief,' muttered Jarman.

Theo grunted, hitching up his black robe. 'And why here?' he went on. 'If you're right, Gabe, what do they want with those within the inn? *With the Company?*' he added in a hiss.

'We come back, I believe, to the secret matter that drove Francis Heron to flee London in fear of a terrible death,' I said. 'I wonder if . . .'

But then my head seemed to fill with mist, and I couldn't remember what I'd been wondering.

It was alarming – no, worse than that, it was very frightening – and I thought, *I'm tired. Beyond tired. And very hungry.*

I braced myself stood up straight and said, 'I'm exhausted. I'm going home.'

And, with a grin, Theo said, 'That's the most welcome remark you've made all evening.'

I had said goodnight to Theo and Jarman at the place where the road to their homes this side of Warleigh Point diverged from mine, beside the Tavy as it curved away from the Tamar and the estuary. Now I was riding alone, it was very dark – clouds had built up, and the moon and the stars were obscured – and I thought it must be late.

I tried to go through the events of this endless day, but I was too tired. And, besides, when I attempted to remember what had happened, I kept being diverted to how I'd felt, what impressions I'd had. For a man of science, as I always told myself I was, this was very disconcerting.

I rode on.

But I'd allowed the memory of the day's moments of unease – of downright *fear* – to get into my mind. And now they were running riot and I was hearing strange noises in the darkness, seeing movements in the deep shadows beneath the trees that lined the road. I kicked Hal into a smart trot, then a canter. He had picked up my apprehension and his ears were laid back. I ran a hand down his neck under the thick mane, talking to him, but even I could hear the doubt in my voice and his hearing was far more sensitive than mine.

We rode on.

I found I was counting the distance to home, to safety, trying to drive out the fearful images by replacing them with pictures of my own hall, my library, my study, my chamber and my warm, welcoming bed.

But then with shocking suddenness a light shone out right in front of me. Hal gave a whinny of alarm and I struggled to control him, to calm him, but I was too shaken myself, and he knew it, and, shaking his head, he reared up, beating the air with his fore hooves as if he was battling an attack.

And I fell off.

I fell hard, managing to twist round at the last moment so that I landed on my side and not flat on my back. Somehow I kept my head from crashing too hard against the firm ground of the track, which was good because a head injury or unconsciousness would have been bad when I was alone and unlikely to be found before morning, but *not* good because knocking myself out would have meant I didn't have to endure the instant agony of all the body parts I'd damaged.

I must have been more affected by hitting my head than I'd thought, because it was only as I was trying very tentatively to sit up that I remembered the brilliant light.

I was facing away from the way I'd been going. But even before I turned round, I knew it was still there: I could see my own shadow on the ground in front of me.

It took more courage than I like to admit to face it. Already I was trembling, and it wasn't from the shock of the fall.

The light was in the shape of a rectangle, about four feet high and three across with a curved top, and its base seemed to hover just above the ground.

It was reflected light, and the reflection was blasting out at me from the shining surface of the Company's antique mirror.

But if the mirror was reflecting the light, its origin must be behind me, so why hadn't I already seen it?

I spun round to search for it, but the quick movement made my vision go wobbly and sent a stab of agony through my head, and for a moment or two I felt the horrible vertigo that used to affect me after the injury that ended my days at sea. I closed my eyes, and at first the spinning sensation and the nausea got worse. Then they eased.

When I opened my eyes again, the light had gone out.

Slowly, shakily, I got to my feet. I couldn't see anything; the dazzling light had ruined my night vision. I crept forward, testing each footfall, and presently I felt a big, warm shape materialize beside me and I smelt Hal's familiar smell.

I put my arm over his neck and leaned against him, breathing him in. 'I'm very glad you're here,' I murmured. He gave a

soft whicker, which I took as his apology for having reared
and thrown me off. 'You're forgiven,' I told him.

Together we moved forward. I was very grateful for his
support; for his warmth, for the fact of having a living,
breathing being beside me, heart beating, blood pumping.

My sight was slowly improving, although I still couldn't
see much. Couldn't see the mirror, but I knew we must be
close to it now. I put out my hand, not wanting to walk right
into it, but then I thought, can Hal see it? Surely he'd stop if
he could?

I moved ahead of him, walking repeatedly from side to side
across the track. I blinked and rubbed my eyes, and now I
could no longer tell myself I was still night-blinded, for I made
out the track like a pale ribbon ahead of me, the black outlines
of trees and bushes on either side.

The mirror wasn't there any more.

Quite a long time later, I mounted up.

More than ever I wanted to be home; needed to be home,
the heavy old door closed and barred, the strong walls
around me. I'd had enough of the night, of people intent on
frightening me, of the growing feeling that these visions and
hallucinations did not in fact have a human agency after all
but were the work of ghosts, poltergeists, spirits, ghouls . . .

'I don't believe in evil spirits,' I said aloud.

But even in my own ears, it sounded unconvincing.

We were almost at the junction where the path down to
Tavy St Luke's branches off the track that leads towards
Rosewyke. I was nearly home.

But then I saw something dark stretched out on the ground.
It was a man, lying face down, his head towards me as if he'd
come from the village and was heading off to Plymouth.

I dismounted. Hal was dispirited now – as exhausted as I
was, probably – and stood with his head down. I walked up
to the body.

The man was dead. There was a knife sticking out of his
back, over his ribs on the left side, and a small amount of
blood had pooled beneath him.

Very gently I turned him over, just enough to look at his face. The clouds had thinned a little, and there was enough light to see by.

But I already knew who he was, for I recognized the garments he was wearing.

It was the body of Fallon Adderbury.

I knelt beside him for some time. I had disliked him virtually on sight, seen my sister's infatuation with him as dangerous to her happiness, burst in on the two of them in Celia's workroom and hurled accusations at them. Yet it seemed I had misjudged my sister; given far more importance than I should have done to a brief flirtation with an attractive young man who inhabited a seductive world of colour, glitter and fantasy.

Sallie had understood far better than I. She'd told me that when Celia finally left Rosewyke with a new husband to love and care for, it wouldn't be any footling actor.

And now that poor young actor lay dead on the track. Overcome with pity, I put my hand on his cheek. He was still warm.

Very gently I raised him up, hefting him up over my shoulder, silently apologizing to him for the indignity. But I had no choice; I couldn't leave him where he lay because this road was used by heavy traffic, and the image of cartwheels crushing his body in the dim early morning light was intolerable. There were two deep wheel marks on the track even now, I noticed, crisp enough to suggest they were recent, although they must have passed before Fallon died.

I laid him in the dying grass and bracken at the side of the track, rolling him beneath the cover of the bushes. The position of the body would be easy to describe to Theo's agents because we were right by the Tavy St Luke turning.

As I walked back to my horse, a very bad thought swam up to the surface of my mind; I'm quite sure it would have occurred to me earlier, instantly on finding the body, but I was so tired. From the position of the body, Fallon had been slain on his way back to Plymouth. And he was at the place where the road came up from Tavy St Luke. And its church. And its vicar, and my sister.

I flung myself up onto Hal's back, kicked him to a canter and thundered down the hill into the village.

I tethered Hal and approached the church door. I'd expected it to be closed against the night, but it was open, just a crack. I pushed it back and went inside.

'Jonathan? Celia? It's me, Gabe.'

There was no answer.

The main body of the church was in darkness but, looking up, I saw that the five glass panels set high in the side wall of St Luke's Little Chapel were glowing faintly. At least one candle was burning in there.

I raced across the stone floor, and as the arched entrance to the chapel came into view, I saw the golden glow again. '*Jonathan!*' I yelled. '*Celia!*'

Why weren't they answering?

Three candles burned on the simple altar. They gave more than enough light to see that the chapel was empty.

I stared round, telling myself there was a sensible explanation for their absence but feeling my heart beating rapidly in dread. Then I looked into the corner towards the low wooden door to the vestry, hidden in the deep shadow behind a heavy column.

It had been kicked open, and the wood of the frame around the heavy old iron bolt was splintered and jagged.

I ran over, pushed the ruined door aside and went in. There were the remains of a fire dying down in the small hearth, two narrow pews had been drawn up before it, there were candles set around them, one of them alight, and a stack of old pieces of paper lay scattered on the floor. Many were heavily stained with ink; an inkhorn lay shattered amidst them. Picking up one of the least damaged pages, I recognized Celia's hand. She'd been in a hurry, for it didn't have her usual neatness. A sudden, agonizingly vivid picture filled my head: my sister, bent over a piece of work, quill flying as her writing hand raced to keep up with her mercurial thoughts. I picked up another page, and this one was covered in a different hand: Jonathan's.

They'd been working on the coded notebook. I knew it, as if one of them had been standing there and told me.

I didn't seem to be able to move.

With painful slowness, I tried to put it together.

Fallon Adderbury had come out here. For some reason he'd needed to speak to Celia, or maybe Jonathan – Celia, probably. But how had he known where to find her?

Had it been him who broke down the vestry door? But no, if it had been locked he'd have called out, identified himself, and they'd have let him in.

Someone else had also come here.

And this second person would have known where to come because he'd have been trailing Fallon Adderbury – my mind seemed to be working better now – so it was quite possible that Fallon had been his quarry and not Celia, especially given the fact that the poor young man was now dead.

The brief surge of hope that had raised my spirits as I worked that out faded. Because Celia and Jonathan weren't here. Fallon had arrived, then someone else hunting for him had broken the door down and . . .

I shook my head violently, trying to dispel the dreadful thought. In the brief dizziness that followed, I stared hard at the red embers of the fire, and focusing my vision stilled the sensation.

Something lay at the edge of the hearth. It had been thrown into the flames when the fire was going well, and it had largely been burned away. But a small fragment of it remained.

It was white, and I thought at first it was a piece of paper, crumpled up in frustration and hurled into the flames. I bent down and flicked it away from the burned, blackened wood. It was soft, and one corner was dotted with patches of scarlet. I picked it up, holding it to the candlelight, but I already knew what it was: the remains of the white silk handkerchief embroidered with strawberries that Celia had made for Fallon Adderbury, to be used in that magical, confounding, highly charged and dangerous play that Celia, Jonathan, Judyth and I had so innocently gone to see less than a week ago.

The confusion was back, my wild, conflicting thoughts crashing around my head like a gang of unruly children. Where had I last seen that handkerchief? In Raphe Wymer's hand, and he had been standing, grief-stricken, in Francis Heron's room, and he'd told me it had to be burned because it had magic in it.

My imagination flew to turn that magic into reality, and I thought I felt the soft silk leap in my fingers, as if it danced at the command of the person who had imbued it with power. Not my sister – oh, God, no, not Celia – for she had done no more than measure and cut the silk, hem it with those tiny stitches and embroider the beautiful strawberries that looked so like gouts of blood.

No – the magic came from quite another source: from the two-hundred-year-old witch who had gone into a trance and woven the silk from holy silkworms, dyeing the cloth with a dye made from the embalmed hearts of dead virgins . . .

My head was spinning and I felt very sick. I thought there was a very faint scent coming from the scrap of silk, and I leaned closer to see if I could identify it. If it had magic power, then maybe it would make me feel better . . .

I tried to go on with my reasoning.

Celia had made the handkerchief, and given it to Fallon, and Raphe had given it to me to bind poor Frances's brow and ease his headache. Celia hadn't put the magic in it, and I didn't imagine Fallon had either, so it must have been Raphe. And – yes! yes! I thought, it all made sense – and it had been Raphe who was so desperate to burn it, because he knew it was perilous with power and must be destroyed.

But he hadn't. He had died, been strangled with a length of cord, left on a trestle in a secret underground room, and somehow Fallon had taken charge of the handkerchief, and brought it out here to Celia, because she had made it, and, just like Raphe, Fallon had feared that the power it contained would bring trouble of the most unimaginably awful kind to anyone involved with it. It was what I'd thought when the terrified Raphe faced me in Francis's room, and I'd raced away to find my sister and take her to safety, leaving Raphe all alone . . . And now he was dead, and so was Fallon, and Celia had gone.

I felt myself sliding to the floor. I had just enough presence of mind to put my arm up to protect my head – I'd already suffered quite a hard blow this evening – and then I was down, my head spinning, fearing I would throw up and dreading it because it would only make the agony behind my eyes far worse.

The fire must have finally died, because I couldn't see its glow any more. Still holding the fragment of silk, I felt the world fall away.

EIGHTEEN

E ven before they heard the alien voice call out softly, 'Is the vicar within?' Celia had silently doused the lights and Jonathan had crept over to the vestry door and, equally noiselessly, slid the iron bolt into its hoop. In the soft light from the little fire, they stood absolutely still. Then there came a second set of footsteps, slightly heavier, and a man's voice muttered, 'I've been to the Priest's House. Or I'm guessing it's that, it's right next door and it's a poor sort of place. He's not there. I banged hard on the door and went round the back, and nobody's in. There's a horse there, a bay gelding with a blaze.'

Celia, angry on Jonathan's behalf at this slur on his dwelling, shot him a glance, but he gave her a quick smile and shook his head, as if saying it didn't matter.

'Keep your voice down,' the other man said. His own voice was a harsh whisper, and he sounded as if he had a sore throat.

'He's coming here. He *must* be,' the second man said. 'The skinny lad with the long neck said he was looking for the woman, and that stupid giggling fool of a friend heard the brother say he had to get her to sanctuary, and this is their church, but it looks like she got it wrong and they went somewhere else.' His voice rising again, he said, 'But *he* wouldn't know that, he'd have thought what we thought – he's *got* to be here!'

After a long and tense pause – Celia found she was hardly breathing, and Jonathan stood so still that she could barely make him out in the shadows – the first man said, 'I believe you're right. In any case, we have nothing else to go on. We'll wait.'

Then a long, slow, metallic noise rang out, loud in the silence, resonating up into the high roof of the church: it was the sound of a sword being drawn from its scabbard. The second man said, 'A blade, Garrett? In a church?' And the harsh-voiced man said, 'Yes, and you keep your weapon to hand too. We must not fail in this.'

Two pairs of footfalls echoed through the church – they didn't seem to be bothering so much about being quiet now – and one set, those of the heavier man, came agonizingly close. *He's in St Luke's Little Chapel*, Celia thought. She began to pray feverishly that he would have a quick look and return to the main church. She hoped Jonathan was doing the same. *He's a priest*, she thought wildly, *his prayers will carry far more weight than mine.*

The footsteps went inexorably on. Then another profoundly incongruous sound filtered through to them: the man was humming a tune, and it was one of the crude songs favoured by drunks and merrymakers in the lowest of Plymouth's quayside taverns.

The humming stopped – the man had started to sing the words, and perhaps even he realized this was not the place for them – and the footsteps began to fade away. Then everything went quiet.

With infinite care, Jonathan moved silently over to her.

'The man in the chapel didn't spot the door to the vestry,' he said, right in her ear. She nodded. Then he stepped cautiously away from her and beckoned to her to follow.

She liked the fact that he didn't put a finger to his lips in warning. She thought Gabe probably would have done.

Silent step by silent step, they went across the little room to the dark alcove on the other side of the narrow chimney breast. Jonathan bent down, and she saw that there was a low door, not much over shoulder height and perhaps a foot and a half across. It looked even more ancient than the main door of the church, its wood warped and twisted, the iron hinges and latch showing the workmanship of an earlier age, and she was quite sure it wasn't going to open, that Jonathan would have to force it and that would inevitably make a lot of noise and bring the men running, and the heavy iron ring that formed the handle would squeak when he lifted it, and—

But the door had opened easily, without a sound, and there was a narrow path outside that led in a straight line to the rear of the Priest's House, and she thought, *Of course it opens easily, he probably uses it several times a day.* She could see the dark night outside, hear the distant scream of a fox, and that was the only sound. Jonathan went through, held out his hand for her, and she went after him. He pushed the door to, but did not risk fully closing it.

Then he said, pointing towards the Priest's House, 'My horse is round the back. We'll be away from here in no time.'

I opened my eyes, just a crack.

There was a soft glow of gold; turning my head slightly – which both hurt and made me feel very dizzy – I saw three candles on the altar, and their shimmering light made the colours of the five stained-glass panels dance.

My backside hurt, too.

'Ouch,' I said.

A cool hand brushed the hair off my forehead. I realized my head was resting on something soft. And warm.

Judyth said, 'Stay still, Gabe. Rest a while longer.'

I opened my eyes wider and looked up at her. 'You look beautiful,' I said.

She smiled. 'Thank you.'

I went on looking, smiling back at her. After a while – I have no idea how long – I said, 'We're in St Luke's Little Chapel. I recognize the panels.'

'We are,' she agreed.

'But I was in the vestry . . .'

'Yes. I dragged you out by your feet and shut the door. I'm afraid I might have hurt you – the flagstones are very uneven, and I had to hurry.' That explained the sore backside. And perhaps the continuing headache too. 'But I pushed the little outer door wide open, so with any luck it will soon have dissipated.'

'Yes, I expect it will.' Then, as it dawned on me I had not the least idea what she was talking about, I said, 'What will?'

'The poison from the fumes. You must have breathed in quite a large amount, for you were unconscious when I found you.'

'You found me?'

She nodded. 'I was in the village. The blacksmith's wife has a fine new baby boy. As I was about to leave, I noticed that the church door was ajar, and that seemed odd for this time of night. I came in, and even from the main door I smelt it. I hurried on inside, because I know how dangerous it can be, and searched through the main church and the chapel, and finally I found you in the vestry, lying in front of the hearth and breathing more of it in with every breath.'

'*What?*' I asked again.

She hesitated, and I thought I saw her look around as if making sure we were alone. Then, leaning down right over me, a lock of her soft dark hair brushing my face, she said very quietly, 'There was a fragment of silk, the remains of something burned on the fire. It was the source of the fumes. Putting it on the fire had the effect of sending them spreading through the room, although the odour is not readily detectable.'

'We're speaking of the white handkerchief that Celia made?' I whispered. 'That's been burned here, on the fire?'

She nodded.

'You're saying it was giving off deadly fumes?' I tried to focus my thoughts, but my mind didn't seem to be working very well.

'It was,' Judyth said.

'Celia didn't put drops of this toxin, whatever it is, on it!' I shouted. Too loudly: the noise made my head start spinning again.

'Not just drops, for it was soaked in it,' Judyth said darkly, 'and no, I know full well she didn't.'

Vital questions battered inside my head – who did, then? and why? and what in God's name is it doing here? – but my fuddled, nauseous, aching head shied away from them. So instead I asked, 'What is the substance? And don't say you don't know, because you just said you recognized it when you came into the church.'

'Oh, Lord, you're starting to notice things again,' she murmured, 'you must be feeling better.'

'I am. Go on,' I said firmly.

Once again, that hesitation. Then she said, 'The art is known as veneficium, which means magic effected via poison. It is said that – that people mix toxic herbs, plants such as hemlock, henbane, mandrake, deadly nightshade, wolfsbane, ergots, that they make an ointment, or perhaps burn the herbs and inhale the fumes, and that this produces visions, illusions, a sense of indomitable power, the ability to fly, the opening of channels for communicating with the spirits.'

'And does it?'

'Never having tried,' she replied, 'I cannot say.'

'How do you know about it if you've never tried it?' I demanded.

'Have you sampled every single remedy and treatment that you mete out to others?' she countered sharply.

'No, of course not!'

'Yet you know about them, and you know they are efficacious.'

'Yes,' I said slowly. 'Yes, I see.'

I wanted to ask her *how* she knew, but for one thing I didn't think she'd tell me – such matters were deeply secret, for the very knowledge of them, even for those who would not dream of using them, was perilous in the extreme and highly likely to lead to an agonizing death.

Agonizing death . . . Why were those words already in my head? Where had I heard them recently?

But I had something more urgent to think about.

The second reason why I wasn't going to ask Judyth where she had come by her dangerous knowledge was because I already knew. Her teacher had been Black Carlotta, whose skill, and open-minded approach to medicine and healing, and vast, extensive knowledge had come to my aid so many times. I did not begin to understand her, and if I'm honest I feared her more than a little, but she was a power for the good – no doubt of that – and, in our increasingly narrow-minded and circumscribed world, people like her were to be treasured.

'And someone doused Celia's silk handkerchief in this mixture?'

'Yes. I could detect it on that last remaining fragment. It's gone,' she added, 'I poked up the fire until it was eaten up.'

'Who brought it here and put it on the fire?' I wondered aloud.

She started. 'I assumed you did?'

'No. It was all but burned away when I got here.'

She was frowning, thinking hard. 'It was – it had become, rather – an object full of peril,' she said. 'Celia made it in all innocence, her intention, I think, to impress that attractive young actor, and—'

Then I remembered the track, and the body.

'He's dead,' I said.

'*Dead?*' The one word was full of all the horror I should have expressed at the killing of Fallon Adderbury. My only excuse was that I'd had time to get used to it.

I told Judyth how I'd found his body. 'I do not relish the prospect of telling my poor sister,' I went on, 'she—'

But Judyth smiled faintly, and, echoing Sallie, said, 'Oh, Celia wasn't really interested in him. He's – he *was*' – her expression grew sad again – 'too superficial for a woman like her.' After a moment she said, 'So somebody must have turned the handkerchief from an object to be used in a play to a means of harm, not to say death, and—'

'Francis Heron!' I shouted, making her jump.

'Francis?'

'He was poisoned. I thought it was belladonna. I haven't had the time or opportunity to work out how it was adminis-tered, and I've been assuming it was added to something he ate or drank – drank, probably, as the poor man didn't want to eat towards the end.'

Judyth was shaking her head. 'The substance on the handker-chief wasn't belladonna. I just told you, it was a vision-inducer. And besides, the handkerchief was nowhere near him.'

'Yes it was.' And I told her about Raphe Wymer – who, I thought, a potent mix of sorrow and fury rising up in me, was also dead – and how he had offered the white embroidered handkerchief to bind Francis Heron's brow and ease the pain in his head.

And, when I'd finished, she asked what I'd earlier been asking: 'Why?'

I was feeling a great deal better, and the nauseous dizziness had quite gone, so that I was sure I'd have been quite all right to sit up. But it felt so good to be lying with my head in Judyth's lap that I wasn't going to admit it.

'It would be a certain way of getting someone – or even a group of people – into very grave trouble,' I said presently.

'To ensure that a handkerchief now soaked in a dangerous and probably highly illegal magic-working drug was found in his or their possession?' she demanded.

'Exactly that. Which suggests that someone knew, that they were trying to return it to its maker – Celia.'

And I heard Raphe's voice, his desperate, terrified voice, saying that the handkerchief must be thrown into the heart of a fire – before it was discovered and linked to whoever made it? To my sister? – because it had magic in it.

'Perhaps,' Judyth said slowly. 'But, Gabe, perhaps whoever it was knew it wasn't safe to destroy it within the Saracen's Head, or anywhere there were people about.'

'Why?'

She gave an exclamation of impatience. 'Look what it did to you! What better way to bring the very forces you were trying to hide it from right to your door than to burn it and fill the air with potent and deadly fumes that anyone who knew about it would instantly recognize?'

'But to come all the way out here?'

'Perhaps it was simply in order to let Celia know she was safe.'

In the absence of any suggestion from me, it seemed the best we were going to come up with.

Then Judyth said, 'If what you just said is right, why should someone want to make such grave trouble for the Company?'

I didn't respond straight away. My mind was much clearer now, but the questions I'd been grappling with these past days confounded me so deeply that I hadn't come up with any answers. But Judyth wanted me to respond: I sensed a new tension in her.

'Not everyone in the Company is down here in the West purely because they're an actor, or a carter, forced to make a living out of London while plague has shut the theatres in the capital,' I began. 'Two of them carried a deadly secret, and both are dead, so it was indeed fatal. We said, you and I, that there was something strange about the Company. You said that the plays they performed were weighted, and that—'

'That there were hidden layers of meaning, and something very dark and dangerous was being hidden.' She nodded. 'Oh, yes, I remember.'

'The four senior players are party to the secret,' I said. 'They showed particular anxiety when Francis Heron was dying. And the determination to confuse and mystify us is still going on' – suddenly I sat up, as a vivid image of what I'd seen earlier flashed before my eyes – 'because on my way home this evening I came across that cursed, malevolent mirror, standing alone on the track, and suddenly it was full of brilliant light and Hal shied and I fell off and banged my head.'

After a short, shocked pause, she said, 'Are you quite sure you fell off *after* you'd seen the mirror?'

'Perfectly sure. Don't think I haven't also wondered if somehow I was confused and only imagined I saw it. It *was* there. Furthermore, I came across two deep wheel marks, and I'm pretty certain a heavily laden cart had been that way not long before.'

'The Company are moving on,' she said thoughtfully. 'To Exeter, I believe.'

'Most of the players will travel on Monday,' I added. 'Although they told me some of the heavy baggage would be on the road tonight.'

We stared at each other.

'It looks as if they took the inland road,' she said, 'the one that goes up over the moors.' She paused. 'After it has gone past the turning to Tavy St Luke.'

'I thought they were looking for me,' Celia said, feeling the tension and the fear begin to leave her as they gained the concealing shadow of the Priest's House. 'I was so afraid, Jonathan. I'm ashamed of how afraid I was!' She tried to laugh, but it was a dismal failure.

'Of course you were,' he said. 'Gabe believed you were in danger, and that was why he sought sanctuary for you, and when we heard those men out in the main part of the church, it looked as if he was right.' He paused, then added disarmingly, 'I was afraid, too. I don't keep weapons in the vestry.'

'We could have picked up one of your old pews between us and hurled that at them,' she said lightly.

'An unwieldy weapon,' he remarked, 'but effective.'

There was a pause, then she said, 'They're hunting for a man.' She hesitated, not wanting to put it into words, then said, 'A man who was looking for me, but I can't think who they meant.'

'Yes,' he agreed. 'It would seem they only came to St Luke's because they thought he was going to be there. We should warn him, whoever he is, that if he goes to the church he's running into peril, but where should we start?'

'I don't know,' she said. 'Let's hope they're wrong, and he knows full well they're after him and is heading anywhere but St Luke's.'

There was a pause, as if he was waiting for her to make a suggestion, and so she said, 'I do not wish to disparage the Priest's House, Jonathan, which *I* think is the most enchanting dwelling. But even someone who appreciates it would have to admit it is not the most heavily fortified place.'

'It is not usually my aim to keep people out,' he said mildly.

'I know. But I think it would be wise to do so tonight.' She paused, then said, 'Let's go to Rosewyke.'

Samuel came out and took Jonathan's horse, but they managed not to wake Sallie, and it was Celia who crept into the kitchen and, careful not to make a noise, prepared warming drinks. Jonathan, she discovered as she carried the two mugs through to the library, had made up the fire.

They sat at the table and got straight back to the code.

With the letters *a*, *c*, *e*, *f*, *h*, *i*, *n*, *o*, *r* and *s* uncovered, they decoded a series that ran -, *o*, *h*, *n*, -, *e*, *e* as John Dee, which gave them *j* and *d*. H, *e*, *n*, *r*, -, -, *e*, *r*, *c*, - was Henry Percy, which added *y* and *p*, and then it was easy, as Jonathan observed, to uncover -, *h*, *o*, -, *a*, *s* as Thomas Percy, which gave *t* and *m*. Very soon, between them they had enough letters to make clever guesses, and the list grew longer: Christopher Marlowe, Thomas Harriot, Gerard Cuddon, Robert Catesby,

Barnaby Abell, Nicholas Hill, someone simply referred to as
Guido the Mercenary, Thomas Winter, Thomas Lightbodie,
John Winter, Humphrey Brewiss.

As they were revealed, Celia realized that she knew some
of them. She glanced at Jonathan, reluctant to disturb his
concentration – *He's worked so hard*, she thought, *and so
swiftly* – but, sensing her eyes on him, he looked up.

'I know some of these men,' she whispered. It seemed like
the sort of remark that had to be whispered. 'These four' – she
pointed – 'are the elder members of the Company.'

He put down his quill, rubbing his eyes. 'I know some of
the others, too,' he said.

He had been working on something from the book's
flyleaf: four five-symbol groups and one of four. For a quite
a long time, and she had heard him mutter under his breath
in frustration at least twice. Now he said, 'Celia, come and
look at this.'

She went to lean over his shoulder. He had written out *thesc,
holar, softh, enumi, nous.*

'*Hola* is how you greet people in Spanish,' she said. He
glanced up at her enquiringly, smiling. 'Gabe speaks a little.
And *nous* is *we* in French. That was my Grandmother Oldreive,'
she said before he could raise an eyebrow at that too. '*Ennui*
is boredom, I think, but it's not spelt like that.'

He said ruefully, 'If whoever wrote this is a linguist as well
as an encryptor, all of this will take a great deal longer. I have
Latin and some Greek, and a little French, but—'

'*The*,' she said softly. She pointed. 'At the start and halfway
through, and— Oh, *look*!'

But there was no need to show him what she'd just seen,
for he had spotted it too. Swiftly, his hand flying over the
page, he wrote out the twenty-four laboriously decoded letters
again, with different spacing.

And now they read *The Scholars of the Numinous*.

'Have you ever heard of them, whoever they are?' Celia
asked.

'Oh, yes,' he said quietly. 'Many of these illustrious names'
– he ran his finger along the page – 'are associated with it. I
think perhaps—'

They both heard it.

A tapping sound, like a branch rattling against a window.

Celia looked at Jonathan. 'Has the wind got up, then?' she asked.

He went over to the window. Celia had drawn the heavy curtains, and he raised one, looking out into the darkness. 'No. The trees are quite still.'

The noise came again.

'It's coming from the hall,' Jonathan said.

Celia stood up. 'From the front door. People often call on Gabe late at night,' she went on, trying to hide her apprehension.

'The knocking is very tentative' – he was already striding out of the door, through the parlour and into the hall, and she was right beside him – 'which suggests that whoever it is may well be sick, or hurt.'

They went through the entry porch and Jonathan pushed back the heavy bolts, Celia reaching round him to turn the lock. She heard him mutter, 'I hope this is the right thing to do,' and then the door was open.

Someone was slumped on the step, half leaning against the wall, half lying on the ground. Celia thought: *He might be pretending, feigning sickness or injury in order to gain entry into the house*, but then she saw the blood.

She was on her knees in a mere instant, and Jonathan must have seen it too, because he was right beside her, his arm going under the head to raise it from the hard ground. 'We must get him inside,' Celia said, 'he's freezing, and he's been hurt.'

Together they raised the inert form, Jonathan at the head and Celia at the feet, and carried him – for, by the weight, it was a man – into the hall. Celia raced into the morning parlour, flinging open the heavy old wooden chest and extracting blankets and pillows, making a makeshift bed on the floor of the hall, then gently unfastening his garments to see where the blood was coming from.

'What shall I do?' Jonathan asked softly.

'Fetch water from the kitchen. The fire's still going and there's a kettle hanging over it, so the water should still be hot. Then go up to Gabe's study – up the stairs, turn right and it's at the end of the passage on the left – and in a big chest by the door you'll find torn-up cloths – bring an armful.' Hearing her own voice giving brisk orders, she looked up at him with an apologetic smile, and, understanding, he said, 'It's all right,' and she heard him striding away.

She had the man's doublet unlaced now, and was very carefully peeling the shirt away, for it was stuck to his flesh by his blood. He moaned, trying to pull back, and she said gently, 'I am sorry to hurt you, but I need to see where you have taken a wound.' And how bad it is, she added silently.

She had been intent on his chest and shoulder, trying to see where the blood was coming from and if it was still flowing, but now, hearing him mutter what might have been *thank you*, she looked up into his face.

He was bare-headed and he had thick red hair. His face was grey with pain, his eyes dull and half-closed, and the wide, mobile mouth that she had often seen in that wicked grin was now clamped shut as he tried not to cry out.

He had played Cassio, and – brilliantly, magically – Puck. He had played a foolish young man hopelessly pursuing the noblewoman in that ridiculous comedy, and made her laugh with his antics and his tumbling.

It was Quentyn Barre.

He had opened his eyes and was looking at her. 'You came to see the plays,' he said, his voice not much more than a whisper. 'You sewed a silk handkerchief embroidered with strawberries and gave it to Fallon.' His face twisted, and his eyes filled with tears.

'Rest,' she said. 'There will be time to talk when you have been tended. You are safe here,' she added, 'with friends and behind a sturdy door, and we shall look after you.'

But he had turned his face away.

Presently Jonathan came back with hot water and dressings, and, by saturating the blood-soaked, stiff, sticky fabric of the shirt, Celia was able to pull it free.

Quentyn Barre had been stabbed in the left shoulder, a couple of inches below the collar bone. The wound was not large but it was deep, and it was still bleeding. When it was clean, Celia padded up a thick wedge of soft, clean cloth and pressed it against the cut, holding it very firmly.

'Will that stop the bleeding?' Jonathan asked.

It was so good to have him there beside her. She had learned a little about such wounds but not nearly enough – she was quietly praying for Gabe's return – and Jonathan's quiet assumption that she knew what she was doing gave her confidence.

'For now,' she whispered back. 'Gabe would undoubtedly stitch it, but I have not the skill.'

He said – and she could tell he was smiling – 'I find that surprising, knowing as I do how deftly you sew.'

She smiled too. 'Cloth is one thing, human flesh quite another.' Then, as Quentyn stirred and cried out, she muttered, 'Oh, come soon, Gabe.'

And she and Jonathan settled on the floor either side of their patient to await the doctor's return.

NINETEEN

Judyth and I were riding side by side out of Tavy St Luke's, and I was trying to persuade her that it made sense to return to Rosewyke with me.

'If you insist on going home, I will go with you,' I said, 'because peril is out walking the darkness tonight, and none of us should travel alone.'

I was bracing myself to counter whatever argument she came up with, but to my surprise she said, 'That's what the blacksmith said. Well, not in those words, what he actually said was, *There's devils and demons out a-screeching and a-screaming, and for sure they don't mean us any good*, and he was all for me staying the night with them until I told him I'd be quite safe as I would be with Doctor Taverner.'

I appreciated the blacksmith's faith in me. He was huge, and looked on most other men as weaklings.

'So?' I asked.

'So?' she echoed.

'Do you want me to see you safely home?'

There was a long pause; I knew full well she was teasing. Then she said, 'No, Gabe. I'll come back to Rosewyke.'

I tried to make no sound as we rode into the yard, but Samuel's bat ears heard us and he was out there even as we dismounted, and Tock was right behind.

'Mistress Celia's been back awhile,' he said, 'and she has—'

I spun round. 'She's *here*?' I demanded, my anxiety-born anger surging as I took in what this meant: that she'd left the safety of St Luke's. 'Jonathan let her leave?'

Samuel was muttering, but I ignored him and strode into the house. Judyth was beside me, and she was saying something about Celia and anybody *letting* her do things, and she sounded very nearly as cross as I was.

But when I burst into the hall, everything looked different.

There was a man lying on the floor. The light was sufficient for me to see his face and recognize him as one of the Company's players, and a name flashed into my mind: Quentyn Barre. He was well wrapped in blankets against the night chill, and there was a large bloody pad of cloth on his left shoulder. Jonathan sat on one side of him, Celia leaned over him, bathing his face. The man was either unconscious or asleep, but Celia and Jonathan both looked up at me.

And, very sensibly going straight to what really mattered, Celia said calmly, 'He has had a blade thrust in the upper left shoulder. The wound is deep and will not stop bleeding, and I imagine it needs to be stitched.'

I was already rolling up my sleeves.

Occupying myself with tending the wound would postpone the moment when I had to tell Celia that Fallon Adderbury was dead.

It took some time. The incision was indeed deep; it was lucky for Quentyn Barre that the knife had not entered a few inches lower, or at a downward angle, for it would have reached his heart and he would have died where he was attacked.

There was much I wanted to ask him, and it took considerable effort to set my questions aside and concentrate on my proper job. He was unconscious for most of the time that I laboured on him, although by the time I was putting a line of stitches in the top layer of his wound, closing up the skin, he was beginning to stir. Very quickly it became obvious how much I was hurting him.

'Hush, now, it is almost over,' said a calm, low-pitched voice.

Judyth's voice.

Judyth?

I had lost myself in my work more thoroughly than I'd thought, for I had not noticed that Judyth had taken Celia's place. I looked up, just one swift glance, and she said quietly, 'I have prepared a cleansing wash, and also a draught that will both ease the pain and help him sleep.'

'Thank you.' I inserted the last two stitches and tied off the thread. Then I sat back on my heels and, closing my eyes, eased the ache in my shoulders. I became aware of the smell of lavender, accompanied by the sweet aroma of something else I did not recognize. Opening my eyes again, I watched Judyth wipe all around Quentyn's wound with a clean white cloth drenched in some oil-based mixture that made his skin glisten. When every spot of blood had been removed, she folded a fresh piece of cloth into a pad and pressed it over the stitches. Without looking up – somehow she knew I was watching – she said, 'As soon as he can sit up, we shall wrap a bandage round his chest and over his shoulder to keep this in place.'

I had noticed before when I'd worked with her this insistence on cleaning wounds, and I'd even seen her give her medical instruments the same treatment. I'd asked her about it once, but she had been reluctant to respond, merely saying briefly that someone had told her it was beneficial. Knowing her better now, I was sure it was Black Carlotta, and that Judyth had held back from mentioning her by name because, to so many people, she was a witch and should be taken out and hanged. But my respect for Black Carlotta and her methods led me to try the wound- and instrument-cleaning procedure myself, and, yet again, the strange old woman had been proved to be absolutely right.

Why did we do it? I wondered now, watching Judyth prop up Quentyn's head in order to feed him the draught she'd prepared, drop by slow drop. Why did we see someone different, who lived their life according to other standards and priorities, who believed in another faith, other gods, and instantly want to shout out at the tops of our voices that they were *wrong*, they were *bad*, they were an evil abomination and an insult to our God, and, since he was the sole true God, these *different* people must be hunted down, hounded out of wherever they lived their quiet lives, imprisoned, tortured, put to death in whatever horrible way a sadistic executioner chose to inflict upon them?

In the name of the loving god we worship, why were we so intolerant?

Because we are afraid, a voice said inside my head.

My own voice? I wasn't sure, and I was now so far beyond

exhaustion that it was easier not to question it but just to listen as the voice continued.

Because we invest so much of ourselves in our beliefs, and the thought that these may be less than the whole truth – that we may have to recognize our ignorance and think again – becomes more and more intolerable as our intransigent, unquestioning obedience deepens.

I nodded, as if in response to my inner voice. It was why I would never speak of Black Carlotta. What might happen if she was ever betrayed was not to be contemplated.

I'd thought I was keeping my musings to myself, but Judyth was looking up at me, a smile quirking her mouth, and I wondered if perhaps I'd been speaking aloud.

Very gently she laid Quentyn's head back on his pillows. The cup was empty, and already his eyes were closing.

'Go to bed, Gabe,' she said. 'I know you're aching to question your patient, but you won't be able to do so until morning because he'll be asleep.'

Yes, she was right. And I also had to break the news of Fallon Adderbury's death to my patient, as well as finding a gentle way to tell my sister. Strange, I thought, how I'd managed to forget about it until now; strange how all the events of this whole interminable day seemed to be moving in and out of my memory . . .

But I had more immediate matters to deal with.

'I should stay with him, in case—'

'No you shouldn't,' she said, cutting off my objection. 'You are no use to anyone as you are now, and won't be until you too have slept long and deeply. I will watch him, and I'll wake Celia when I need to rest and she'll take over.'

I looked round. Both Celia and Jonathan had gone. 'Where's Jonathan?'

'Gone back to Tavy St Luke's. He's uneasy, being away from his flock when they need him, and I think he only left the village to make sure Celia got home safely.' She frowned, biting her lip. 'There was something he said to tell you . . . Yes! The message was that he and Celia have found out what's in the notebook and you'll be very interested.'

'Have they?' I was pleased and very surprised, for I'd been

quite convinced it would defeat them. I stood up, thinking to go and ask Celia to tell me what they'd found out, but Judyth must have realized because she grabbed hold of my sleeve.

'Don't,' she said. 'Let it wait till morning. Sleep.'

As she said the last word, drawing it out a little, she fixed her large silvery eyes on mine. And, as if she'd cast a spell on me – administered one of Puck's potions perhaps, or Juliet's sleeping draught – suddenly I had the strange sensation that I was falling asleep where I stood.

She laughed softly, and the sensation went away. I smiled at her – she really was the most lovely woman – and headed for my bed.

I stood at the window of my bedchamber, looking out at the mist swirling up out of the river in its deep cutting over to my right. Turning to the left, I saw the gold disc of the early sun rising up out of the moors, hazy behind a screen of white. I was still dazed with sleep, and I wondered if whatever I had breathed in last night in the vestry was still affecting me.

I couldn't allow it to. I had three people to speak to as soon as I could, and the tally of all that I must do this day was depressingly long.

'Then get on with it,' I told myself.

I washed, dressed and hurried down the stairs. Celia was sitting on the floor beside Quentyn, who was now propped up against a chair turned upside-down to provide a leaning slope, its back padded with cushions. He was still cocooned in blankets, the dressing was now fixed in place with a bandage, and he was eating a thick piece of fresh bread spread with butter and honey.

I was very relieved to see that there was no blood permeating through the pad and the bandage.

They heard my steps on the flagstones and looked up at me. Celia said, 'Sallie's good bread and the honey of our Rosewyke bees is putting the colour back in Quentyn's cheeks.'

Quentyn smiled at me. Not the wide, mischievous grin I recalled, but then he had received a grave wound only yesterday.

'You have cared for me very well, Doctor,' he said. 'I have

but a vague memory of last night, the highlight – or perhaps that is not the word – being the very long moments when you were sewing me together again.'

'I am sorry, but it was necessary,' I replied.

'Of course, and I am most grateful, as I am to your sister and the woman who nursed me last night – Judyth?'

'Yes,' I confirmed. I wondered where she was, then realized that undoubtedly she had gone home to set about her day's work.

'She makes a powerful draught,' he remarked, his brown eyes watching me.

'She is a midwife,' I said coolly. There must be no question of Quentyn picking up the notion that Judyth's skills were in any way suspect . . .

He laughed, wincing as the movement of his chest caused him pain. 'Ouch! Then I shall be sure to remember her if ever a wife of mine is about to give birth.' His eyes crinkled as he smiled widely, and for a moment the hall seemed to be besmirched, as if someone had just told a dirty story.

I crouched down beside him. I looked at him, then at Celia. I said quietly, 'I am afraid I have ill tidings.'

His face straightened in a flash. His mouth tightened, then he said, 'Fallon.'

He knew.

But Celia did not. Could not.

'Fallon?' she repeated, in a very different tone from Quentyn's.

'Yes. I am sorry to tell you both, but he's dead. I came across his body last night. He had been stabbed in the back, and he would have died almost instantly.'

I heard Celia draw a short, sharp breath. Very softly she said, '*Oh*,' and there was a depth of meaning in the drawn-out syllable.

Quentyn's face had fallen into deep lines, and I saw now that he was probably older than I'd thought. 'Where is his body?' he asked dully.

'I left him beside the track, well hidden. This morning I shall go to the coroner's office and report the death. He will be respectfully treated and decently buried, you have my word.'

He nodded.

I waited to see if he would speak, but he didn't. So I said, 'The coroner will want to know how he died. Will you tell me, so that I can pass the information on?'

Quentyn sighed deeply, and briefly put his hand up to hide his face. Then, removing it, he said, 'We were running away from them. We thought we'd taken the right short cut – Fallon said he had a good sense of direction and swore we'd catch up with the wagon, where the presence of the others would ensure they couldn't attack. But we got lost, and when we found the track again they were waiting. They jumped us, and one fell on Fallon from behind. I spun round to face the other one – I think there were only two of them – and he stabbed me. It didn't hurt for a moment, then it did, and I fell, and I think they thought both of us were dead.'

'He aimed too high,' I said.

'Yes.' But I don't think he heard; he was gazing across the hall, his eyes unfocused. 'I think' – he frowned as he tried to remember – 'I think I crawled away, perhaps hoping to hide. I passed out, I believe. Then I got up. There was no sign of the assailants. No sign of Fallon, either, and I did not know what had happened to him. I came here.' He stared at me, and now his eyes were bright with intelligence; with calculation. 'That is all I can tell you.'

'What were you doing out here?' He had mentioned a wagon, but I decided not to ask about that yet.

He smiled faintly. 'What were we doing,' he echoed. 'What indeed.' There was a pause, then he sighed again and said, 'Our purpose was twofold. We were continuing with what we've been doing ever since we left London, which is – or was, until it turned serious – a matter of misdirection, of the deliberate confusion of all whom we met and before whom we performed, of making people believe one thing while all the time concealing another.'

'And you coloured every play – you *weighted* it,' I amended, recalling Judyth's word – 'to blind your audiences with the thrill and the magic of what you were putting before them.'

'We did,' he agreed. 'And what a time we had! It's so easy. Doctor Taverner, to make people believe the unbelievable. To convince them that ghosts are real, to hack a character to pieces with a pretend sword and make them think he is truly dead, to set a mysterious old mirror at such an angle that those who peer so nervously at it believe they are seeing into another world.' He shot me a rueful look. 'It was on the wagon last night,' he said. 'We couldn't resist one last trick, and we'd never used it out in the open before.'

'But why?' I asked, mystified. 'What was it all *for*?'

His eyes had slid out of focus again, and he didn't answer. 'But then people started dying,' he whispered. 'Poor old Francis, who began it all, and then the young man Daniel, who we believed was one thing and turned out to be another. Who was, as we found out too late, one of that group of ruthless, efficient bastards who dress themselves up in fancy cloaks worthy of one of *our* productions and keep to the shadows as they go about their masters' dirty business, and who have been watching and waiting pretty much ever since we left London. Oh, none of us mourned *Daniel*.' He glanced over at Celia. 'And then Fallon had to go and involve you, mistress, and everything really turned serious.'

And Celia broke her long, sorrowful silence with a gasp.

'What do you mean?' I demanded.

He frowned at me, then turned back to Celia. 'You made that pretty silk handkerchief, more than worthy to grace Desdemona and her tragedy. And it changed – it *was* changed – from something beautiful to something deadly.' He paused, and the frown deepened. 'I should have noticed, how people were strangely affected when they'd been near Francis, saying they'd seen weird visions, experienced odd sensations.'

As did I, I thought.

I was a doctor. Dear Lord, if Quentyn was reprimanding himself for not perceiving the source of that puzzling mental confusion, how much more should I?

'Then not only did it kill poor Francis,' Quentyn was saying, 'it threatened, in a different but equally lethal way, to bring untold harm to you, mistress, who had made it with nothing but generous intentions. So we knew, Fallon and I, that we had to destroy it, for Raphe Wymer lacked the balls to do so, despite his protestations and his weeping, and—'

'But why take it out to the church in Tavy St Luke's?' I interrupted furiously. 'Why not set fire to it in some back alley behind the Saracen's Head?' Then I remembered Judyth's sound reasoning of last night, and what had happened to me when I encountered the fumes from its immolation. 'You had to be away from crowded streets,' I said.

'Yes. Oh, yes.' His mobile face twisted into a grimace. 'We loathed what the thing had become by then. Scared ourselves into believing we had something truly devilish in our possession . . .' He paused. Then he said softly, 'A church seemed a good place for the burning. We knew you were taking your sister to sanctuary, Doctor – people heard you yelling when you dragged her away from the inn – and Fallon said St Luke's was the nearest church to your house.'

Then, looking straight at Celia, Quentyn added, 'I think, too, that Fallon wanted to make sure you were all right. He really cared for you.'

There was a brief silence. Celia made no sound, but, watching her, I saw tears in her eyes.

But my thoughts were flying, and I did not pause for a kind word.

Trying to make sense of the timing of last night's events, I said to Quentyn, 'So you got to the church and found Celia and the vicar there?'

'We did hear two men out in the main church,' Celia said – and she sounded surprisingly calm – 'and one of them walked heavy-footed round the chapel. But they were not you and – you and Fallon.' Her face creased in distress as she spoke his name.

'Nobody was there when we arrived,' Quentyn said.

'Celia and Jonathan Carew – he's the vicar – must have already left,' I said slowly, 'because they heard the assailants arrive.' I turned to Celia. 'If that was who you heard?'

She was sitting with her head bowed. Now she looked up. She was pale, and tears still glittered in her eyes. 'It was,' she said dully. Then she gathered herself and added, 'They had weapons. They drew their blades, right there in the church, and one said, "We must not fail in this".'

I tried not to think about how close my sister had come to violence last night. I had much for which to thank Jonathan.

'You and Fallon found the church empty, you burned the handkerchief in the hearth, you fled, and—' I said to Quentyn.

'We fled the instant it caught, running as hard as if half the occupants of hell were on our heels!' he interrupted.

'You tried to catch up with those of your Company who were setting out across the moors in the wagon,' I continued, ignoring the interruption, 'you got lost, you regained the track and the killers attacked.' I shook my head violently to clarify my thoughts. 'And the assailants . . .' But I couldn't concentrate.

'It was the assailants' arrival that drove Jonathan and me to get away' – Celia picked up the narrative – 'and presumably they settled down to wait.' She frowned. 'But the church was empty when you and Fallon got there . . . *Yes!*' she cried sharply. 'They – the assailants – must have become suspicious, perhaps thinking whoever they were waiting for knew of their presence and wasn't coming, and so they left the church to keep watch outside instead, careful to conceal themselves. Then you and Fallon turned up, and they watched you go in and leave again, and they set out to follow you but you—'

'But we took Fallon's wretched short cut, we got lost, and they were waiting for us when we got back to the track!' For just a moment Quentyn's expression was bright with the satisfaction of working it out, but then, no doubt recalling what had happened when the assailants finally found them, his face fell once more into lines of grief.

I got up. 'I'm sorry,' I said. He probably didn't know what I was apologizing for, and I'm not sure I did. 'I must go. I shall call in to see Jonathan,' I went on, looking at Celia, 'and then I'll carry on to Theo's office.'

'Very well,' she replied. Then she said, 'Ask Jonathan about the code,' and I remembered what Judyth had told me last night.

It was a great relief to be outside in the cold, clear air. Samuel had Hal ready, and did not hold me up with more than a brief, 'Good morning.'

I was already cantering off down the track before I recalled that I hadn't had any breakfast.

Jonathan was in the Priest's House. From his air of slight preoccupation, I picked up that his mind was already on the service he would be conducting soon.

'I'm sorry to interrupt,' I said, refusing his courteous invitation to go in. 'Quentyn Barre is sitting up and has eaten some food. He has been able to tell us quite a lot about last night, and he has a fair idea of who attacked him and killed Fallon.' Briefly I told him what Quentyn had said, adding that it was likely that Theo, Jarman and I had seen three members of the group in the street outside the Saracen's Head last night, and, as often in the course of conversations with Jonathan Carew, I had the feeling that he had already worked out for himself what I was revealing to him.

'These men he speaks of who do their masters' dirty business . . .' he began. He stopped. He met my eyes, then looked away. If I hadn't known and trusted him, I'd have said he looked furtive, or even guilty.

But then I remembered what he'd told me of his past. How he'd been at Trinity Hall in Cambridge, studying canon law and, presumably, was stimulated and fulfilled by a subject so well suited to his keen mind. How the potential of that mind had been spotted by the sharp eyes of the unobtrusive men in the shadows who were ever on the lookout for new recruits. How he had been drawn into the great spy network created by Francis Walsingham and which was his greatest and long-enduring legacy. How Jonathan had sickened of the work he was ordered to do, turned away and been hurled out of the band of the select few, punished by being sent to a small parish in a remote region in the far west of England.

It had occurred to me, once I knew Jonathan's story,[2] that he'd probably been lucky to escape with his life.

'You have an idea who they are,' I said, dropping my voice. There didn't appear to be anybody around, but such matters were not for open discussion.

He shrugged. 'I once knew men very like them. They are

[2] See *The Angel in the Glass*.

recruited to the cause, they carry out a mission or two, gradually they find themselves willing to perform tasks they would not have thought themselves capable of, and their belief in the cause they work for deepens into fanaticism as, step by step, they leave their conscience and their humanity behind.' He paused, his face riven with the deep lines of old grief. 'How else may a man excuse his worst actions in his own eyes, other than by telling himself that the dubious end justifies the terrible means?'

I nodded. 'Either that,' I added, 'or the old faithful excuse: *I was just following orders.*'

He sighed. 'Yes. That too can work.'

'So, you think these men killed Fallon as part of a wider mission?' I asked.

'Undoubtedly,' he replied. 'They are professionals, and so good at what they do that hardly anybody has seen them or even suspects their presence here, save by the evidence they leave behind.'

'The dead bodies,' I said.

'Yes. But what purpose can it be that makes them dog the steps of a theatre company, touring down here far from the capital while plague shuts the theatres of London?' He paused, frowning. 'Yes. The fact that they have come so far, that there was originally a number of them and they kill without hesitation, does indeed suggest they are on a mission, and, moreover, that it is one deemed to be of no small importance.'

After a moment's stunned silence, I said, 'Celia said to ask you about the code.'

Slowly he turned to face me; he had been staring across at the church, perhaps seeking strength. His expression cleared – lightened, even – and he said, 'Ah, yes. The code. Names, Gabriel, such names, a long list of them in a notebook found in the possession of a dead assassin who stole it from a man hiding among a band of players. Scholars, explorers, adventurers, scientists, men of power and influence, magicians. And actors,' he added softly, 'those four older men in the very Company with which we have become entangled.' He paused, his expression deeply troubled. 'All Scholars of the Numinous,' he added, leaning close and speaking hardly above a whisper. 'And you have already asked me about that secretive organization, because the man known as Daniel muttered its name in his sleep.'

My head felt too full. I was trying to understand a mystery, but I only had half the pertinent facts. If that.

I felt time pressing; Theo would be in his office, might even now be about to go out in response to some urgent appeal. And Jonathan was needed in his church: for a few moments, I wished very much that I was in Tavy St Luke's that morning purely for the consolation of attending the service.

'I must go,' I said. 'I have yet to report Fallon Adderbury's death to Theo.'

Jonathan nodded, stepping back inside. As I hurried away, I thought I heard him bless me.

'There is another body for you,' I said to Theo not long afterwards. We were in his inner office, and, outside, the corridor and the outer office were busy with his agents; for all that it was still early, they were already deep in the demands of the new day.

Theo sighed. 'And there I was thinking you had brought me good news,' he muttered. 'Where is it, who is it, and how did he or she die?'

'The body's concealed in the undergrowth beside the track where the Tavy St Luke track joins the road into Plymouth. It is that of Fallon Adderbury, he died from a knife to the heart and he was killed by one of a band of agents, spies, whatever we are to call them, who appear to have followed the Company down here to carry out some important mission.'

Theo was already getting up, reaching for his black robe. 'And just why you think that this band of secret agents are down here in my town, and that this mission includes the killing of that rather dashing young actor, you can tell me on the way.'

Our little procession of Theo and me on horseback and one of his agents on the flat-bedded cart did not take long to reach the junction where I had found Fallon's body, for there was as yet not much traffic on the roads. The spot was deserted, and it was swift work to find where I'd hidden the body in the bracken and load it onto the cart, covering it with a white sheet and a blanket on top of that. We went straight to the house along the road from Theo's office, and Theo and I bore the body down into the cellar.

I removed the doublet and the shirt, then turned the corpse onto its side. I did not need more than a glance to confirm what I'd thought last night: Fallon had died from a very accurate knife thrust into his back, between the ribs and into the heart.

At least it would have been quick.

I stood looking down at him, this young man who had briefly burned so brightly across our small town, he and his fellow players vividly coloured in contrast to the dun shades of our modest everyday lives. I stared at his handsome face. He had been young and exuberant; arrogant, aware of his good looks and his charm, and, undoubtedly, of his effect on women. But I understood suddenly that this last would not have provoked such anger in me had one of those women not been my sister, with the dark shadow of her past still far too close. And instantly, straight on the heels of that realization, I thought how unfair it was, that all his vitality and talent, all the promise of the life ahead, should have been stamped out.

And I thought of the other deaths: of Francis, slowly succumbing to the subtlety of poison, the confusion of a sinister hallucinogen. Of Daniel and the spade-bearded man in the barn – the London spy, if Jonathan was to be believed, and I was sure he was – the one stabbed in the heart like Fallon, the other with his neck broken. Of Raphe Wymer, strangled with ruthless efficiency and laid out like a sacrifice.

I had absolutely no idea why they had all had to die; what deadly secret had come with them from London, their fates decided by those with the power to rob men of their lives for their own deep and mysterious reasons.

But, as I felt the anger stir deep within me, I vowed to myself that I was going to find out.

TWENTY

I found Theo's office alive with activity, and the buzz of alarm was apparent even as I went through the street door.

'. . . *would* have done, given half a chance, but they were off and away before we got the chance!' a loud voice shouted with a definite touch of defensiveness.

'The buggers were heavily armed!' cried another. 'And besides, we weren't—'

'Couldn't you have managed to hang onto *one* of them?' Theo's angry voice blasted out. 'And where the hell's Jarman Hodge?'

'They didn't give us the chance,' a third voice muttered. 'Like we just told you, one of them came in here, the other one stood in the doorway, and the first one, he demands to know where you are, and we says you're not here, and he says, cool and smooth as you like, "Tell him I shall return, for there are matters he should know, and we are aware he has information for us." Then he added something about it being an offence not to inform him of things that—'

'He said it was dangerous!' one of the others interrupted. 'He said it with real menace, like he was warning us not to cross him!'

'And you meekly let him stroll away.' Theo returned to his main gripe. He glared round at the four men in the outer office. 'Did this smooth-speaking well-armed man give his name?'

'Robert something . . .' one man said.

'Robert Fox,' supplied another. 'The other was Ashe, Martin Ashe. Nondescript sort of a fellow, lean like a whippet.' He glanced round at his companions to see if one of them was going to speak, and when nobody did, he leaned closer to Theo and said, 'We all reckon they're . . . *officials*.' He looked earnestly at Theo as he spoke, as if hoping Theo would pick up what he meant without him having to say it out loud. 'From London,' he whispered.

Theo stared at him, frowning. 'You think they are here to make sure nobody is acting against the interests of the King?' he said. 'That they're spying on us?'

'Spying on somebody,' the man muttered.

Theo thumped him on the shoulder, heavily enough to make him quake slightly. 'Well, Matthew, I reckon you're absolutely right,' he said. 'All the same, I wish you had—'

There was the sound of hoofbeats outside, and a voice yelled, 'Will someone tend the mare? I have urgent business here!'

Matthew, looking relieved to have an excuse to get out of Theo's reach, hurried to comply.

And Quentyn Barre stumbled in.

'You should be resting!' I said, hurrying to support him. He was pale as death, his face drawn with pain.

'That's what your lovely sister said,' he answered, grimacing as I led him along the corridor and into Theo's office, hooking a chair with my foot and helping him to sit down. 'She refused at first to let me borrow her mare, but I said I'd walk if she didn't.'

Theo had joined us. 'Better news,' he said to me. 'Tomas just told me Jarman's gone after Robert Fox and this companion.'

'Good. This is Quentyn Barre, another of the Company,' I went on.

'Puck,' Theo said, glancing at him.

'He was injured in the same attack that killed Fallon, and managed to reach Rosewyke, where we tended him. And where he still should be,' I added reprovingly.

'I wish I was, Doctor, believe me,' Quentyn said. 'The wound hurts like the devil. But I had to come, because—'

'Be quiet,' I told him. 'I don't want to hear another word till I've had a look.' I was very afraid that riding from Rosewyke would have torn the stitches and opened up the cut, but a swift check showed everything still in place, and no new bloom of blood on the pad and the bandage.

I stepped back. 'You're all right. For now, anyway. Go on.'

He nodded his thanks, took a breath, which clearly hurt a lot, and said, 'There are things I have to tell you. I don't want to. For so many reasons, I – we – would so much rather keep silent, but it's not safe any more and I no longer have a choice.' He took another breath, this time groaning softly. 'You see, when the Company left London, it wasn't only to come down here on our Plague Tour, as people call it, although that was a fine excuse, a first-rate disguise, and should have afforded all the necessary protection. It *would* have, if only Robert Fox and his band hadn't picked up our trail, because of all the agents, spies and private killers in London, they are the most efficient, the most ruthless and the most fanatical.'

Theo and I exchanged a glance. We had only recently heard the name Robert Fox.

'Who are they?' Theo asked, after a quick glance at the door to make sure it was shut.

Quentyn sighed. 'Who knows? We never really do know, do we? The rumours and the whispers say this or that man is one of the shadowy band the normal rules don't apply to, who can strike where they like, make men vanish without a trace, have them killed, and give no more reason than that they're acting in defence of the State and it is not in anyone's interests to ask.'

Quentyn was younger than Theo or me, I reflected, and unlikely to have been old enough to experience the paranoia that affected England in the reign of Elizabeth, especially towards the end.

'What was this other purpose?' Theo asked.

'With us there was a man with a dangerous secret,' Quentyn replied. 'And let me tell you straight away that I don't know what it was, so it's no use asking me.'

Theo glowered at him.

'He wasn't one of the Company,' Quentyn went on, 'but we had to pretend he was. He was accompanied by a man who took on the guise of a luggage-hauler.'

'Daniel,' I said.

'Yes, that was what he called himself,' Quentyn agreed, 'and the man with the secret was, as I'm sure you've guessed, Francis Heron. He was desperate, poor man. He was a close friend of Thomas Lightbodie and the others, and—'

'The other older players?' I asked. 'Barnaby Abell, Humphrey Brewiss and Gerard Cuddon?'

'*Yes*,' Quentyn said, clearly impatient to continue. 'They said we had to take care of Francis, and, since they're the men of power in the Company, the rest of us didn't have a choice. Well, we could have quit the Company, but with the theatres all closed while the plague rages, there's no work in London and no way of earning a living, and nobody was prepared to give up on the tour.' He sighed, shaking his head. 'Besides, we all thought it was a grand adventure. We were already afire with the excitement of getting on the road, and the prospect of having a real-life drama in our midst, of having this wonderful opportunity to hide a man in full sight, was just too good to miss.' He paused. 'Of course, we were soon carried away with our own cleverness. It would have been wiser not to draw attention to ourselves so blatantly, but once we discovered how good we were at playing with people's minds, we fell over ourselves trying to come up with even more outlandish ideas.'

'You did it very well,' I said wryly, remembering how I'd been mystified – fooled – by the tricks. How hard I'd had to fight to conquer my fear in the Saracen's Head at night.

Quentyn looked at me. 'We'd have plenty of practice by the time we reached Plymouth,' he said. 'Fallon had come up with the idea of having different people appear dressed in the same rust-red velvet costume, and using the mirror in all the plays. We were subtly shading every production by that time too, finding all manner of ways to make our audiences think what we wanted them to think.'

'It wasn't the plays I was referring to,' I said.

'Ah.' He nodded. 'I'd forgotten you were in the inn during the night. I'm sorry, Doctor. We knew you were one of the good men, but we couldn't stop what we'd begun.' He paused. 'Not that we had to do much.' Then, in as casual a tone as if he were commenting on the weather, he added, 'The Saracen's Head is haunted, you know.'

'I do not believe in ghosts,' I said coldly.

He raised an eyebrow. 'Perhaps you should.' His dark eyes held mine. 'There are more things in heaven and earth than are dreamed of in your philosophy, Doctor. Our Will wrote that,' he added. 'He *knows*. It's a shame he didn't come on the Plague Tour with us. He'd have been in his element.' He smiled, his face suddenly softening.

'Francis Heron was killed for his secret.' Theo spoke coldly. 'He was told he'd be safe with the Company. He wasn't.'

'Don't remind me,' Quentyn said heavily. Briefly he covered his eyes with his hand.

'You said Daniel took on the guise of a luggage-hauler?' I asked.

Quentyn looked up. 'We thought he was there to look after Francis. We reckoned Daniel knew there was a secret, although probably not what it was. But we quickly grew suspicious of him, for Daniel wasn't what he seemed to be.' His eyes narrowed. 'The younger players who were protecting Francis and the senior men decided it'd be a lark to follow Daniel and see where he went. I know it sounds foolhardy and as if we didn't take it seriously,' he said before either Theo or I could, 'but truly, we had no idea what we were dealing with, no idea how serious it was. We thought it was just a game, an excuse to see how far we could take our misdirections, our illusion that the places we stayed were full of unquiet spirits, our efforts to make our audiences uneasy and persuade them that our stage magic was real. It was all to aid the confusion, don't you see?'

He seemed to recall what he'd been saying.

'Then it all changed. It was our turn to follow Daniel, Fallon's and mine, and we trailed him out onto the moor, to a ramshackle old barn. When we got there he was fighting with a man who was so very much better at it than he was, poor sod, although Daniel did his best. But the man stuck a knife in Daniel's side, and he went straight down, not even time to cry out.' He paused, eyes momentarily unfocused. 'The other man had this carefully tended little beard,' he murmured, 'and I remember thinking, he's just killed a man and he hasn't a hair out of place.'

There was a brief silence.

'I don't know what made Fallon and me dash in,' Quentyn went on. 'Stupid, really, we're players, we only fight with blunt swords, and when we hit each other, that's pretend too, and the sound of fist on flesh is achieved by the fellow in the wings thumping a haunch of pig. Anyway, in we went, Fallon yelling like a banshee, and the man eyes us with cold humour and says, "And what do *you* propose to do, my pretty boys?", looking us up and down as if we were girls, and Fallon does a sort of growl, and the man laughs aloud and says, "You think to avenge him, is that it? Too late, I fear. He brought me what he was ordered to find, but he betrayed those to whom he owes his loyalty and obedience – said he wanted to join your pathetic little company for real, would you believe it! – and he's paid the price for his treachery." Well, something in all that really affected Fallon, he leapt on the man and I did too, and we were punching him, and it wasn't at all like on stage, and we managed to drive him a few steps backwards and he fell, he tripped over something lying on the ground, and he yelled as he went down, and we ran for it, and somehow –' he eyed us nervously – 'somehow we must have killed him, because soon word spread back in town that *two* bodies had been found out on the moor.'

There was dead silence in Theo's office.

There had been something in Quentyn's account that snagged my attention. I murmured, 'Francis and the senior men.'

Theo shot me a questioning look. Quentyn said softly, 'Ah.'

'Well? What did you mean?'

He didn't answer straight away. Then he muttered, more to himself, 'Why not?' and, looking first at Theo, then at me, said, 'They are all involved, all four of them. It was only Francis who knew the dangerous secret, and he refused to tell them for their own good, or that was what he said. He told them – and I overheard the whole conversation, because it was my turn to watch over them that night and I think they'd forgotten I was there – he told them he was haunted by what he knew, and it would not leave him alone. He could not believe such evil could be countenanced, he said – and he was sobbing by then – and he wanted no part of it. And he said those who were after him would make him reveal what he knew, they'd force him to give up the names of his fellow conspirators – and they would, of course, because they're masters at the extraction of information – and it would condemn him to the most terrible death imaginable.'

'So Francis knew something the others didn't,' I said slowly, 'although all of them were mixed up in it?'

Quentyn shrugged, wincing. 'I assume so, yes. As I told you, we were protecting them, making it look as if we were no more than what we appeared to be on the outside: a London theatre company touring the West Country because the plague stopped us earning our living in the capital. We wanted to go to the Midlands,' he went on, speaking rapidly now, 'and Will did especially, he really tried to force us because he had to go back to his family in Stratford and if we'd gone the way he wanted he could have been with us, but Thomas stood firm and the others sided with him, said it had to be the West Country and we had to finish in Devon, because down here you're almost as far away as you can be, with only Lyonesse beyond.'

'Lyonesse?' Theo echoed. 'What is Lyonesse?'

But I knew.

Lyonesse was the ancient name for Cornwall and the lands of legend that lay beyond; lands now drowned beneath the sea, existing only in mankind's long memory. And, perhaps, in the minds of a mysterious group of men to whom such a myth would appeal, and who called themselves the Scholars of the Numinous.

'What is their purpose?' I asked Quentyn.

He looked at me, a sad smile on his bright face. 'Now that,' he said, 'you'll have to ask them.'

He refused to go with us. 'You don't need me to show you the way,' he said ruefully, 'for you have managed to discover for yourselves what we believed had been so carefully concealed. I'm hurting,' he added, his face twisting in pain. 'I shall make use of your sister's horse for a while longer, Doctor, and make my way back to my bed at the Saracen's Head.'

Theo and I took the secret way, although, having experienced it once, neither of us wanted to. But it was quicker, and going by that route meant the sight of the coroner and the doctor hurrying on some urgent errand would not be seen and gossiped about by the townspeople of Plymouth. It was as unpleasant as we'd anticipated, and we made our way largely in silence: as before, it was a great relief to emerge onto the shore at the far end.

Theo stood frowning up the track that ran past the row of hovels. 'Come on, then,' he said. I followed as he strode off, and stood beside him as he raised his hand and knocked on the door.

For some moments nothing happened. I tried to peer through the gap in the warped shutters, but something had been hung behind it. Theo knocked again, harder this time. And with a creak the door began to open. Just a crack, but it revealed the long, pale face and silver beard of Thomas Lightbodie, his smooth hair covered by a close-fitting black cap.

He stared at us, he stared *beyond* us, in a swift glance with fear clouding his eyes. He said softly, 'You are alone? Nobody has followed you here?'

'I very much doubt it,' Theo said. 'May we come in?'

Very quickly Thomas opened the door, almost dragged us inside and then closed it again, pushing the bolts across. The squalid room had been crowded before. Now six of us stood in the small space, and the tension in the cold, damp air was tangible. In the first quick look, I saw the others – Barnaby Abell, Humphrey Brewiss and Gerard Cuddon – standing with their backs to the far wall. In each face I read the same expression: fear, most certainly fear, but also a glow of excitement, of . . . of *hope*.

My eyes ran on round the dark little room. I saw the carefully tied bedrolls. The four modest travelling bags. The water flasks, the large bags of what looked and smelt like provisions. And I'd already observed that the four men were dressed in warm, heavy cloaks and thick boots.

'Wherever you're bound,' I said quietly, 'it isn't Exeter.'

Thomas was staring intently at me. He hesitated, perhaps preparing a lie, then he seemed to relax. 'No,' he said with a gentle smile. 'The Company will have to manage without us from now on.'

Something about the four players had changed. I had seen them in a variety of costumes, subsuming their own natures

in the roles they portrayed. Now they were different again.
But this time they were not mere costumed characters in a
play. It was as if each of them had stepped into another aspect
of himself and left the old one behind, discarded on a path he
had already trodden.

Theo said bluntly, 'Wherever you're going isn't my concern.
But five dead men are. I am certain you have information for
me, and—'

There was a very quiet tap on the door.

The four players looked at each other, aghast. I said quickly,
'I will see who it is.'

I opened the door a fraction. Jonathan Carew stood outside.

'I went to Theo's office,' he said. 'His man Matthew said
where you were.'

I admitted him, quickly bolting the door again.

'I believe I have uncovered some valuable intelligence for
you,' he muttered to me, 'but, having found where you are
and who you're with, I imagine you are about to hear it from
those who concealed it.'

Thomas had heard. His expression and his sudden pallor
gave it away, and he said urgently, 'What have you uncovered?
Who have you told?'

'I have told nobody,' Jonathan replied calmly. 'One other
person knows, Doctor Taverner's sister, but only because she
was involved in the uncovering. Indeed,' he added with a smile,
'she provided the key.'

'*What do you know?*' Thomas repeated, the words a hiss.

'That you four and your old friend Francis Heron were
members of a private, clandestine group called the Scholars
of the Numinous. That men of renown are of your number;
men of power and influence such as Sir Walter Raleigh, John
Dee, Thomas Percy, Henry Percy; men of letters such as
Christopher Marlowe and Thomas Kyd. That your interests
range widely and include astronomy, geography, cartography,
mathematics. That you aim to explore both the realm of the
tangible and the inner realm of the mind and, in the words of
John Dee, uncover the secret of the world.'

'John Dee is a spent force,' Gerard Cuddon murmured.

'He's not had the power nor the will since Edward Kelley died and his access to the spirits ceased.'

'Since he returned from Poland to find his library ransacked,' Humphrey Brewiss corrected. 'That's what broke him.' He looked at Jonathan. 'Francis had one of his work books,' he said conversationally. 'And that mirror of ours belonged to him too. It's bursting with the old man's magic, you can't see your own reflection for all the spirits floating round in it, and—'

But I stopped listening.

John Dee's mirror. His notebook.

In my mind I saw that strange symbol again, and I knew now it hadn't been Francis Heron's; it had been John Dee's. And yes, of course, they'd known each other. I'd thought Francis was rambling, deep in delirium. He'd spoken of someone whose library had been ransacked, and I'd assumed he was referring to the Wizard Earl, since he'd just been talking about him. But he wasn't.

It had been his friend John Dee who was in Francis's thoughts as he lay dying.

'Who killed Francis?' I asked harshly across Humphrey Brewiss's stream of words. 'He had a very powerful secret, and he died for it. He was poisoned with belladonna, I'm sure of that, but there was another deadly substance, and that silk handkerchief was soaked in it.'

Barnaby Abell spoke up. 'We had the misfortune to be pursued by the most efficient of State spies, a man called—'

'Robert Fox,' Theo said. 'Yes, we know.'

Barnaby nodded. 'We believe he placed a man within the Saracen's Head, for only by so doing could he have reached Francis. We guarded him so well, or so we believed,' he added sadly. There was a quiet moan from Gerard Cuddon, who had put up his hands to cover his face.

'Among the many talents of Fox and his men is the ability to kill in a variety of ways,' Barnaby went on. 'It would be no surprise if these included a wide knowledge of poisons. And, of course, a company of players will always have belladonna in their luggage.'

'I don't understand how Fox penetrated our guard!' Gerard burst out, dropping his hands to reveal a tear-stained face. 'They looked after the five of us so well, all those young players, they threw themselves into it with such joyful enthusiasm, as if it was the finest of games! And they'd got us all the way here, on the very fringe of Lyonesse, without mishap, and we were *so near*, we had only days to wait, and Francis tried and tried, for he knew that once we were away the powers would stretch out to greet him and he'd be saved, but he couldn't find the strength and – and he died.' The last words were no more than a whisper.

'What was this deadly secret?' I asked.

None of the four men answered straight away. Then slowly, one by one, the other three turned to Thomas Lightbodie. And with a deep sigh he began to speak.

'It is twofold. One part I cannot reveal in full, for I do not know it all. You are right, Francis and the four of us were indeed among the Scholars of the Numinous, and for many years our association with our fellow students of the world was nothing but a joy. Imagine it, my friends!' he declaimed dramatically, and I thought, ever the player, even to an audience of three. 'Men from all professions, all walks of life, united by our common love of learning, our hunger to further the sum of human knowledge! And *nothing*, no subject however obtuse or unlikely, however frowned on by the powers who would control our thoughts, was forbidden, and we talked and argued about magic, the occult, the truth there may be in the ancient legends, just as we pondered geography and physics!' He paused, gazing at Theo, Jonathan and me. Then abruptly his expression changed, and the light seemed to leave his face. 'But then the focus of our school began to change. An element of our brethren began to speak more urgently of matters of State; specifically, of our new King and his attitude to Catholics, and whether he was going to moderate religious persecution. Then came the Main Plot, and the whispered discussions intensified further.' He paused, his brows creased in a frown. 'Now we' – he indicated his three fellow players – 'were not privy to what was going on in the last weeks before we left London, for we were busy preparing for the tour. But Francis was.'

He paused again, for longer this time, and I heard Gerard Cuddon mutter, 'He was in such distress, poor Francis.'

I was about to prompt Thomas to go on, but he seemed to know, for he gave me a quick nod and began speaking again.

'Very late one night, he came to where we were rehearsing. The others had gone, just we four remained.'

'He'd said he'd come if he could,' Gerard interrupted. His face was creased in distress.

'He told us he'd just heard something truly terrible,' Thomas went on, as if Gerard hadn't spoken. 'He said they'd gone too far. He said too many innocent lives would be blasted apart, and the very thought disgusted and sickened him. He said he could not believe that decent men – men who had been his friends, who he had admired, talked with on everything under the sun – could contemplate something so dreadful, and at first he had believed it was no more than wild talk. But then he said – and I remember the words perfectly, because I had no idea then what he was talking about and I still haven't now – "It is true, I know it is, because Thomas Percy has already taken a lease on a house right next door."'

I glanced at Jonathan. 'Next door to where?'

And Thomas said, tight-lipped, 'I do not know and I will not guess.'

Francis had been a party to this plan, I thought, and so close to the heart of it that he'd had in his possession a notebook once belonging to John Dee containing the names of his fellow conspirators. But the plot had become too dangerous, too frightening, too dreadful, and he had backed away. He'd thought, poor man, that he could hide, escape with his actor friends and melt away. But that was not the way conspiracies worked. Somebody always suspected. London was full of men trained by Walsingham who in turn were training others, and they never gave up, and nobody ever escaped.

After a short silence, Jonathan said, 'You said the secret is twofold.'

Thomas came back from whatever dark thought had been holding him. 'I did, I did. The second part I may explain in full, for in essence it originated with me; and when very tentatively I first revealed to my four good friends what I had in mind, I discovered with humility and joy that they felt as I did. Straight away they showed me with absolute clarity that they were willing – no, *eager* – to come with me.'

'Where are you going?' Theo asked.

I watched Thomas as he prepared his reply. His face was alight with joy, and the courage, the utter confidence, that I felt pouring off him affected me profoundly.

'We are leaving,' he said simply. 'We are about to take the next step in a plan made a long time ago, before ever we set out on our tour. A ship will call tonight, already carrying others of our kind. We shall sail west, and perhaps, like the mystics and holy men who set off into the unknown, we shall come to the lands beyond the mist, where the heart, the mind and the spirit are still free to soar.'

For just a moment Jonathan looked as if he'd quite like to go with them.

But it was plain that Theo, my dear down-to-earth, rational friend Theo, did not begin to understand. 'Why?' he asked.

Thomas turned to him, smiling gently. 'Because we cannot bear to live in a world that is under the brutal control of the forces of modernity. Men who, with their cold hearts and their total absence of imagination, are working with such ruthless determination to stamp out all that is wondrous in the world, all that stretches human imagination and makes us reach for the stars.' He paused, perhaps searching for words to make us understand; to make Theo and me understand, for I was quite sure Jonathan did already.

'Already we have lost so much,' Thomas went on, his voice soft. 'Miracles, holy shrines, sacred wells, the ancient ways of the deep countryside, statues and images of men and women once worshipped as saints and seen by the people as friends who stand beside them and help them through their hard lives. The Catholic mass' – he met Jonathan's eyes – 'and the daily magic of having Christ's blood and flesh before you, ingesting his essence into your own body.'

'So you seek to find a land where you may openly worship Rome?' Theo demanded.

But Thomas shook his head. 'Oh, so very much more than that, Master Davey. We want to open our minds and our hearts to uncertainty; to *possibility*. We want to mix with shamans and witches, conjurers and weavers of magic, with the undead and the resurrected, and to talk to them, argue with them, as freely as once we did with our brother Scholars.' He leaned forward, his expression intense. 'We want to be free to do all these things,' he breathed, 'all these mind-expanding, thrilling, soul-opening things, without the fear that we shall be arrested, tortured and executed.' He stopped, panting a little, the passion still thrumming in him. 'And we cannot do so in England, for those who have power over us will not permit it.' He paused again, then said very quietly, 'They would remove the magic from the very weave of the universe, and we cannot stand by to watch it happen. And so we are going away.'

The four of them stood watching us, a similar expression on each face. Theo was frowning as he strove to understand, Jonathan looked wistful and, I thought, sympathetic.

As for me, I was sad.

For I knew what would happen when this ship of Thomas's had collected him and his companions and sailed off beyond the western approaches and the Isles of Scilly and out into the Atlantic. I had been there, I had travelled extensively on the other side. I had witnessed the despoiling of virgin lands and the rape of indigenous peoples, all in the name of greed. I had even seen for myself the stamping-out of the ancient religions by those of the young faith who thought they had the one and the only answer; who believed their god was the sole god.

I was still watching the four old players, and as I did so I began to feel that something, some thought, some emotion that was shared by them all, was somehow being communicated to me.

And I found that what I had believed utterly only moments ago was changing subtly . . .

I thought, *I haven't been everywhere. No man has.* And as I held Thomas's brilliant eyes, I felt the very edge of his spirit touch against me. And I thought I heard a soft voice say, *There IS a place. And they will find it.*

TWENTY-ONE

There was an unnatural stillness in the little room, as if the world held its breath to see what would happen next. And into the silence a voice from outside called softly, 'Chief? You in there?'

Theo had the door open in a second, and Jarman Hodge fell into the room. Straightening up, he looked round at all of us within, and nodded as if our presence confirmed his expectations. Turning to Theo, he said, 'I followed Fox and Ashe. They were hunting for one of their number, a man called Bryce, concerned because he's missing. I couldn't get near enough to hear everything they muttered to each other, but seemingly there were six of them. One died in the barn, two went to St Luke's and are now following the Company's wagon.' He paused, chewing his lip. 'I reckon this Bryce was staying at the Saracen's Head. One of them must have been, for without a doubt they had eyes inside the inn. *Must* have done,' he added. He was frowning.

'You did well,' Theo began, 'you—'

But Barnaby interrupted. 'If I may, Master Davey?' he said courteously. Theo waved a hand. 'Thank you. Your man here is quite right: we had taken note of Bryce – that's his name – early on.'

'What does he look like?' I asked.

'Wears a dark wool cap, under which he's bald. Small in height but very powerfully built, with a body like a barrel. Light eyebrows, almost colourless eyes, wears even fine garments as if they're rags.'

He had just described the man I saw appear and disappear in the inn yard.

'He's been busy these past days,' Barnaby went on wryly. 'He poisoned Francis with belladonna in a jug of ale, and when poor Oliver Dauncey spotted him in the scullery behind the taproom washing out the jug, he punched him so hard that he dislocated his jaw, threatening much worse if Oliver didn't hold his tongue. However, he didn't manage to find the underground room and the tunnel down to the cove. We already knew the tunnel was there, of course – I found it when I was down here looking for locations where we could perform, and it was perfect for our purpose. This time, we've always been so careful to keep the old door locked, and when it's closed it's virtually invisible.' He stopped, his face creasing in pain; warning signs. I thought, that something grim was coming.

'But then bloody Bryce started shadowing Raphe Wymer all the time, and he must have followed him through the door. Seems he extracted from the poor lad the information he wanted: where the four of us kept slipping off to. Wouldn't have been hard,' he added bitterly, 'Raphe was soft as putty, and the vicious bastard didn't need to kill him.' He drew a couple of breaths, then continued. 'Bryce emerged on the shore beneath the headland. He was looking round for the hovel – Raphe wouldn't have known exactly where it was, he never came here – and he was down on the shore eyeing the narrow track leading up inland when we jumped him.' He glanced at Humphrey Brewiss, then the four of us. 'We'd been keeping a watch,' he said. 'We took him by surprise. Humphrey said, "I know you! You've been hanging around at the inn!" and Bryce's face twisted in a sneer and he said something about us being the easiest band of foolish fops he'd ever had to deal with. Told us what he'd done to Raphe. That was too much. I was behind him, he'd totally ignored me, so when I hit him with a rock it came as a complete surprise. He wasn't dead, so we rolled him down to the sea and held him under till he was.' He looked at Theo, mouth twisted down. 'Another one for you, Master Davey.'

Jarman had been listening intently. Now he said, 'That Bryce isn't the only one to have found your hidden way. Fox and Ashe have just discovered the door too. I saw them go through, and it's pretty plain they'll be following it all the way to the bay. I reckoned I could get here more quickly overland, and seemingly I was right. But they won't be long.'

And, like actors striding on stage as they hear their cue, the door burst open and Robert Fox and Martin Ashe appeared on the step.

They would be expecting four. Now their eyes roamed round the cramped space and took in eight of us.

'The odds are not in your favour, Robert Fox,' Theo said.

The shock of finding the four men they had surely come to kill in the company of four others had made Fox's long, lean face go pale. Now, hearing himself addressed by name, his thin lips tightened until they were almost invisible.

'There are more of us,' he said coldly.

'If you mean the barrel-shaped bald man, don't count on him,' Barnaby said. 'Several tides have risen and fallen since he went in the sea, and his body will be some way up the coast by now.'

'Bryce,' muttered Fox. 'No matter. He had served his purpose.'

Your spy in the inn, I thought. Who poisoned Francis's ale. Something fell into place in my head. Possibly it was thinking about the belladonna in the jug of ale: suddenly I knew what had killed Francis Heron and how it had been done. 'He got his hands on the silk handkerchief that Raphe gave me for Francis's headache,' I said. 'He soaked it in a very potent and highly effective potion that slowly and inexorably brought about death.' And the most realistic visions and horrific illusions, I might have added, remembering.

Fox's only response was a shrug. But he hadn't denied it.

'I've been wondering how you came by the potion?' I asked, looking at Fox.

He looked at me coldly. 'We interrogate any number of witches,' he said dismissively. 'They talk. Some of them try to buy off their interrogator by offering to give him his heart's desire, whether it's sex, a love potion or a subtle poison to rid you of your enemy. Most men take the bribe and kill the dark-hearted bitch anyway.'

'And naturally,' I said, 'when the nature of this potion came to light, all of those believed to be implicated in its manufacture and its employment would be arrested on the very gravest charges.'

Fox gave another shrug.

The room seemed to grow colder.

With difficulty, I recalled what we had been talking about.

'Another of your number lies dead in the coroner's crypt,' I said. Staring into his intensely dark eyes, I realized something else: I knew how the spade-bearded man in the barn had met his end. 'Two of the young players believe they were responsible, but I have no doubt they're wrong.'

'No bloody use to us with a broken ankle,' Martin Ashe said. 'He'd have slowed us down just when we needed—'

'Be quiet.' The two words were softly said, but Ashe shut his mouth like a trap closing. If we hadn't all realized it already, his expression gave away the vicious cruelty of his superior.

Robert Fox turned to me. 'You are helping these four men.'

'Yes.'

He sighed. 'Like all the simpletons who gaze open-mouthed at their antics on the stage, you have been taken in,' he said. 'They have spun you a tale of intelligent men drawn into a secret society where they feel safe discussing their ideas with like-minded companions. You believe them when they tell you they yearn for freedom of thought, for a place where it is safe to discuss matters which right-thinking men regard as heresy and treason. Of course you want to help them, Doctor.' His eyes raked over Theo, Jarman and Jonathan. 'The coroner and his man know no better than you, but I'm surprised to see you in this company, priest.'

Jonathan met the sharp steel of his gaze. He raised his eyebrows. 'Are you?'

Fox laughed, a sound as harsh and cold as a blade being sharpened. 'Jonathan Carew,' he said softly. 'Oh, we haven't forgotten *you're* down here.'

'Indeed I am,' Jonathan replied. Then his voice changed. 'And you may tell the men who sent you that the stagnant backwater that was meant to make my brain atrophy within six months and have me dead of boredom and despair in a year has failed in its task.'

They held each other's eyes for a few moments. Then Fox turned away.

Theo said, his strong voice cutting the tension, 'What are

they really up to, then? They've fooled us, you said. Taken us in. So why are they running away? What's this secret they've brought out of London, that's so vital that six of the State's spies have come haring after them to confirm what they know and make sure it goes no further?'

Fox turned to Ashe, but Ashe had nothing to say. Facing us again, Fox said, 'Our function is that of our predecessors, who learned their craft from the very best. Just as Walsingham's men were for their Queen, we are the watchmen; we search out plots against the King. We have been accused of killing first and verifying the details afterwards, but we take the view that what worked for a queen will work as well for a king. Men have died here, of course they have.' Suddenly there was passion in his voice. 'One – no, *two* of ours' – he shot a poisonous glance at Barnaby – 'or, indeed, three, for the man you knew as Daniel was ours, sent to pose as a supportive friend for Francis Heron as he made his escape, while in fact keeping us aware of all that happened. And' – the thin lips moved as silently he counted – 'three of the Company. Six lives. A small price, when set against what is at stake.'

'Which is?' It was Theo's voice.

'Oh, not much, you might say, to make the State's finest set out on their long journey. Not much, to lead to the deaths of half a dozen men. But it is our job. It is what we train for, what makes us willing to do what we must to ensure the safety of the man we serve. There was a whisper, you see; just a whisper. A house had been let, the whisper said, hard by the very epicentre of power in the realm. A plot, the whisper went on, that would see an end to the King, his family, his government and every man of power, wealth and influence in the land. Fantastical, you might say? But Ashe and I, we know. We *know* this whisper speaks the truth, and when we have finished dispatching the rats who evaded the trap' – he stared hard and long at each of the four players – 'we shall return to London and see to the rest of them.' He glared round at us all, and now it seemed as if the dark eyes were full of fire. In a voice like a snake's hiss he said, 'Do you still wonder that we acted as we have done?'

I had no idea what would happen next.

Fox had traced his whisper, found his whisperers, and surely he would not leave the four who remained alive. But their ship was due tonight: they had so nearly made it. Perhaps Theo had the same thought; he said calmly, 'We are now eight, Master Fox, and you are but two. You tell us you act for the State, yet what you just told us sounds preposterous and highly unlikely, and I for one am disinclined to believe you. These four, however' – he indicated the players – 'have told us a far more convincing tale.'

I turned to Robert Fox, my hand on the weapon at my belt. 'Are you going to kill us all?' I asked softly.

He held my eyes for a moment, then he looked away. 'Come,' he said curtly to Ashe. As they turned to leave, he fixed me with a long, steady look. 'I know you now,' he said very quietly. 'We have long memories, Doctor Taverner.'

It happened in a flash. One moment, two men in dark cloaks emerging silently into the night. The next, a cry, a flash of steel, a big, athletic, dark-complexioned figure who moved like a dancer and wielded his sword – no wooden model now – as if it were an extension of his own arm. And two bodies on the track, one with a deep cut in his throat, one with a bloom of scarlet on his chest. Both of them dead.

And Harry Perrot – Othello, Oberon, Mercutio, Aaron the Moor – said in a voice breaking with grief, 'He's dead. Raphe is dead. He was gentle, and I loved him. They did not have to kill him.'

It took several days for Plymouth to fall back into its usual ways after the Company had gone. The townspeople, of course, had no idea of what else had been going on, and they missed the simple excitement of having a group of players among them. The chatter in the taproom of the Saracen's Head was of little else for some time, and there were regular and quite heated arguments over who had performed best, which was the most entertaining play, whether comedy was preferable to high drama or extreme violence. The remaining players arrived safely in Exeter, we learned, put on a reduced programme of three very minor plays – they were, of course, missing many of their major actors, and it was quite a surprise they had managed anything at all – and then set off back to the capital.

My sister, my friends and I took longer to put that extraordinary week behind us. We were all relieved and happy that Thomas, Barnaby, Humphrey and poor sad old Gerard had got away. The ship they were expecting turned up as arranged in the cove under the headland, we saw them aboard, Theo, Jarman, Jonathan and I, and they said farewell to us with heartfelt thanks. My three companions had gone on ahead, but I waited on the shore until the ship was out of sight. I still had misgivings, but I was trying to let hope outweigh them.

At home, I watched with secret pleasure as the new bond between Celia and Jonathan grew stronger. Something had happened during the hours they worked on the code, and I thought it was surely something good. But it was none of my business, so I didn't ask. Not that my sister would have told me anyway.

Judyth and I at last had our quiet supper together, in her sweet-smelling little house down by the old quay. What happened that night, I shall keep to myself.

I found the occasion to speak to Theo in private about the extraordinary plot that Robert Fox had claimed was being prepared in the heart of the capital. Theo had wondered if it was our duty to report it (to whom I wasn't sure) on the grounds that the least suspicion of something so unimaginably terrible ought not to remain concealed.

'All those names, Gabe, and that unimaginable suggestion concerning what they're up to!' he said as we sat huddled together late one afternoon behind the tightly closed door of his inner office, a bottle of fine brandy and two mugs on his desk. 'And Fox seemed so certain of the source of his intelligence, so sure that this house which some band of conspirators had rented was even now having a tunnel dug in its cellar to connect it to the undercroft of the Palace of Westminster!'

'Robert Fox was a fanatic,' I replied. 'Look what he did down here! Six dead, one his own man who was killed by another of them.' I paused, for this was still too fresh a memory not to be painful. 'And three of them players, surely no more threat to the safety of the King's exalted person than you or I, yet dead nonetheless.'

'You sound angry,' Theo remarked.

'I *am* angry.'

It would be a long time before Harry Perrot's agonized words faded from my memory. *He was gentle and I loved him*, he'd said of poor Raphe Wymer, Desdemona to his Othello. *They did not have to kill him.*

I thought of the coded list in Francis Heron's notebook. Those men would die too if we gave it up, whether they were guilty or not, for Robert Fox's kind never took the risk of leaving someone alive who only *might* be a threat.

Theo was watching me. 'You are in favour of keeping it to ourselves?'

'Yes,' I replied, 'for I will not have more deaths on my conscience.'

There was a long silence. I thought I could hear Theo turning it over in his mind.

Then he sighed, reached for the brandy and poured a generous measure into the two mugs. He raised his, I did the same, and we clinked them together.

'What should we drink to?' I asked.

He pulled a face. 'To this bloody plot being no more than a fantasy,' he replied.

We drank.

A month or so later, when the weather had turned very cold and several of the townsfolk had suffered painful falls that required a doctor's attention, I paused between visits to a very old man and an even older woman to snatch a hasty meal in the Saracen's Head. I had nearly finished when Coxton the innkeeper sidled up to speak to me.

He looked carefully to see if anyone was listening. Then, leaning close, he said, 'You realize, Doctor, that the Company weren't responsible for *all* the weirdness that went on?'

I stared at him. 'Go on.'

'Something got disturbed,' he said quietly. 'Like as not it was when they unblocked the old tunnel beyond the underground room. It's *old*, see, this inn. Been Coxtons here for generations, like I said, and we *know*.' He paused, and there was sweat on his brow. Dropping his voice to a whisper, he added, 'Whatever was down there woke up. Picked up the mischief being acted out by those young Company fools and fed on it. Grew strong on it. Joined in.' He straightened up. Then with a nod, he moved away.

I found I'd lost my appetite for the last of my pie. I felt cold suddenly, and slightly sick. The tunnel had been bricked up at the far end and the door in the passage turned into a permanent barrier – that had been done as soon as the Company had departed – but it wasn't much of a comfort just then.

I stood up. I had more patients to see, I couldn't afford to waste time trembling in the Saracen's Head taproom.

And besides, I reminded myself as I strode out, I didn't believe in ghosts.

Did I?